Eclairs And Executions

A Terrified Detective Mystery

Carole Fowkes

INK LION BOOKS

Chapter One

"What's wrong with working for Gino again, Claire?" My father, Frank DeNardo, popped a grape into his mouth as if to emphasize the question. I should have known this would be the topic when he invited me over to his house and my aunt happened to drop by.

At least Aunt Lena, a fabulous baker who owns *Cannoli's*, one of the best bakeries on Cleveland's West Side, brought some of her frosted caramel brownies to ease into the discussion. I grabbed one before answering. At 5'2''and 108 pounds, I hardly needed the extra calories. What I needed was a moment to think.

My father was talking about Gino Francini, his second cousin and my former employer, who had left me his floundering private investigation business when he retired to Miami. Good thing, because a Master's Degree in Mass Communications wasn't the most promising career path.

Aunt Lena, my late mother's sister, chimed in. "Your father's right. It'll be safer and he won't have to worry about you." She cut one of the brownies in half and took a bite from the bigger piece. "Granted, you won't see

Brian as much. At least not professionally." She winked at me. "I'll bet he comes around anyway." She wiped the corners of her mouth with her pinkie. "Then Ed can concentrate on his career."

Ed is a full time security guard and my part time muscle. After one of my particularly nasty cases, he also became Aunt Lena's main squeeze.

I ignored her comment about Brian, meaning Detective Brian Corrigan, Cleveland PD, my currently on-again relationship. "You're both right. It would be safer. You know, though, I'd make even less money, if that's possible."

Aunt Lena clucked. "Maybe you would have more money as an investigator, and for what? So we could use it for your funeral after some thug kills you?" She cut the remaining brownie half in half again and took a piece.

My father swallowed another grape. "Your aunt has a point. No parent wants his kid to die before him. Work at your aunt's place if you don't want to work for Gino."

That gave me an idea. One I was not about to discuss. It needed time to develop, just as I did when all the other girls my age looked like women and I still had the figure of a cucumber. "We can talk about this later. Right now I've got to meet a new client."

My aunt opened her mouth to say something else. She stopped when I held up my hand. "This one will be non-violent and resolved before Gino gets here. An author hired me to interview a critic." With any luck on my side, I would have the unbelievable fee of $10,000 in my pocket too.

My aunt's eyes sparkled with curiosity mixed with excitement. "A writer? Who? Is he famous?"

"He's a she. I'll tell you all about her when I have

more time." The author was Iola Taylor, prolific writer of erotica. Given her subject matter, it was better not to tell Aunt Lena.

"Two seconds to tell me who she is. Is she famous?"

"I have to leave now. I repeat. You can ask me about her later." I kissed both my aunt and father goodbye.

My dad couldn't resist having the last word. "We're not done talking about your working for Gino."

"Love you both." I hurried out before we were off and running with more discussion.

Anyway, that was yesterday and I had all evening to think about Gino's homecoming. On this day I needed to concentrate on George Herbert Dixon, since he was the reason Iola Taylor hired me. She wanted to know if Dixon had some career-destroying information on her, as he claimed he did. If so, my job was to get it back and find out his source. That meant my first move would be to talk with Dixon.

To get this interview with him, I somewhat twisted the truth. No. Not twisted, choked it to death. Although 32 and well out of my college years, I claimed to be a student at Kent State University who wanted to do an article on his book reviewing process. Then I laid it on thick about admiring his work. That last part wasn't a lie. In the name of research, I read some of his reviews. He was a clever phrase turner.

My thoughts returned to Iola Taylor, author of numerous erotic books, each one steamy enough to take the wrinkles out of anyone's bed sheets. From her photos, she looked like the kind of woman you wouldn't take home to Mother. With her long, black hair, green eyes and a figure so voluptuous the nuns at Holy Trinity would have automatically prayed for the soul of any man who met her, I got the feeling she wrote from firsthand experience.

In person, though, it was hard to tell if her pictures were accurate. She wore a bright red scarf around the collar of a tent-like black coat much too heavy for Cleveland's late spring. Her hair was pinned up under a floppy hat. Even though it was early evening, she never removed her enormous sunglasses. She kept her head lowered most of the time, never allowing me a clear view of her face. Her voice had been a mismatch too, with its nasal quality, as if she had a head cold.

A shiver ran through me, recalling her response when I asked what the next step would be if he had the information.

Her face was deadpan and her voice calm. "Kill him."

I sounded as if I just sat down naked in a pile of ice. "What did you say?"

Her laugh resembled a donkey braying. "A joke. The only thing I want killed is his exposé of me. If it exists."

"Isn't that something you should discuss with him yourself?"

She waved her hand. "I tried and got nowhere. Besides, someone has to stop him. So find out if he really has the information he claimed in his last article, get it from him, and find out where it came from so I can stop the supply."

Something didn't add up and it wasn't her book sales. "Is this information regarding any criminal activity on your part?"

Head bent writing me a check, she murmured. "Of course not. But if he has what he says he does, it could ruin me. He's merely a little soul in a corpulent body.

Now, would an advance of $10,000 with another $10,000 final payment be agreeable to you?"

That amount would make me sing karaoke on national television. Sober. With her fee, I could start my own PI business. "One more question. Why did you choose me?"

"You were so sweet-looking in your photo. With those enormous dark eyes and tiny stature, George will have no reason to be on his guard."

No argument there. I looked as non-threatening as tapioca pudding. Although the case still didn't make much sense, I was not about to turn down a fee, especially such a generous one.

As a matter of fact, I deposited the check as soon as Iola left my office and planned my next move.

So here I was, 7:15 that same evening, on my way to see George Dixon. The address he gave me was on Cleveland's Gold Coast, an area with stately homes and a great view of Lake Erie. The man was doing pretty well.

I parked on the street and turned off the ignition. A familiar-looking woman in a black coat too heavy for the late spring weather and a floppy black hat rushed out of the house's side door. Her red scarf caught in a strong breeze, and she grabbed on to it. Then looking straight ahead, she dashed into a Mercedes and pealed out of the driveway as if the devil himself was chasing her.

My mind didn't kick into gear soon enough to try and stop her, but I managed to snap a picture of the Mercedes' license plate.

I jumped out of my car, rushed across the street to the house, and skidded to a halt. What if a crazed killer lurked inside? Then again, what if somebody was hurt or dying? I could not let that be on my conscience. Wishing to be anywhere besides this place, I forced myself to make a choice.

Holding my gun in my moist hand, I tried the side door. It was unlocked and I stuck my head inside. "Hello. Mr. Dixon? Anyone home?" Nobody responded.

With the pounding of my heart in my ears, I stepped inside the kitchen. No one there, so I headed into the dining room. "Hello?" Still no answer, except a soft whimper coming from my throat.

I found Dixon bare-chested and bloody, bound to a chair in his library. He had a big lump and bruise on the right side of his forehead. Covering his face, arms, and upper torso were multiple lacerations. I cringed and swallowed hard to keep my most recent meal in its rightful place. Bloodied manila folders lying at his feet told me these were what made the paper cuts. Some cuts were short in length, others, long; all must have been painful. A wadded newspaper was stuffed in his mouth. My whole body trembled as I called 911.

The ambulance arrived in less than five minutes, with the police close behind. I stood back as an EMT leaped from his vehicle. Uniformed officers bounded from their cars. Amidst the chaos, my mind refused to focus. Even when one of the cops escorted me away, my foggy brain could not put what had happened here together in any way that made sense.

The situation grew more complicated. Of all the homicide detectives in the Cleveland Police Department, Detective Brian Corrigan caught this case.

Resembling a kid found smoking in the school restroom, I shuffled my feet, hoping he'd go easy on me. He didn't.

Corrigan sauntered up to me, shaking his head.

"Don't tell me. The victim hired you to protect him."

We had met over similar situations in the past. I crinkled my nose, not wanting to say anything. The detective pulled out his notepad. Knowing he would find out soon enough, I gave him a quick rundown of the events leading up to my presence at the late Mr. Dixon's house.

"Let me get this straight. You came here hoping to talk to the victim but he was already dead." Corrigan scratched his chin. "Did you see anyone going into the house or coming out?"

I coughed and looked around, then down at my feet.

"Who did you see, Claire?" Corrigan's foot began tapping as fast as my heartbeat.

The name stuck in my throat. It took a huge effort to spit it out. "My client, Iola Taylor."

Chapter Two

Corrigan wrote the name down and tapped his pen against the pad. "Doesn't she write that smutty stuff?" He grimaced. "Never mind. Did she have anything in her hands?"

I shook my head, feeling like Benedict Arnold. The only difference was that, instead of betraying my country, I was in the process of doing so with my client. As Gino, my former and perhaps soon-to-be boss, would say, "Life is a series of spinning the wheel and taking your chances." Too bad I chanced upon the scene as she fled. "Not that I could see, but I'll send you the pictures I took of her license plate."

Corrigan noticed my wobbly state, took my arm and led me to a lounge chair on the patio. "Have a seat, Claire. Should've had you sitting before I asked any questions." Out of the corner of his mouth, he smirked, "Think I'd know by now. We've done this so many times."

Once seated, I felt better, but saw no humor in his comment.

He must've gotten the message because he coughed

and continued his questioning. "You didn't see her enter. What time was it when she left?"

"7:15 this evening." I wanted to break out of there and devour some chocolate.

The gods must have realized my need. A uniformed officer approached Corrigan to take him to the body.

"Claire, I'll be right back. Will you be okay?"

"Yes. Can I go?" I stared at him with pleading-puppy eyes, hoping he couldn't forbid me to leave.

He looked up to the sky. "Okay, Claire. You can wipe that dog-in-the-pound look off your face. If you're okay, go." He leaned close, "Call you later."

A little put off by his less-than-flattering read of my expression, I almost told him not to bother. I didn't because if I had given him a hard time, he might have made me wait there.

His voice all business again. "If you hear from your client, call me. Understand?"

"Perfectly." Knowing Corrigan was watching me, I took my time getting to my car. Too fast and he'd get suspicious. Too slow and he'd think I needed assistance.

In the privacy of my office, I covered my face with my hands and moaned. Despite having seen other dead bodies, Corrigan was right. It wasn't any easier.

My client probably committed the murder and I was the only witness. Wishing I had never taken this case was of no use. Then guilt set in. What if I'd gotten there sooner? Would Dixon be alive and my client be just an angry author? My thoughts whirled like a Kansas tornado in my mind.

After my minor breakdown, practicality took over. Did the check clear? With my dire financial situation, it was impossible not to think about it. I had just gotten on my bank's website when my office door opened and then closed.

I wasn't expecting anyone. "Is anyone out there?" When nobody responded, I pulled my gun out and rose from my seat, making my way to the reception area and my office door.

Iola held up her hands. "Don't shoot. It's Iola." Although she was still wearing the dark glasses, she held the hat in her hand.

Even though this wasn't the first time I'd faced a likely killer, it still scared me, making me feel as exposed as a banana without its peel. Just as easy to smash too.

I lowered the gun and steadied my voice. "Why are you here?"

Iola slipped off her scarf, removed her sunglasses, her face level with mine. She didn't resemble her photos at all. She had thinning brown hair, close-set eyes, and without the oversized glasses, her nose appeared to be an unfortunate size. I kept quiet; instinct telling me now was not the time to offer her makeup tips.

Her chin quivered. "I went to see George this evening. He was..." She took a deep breath. "Dead." She covered her mouth with her hand. Still, her sobs broke through.

Unwilling to stand there and watch her fall apart, I put my gun down on my desk and guided her to a nearby seat. Grabbing the tissue box, I handed her one, pulled my desk chair around and positioned it so close our knees almost touched. "Tell me exactly what happened."

She dabbed at her eyes and released a jagged breath. "His review of my book, *Torn Lace,* was online. It was cruel beyond belief. So I went to see him, to demand he retract what he'd written." She put up her hand. "I know.

I hired you to talk to him. It's just that he so infuriated me. How dare he..." She ripped little pieces of the tissue off, leaving what looked like crumbs in her lap.

I leaned in and as gently as possible, urged her to continue.

Iola sniffed and stared down at the shredded tissue. "His door was unlocked. I knew not to go in. I did anyway. George was tied up, covered in blood. Terrified, I ran out without even checking to see if he was alive." She squeezed her eyes shut and her body jerked with a silent sob.

My natural reaction would have been to hug and comfort her. In this case, though, my instincts told me that would be the wrong thing to do. She might just be putting on a convincing act.

As if some unseen timer had run out on her remorse, she detached herself from George's death as fast as she'd fallen apart over it. Her spine straightened and she tilted her chin "I thought it best to get to my car and leave before anyone knew I'd been there."

I knew you'd been there.

Tempting as it was to demand why she hadn't bothered to call 911 for the man, it wouldn't have helped me obtain more information. "Was anybody else at his house?" That was assuming she, herself, wasn't the killer.

She closed her eyes. "No." Then blinked and opened them. "I got two blocks away before turning back to help him."

Knowing the answer, I still asked, "Did you help him then?"

Iola stared over my shoulder. "Someone was already there, and I heard the sirens." She adjusted her coat's collar. "Yes, I happened to be in the wrong place at the wrong time. That doesn't mean I killed him. Someone else did. You must believe me."

I cast my eyes up to the sky. Of course she killed him. Before that thought cemented itself in my mind, another little voice inside me whispered, "What if she didn't?"

Even if she was telling the truth, it did not look good for her. She was the last one spotted at the scene of the crime and had a strong motive.

I chose my words carefully. "Iola, at this point I believe the best thing for you to do is—"

A deep voice interrupted. "Police. Open up." My door rattled from the force of the cop's fist rapping.

Iola turned the color of fresh fallen snow. "Is there a back door?" She clutched my hand with her icy one.

The pounding became more insistent. I reclaimed my hand and rose to let the police in.

Iola's tortured expression punched me in the stomach. Expecting her to bolt, I was shocked when, instead, she put her hat and sunglasses on. "If I must. I'm ready."

The police scrambled inside my office and threw the cuffs on Iola. Rather than sobbing or panicking, she tilted her head down. When the cop asked her if she understood her rights, she murmured. "Yes. Now can I call my lawyer?"

"Claire." Detective Corrigan made his entrance as the uniformed cops escorted Iola out. Was I in trouble? I didn't have to wait long to find out.

He pulled up a chair and sat down. "Have a seat." His words were casual. It was the way he said it that put me on edge.

Once we were both seated, he leaned over, his forearms on his thighs. "How many murder cases have you worked, Claire?"

I folded my hands in my lap as if I was a wayward school girl waiting for the principal. "Why?"

"So, am I correct in thinking you would know what to do if a suspect contacted you? Even if that suspect was your client?"

"She just showed up—"

"And despite seeing her flee the crime scene, you didn't think to let the police know?"

"She claims he was already dead when she got there."

"And of course, you believed her." He rubbed his face. "Wouldn't you say that's a little naïve?"

"Iola Taylor is my client."

"You should be saying, *was* your client. She's going to need a good lawyer, not a private investigator. Besides, since you're the chief witness, you should remove yourself from this case."

For the first time in memory, I had to agree he was right. Not that I wanted to. What would losing her fee do to my business plans? Then I realized Iola had hired me to find out what Dixon knew and try to get it from him. Now that he was dead, it didn't matter. Case closed. Fee to be paid-in-full. "You're right."

Corrigan's eyes narrowed. "What did you just say?"

"I'm done with this case."

His smile beamed so brightly, the room didn't need a lamp. "Best news today." That smile turned mischievous. "What do you say we get one of Iola Taylor's books and act out the sexy parts together?"

My eyes opened wide and I pretended to be offended. "Why Detective Corrigan! How can you even think of saying such a thing?"

His eyes raked over my body. If he had a mustache, I'm sure he would have twirled it. The moment he swept me into his arms my office phone rang.

Willing it to stop didn't work and the caller's voice distracted me. It was Aunt Lena.

"Claire, if you're there, pick up. Your father heard from Gino and—"

I almost tripped grabbing the phone. "Hello? What did Gino say?"

"Sure, now you answer." She huffed and then continued. "Gino will be back in Cleveland the end of this month. I thought you should know."

That gave me three weeks to implement a plan. "Thanks so much for telling me. Wonder why my father didn't call."

"I told him I would since I needed to talk to you anyway."

Here it comes. "Why is that?" If I hadn't asked, she would have told me anyway.

"Can you come to my house Wednesday around 6? I need your help."

I tilted my head, puzzled. Aunt Lena seldom asked for assistance if it didn't involve *Cannoli's*. "I'll be there. Care to tell me why you need my help?"

"Ed and I are in a dance competition."

I closed my eyes, trying to picture them, my ample-waisted, short-legged aunt with the tall, wiry Ed. "Dance competition?"

"He cuts quite a rug."

"I don't have any pressing business, so okay."

"Thanks, Sweetie and say a prayer we win. Grand prize is two custom-made bowling balls."

I glanced over at Corrigan, who was reading his text messages.

"Someone's here, so I better go. Thanks again for the information, Aunt Lena."

To my hormones' disappointment, Corrigan was almost on his way out the door. "Sorry, Claire. Duty calls. We'll read that book another time."

Left alone, Iola's statement about being in the wrong place at the wrong time bounced around in my head. Except for the final billing she was no longer my client, but I was curious and decided to delve into George Dixon's background.

He'd been an M.P. during Desert Storm, went to Brown University, an Ivy League college, for his graduate degree. Never married. One sister, Felicity Dixon, also never married. Lived in New York for a time before moving to Cleveland. Became a critic for the *Cleveland Plain Dealer* and branched out to other newspapers and magazines before the Internet.

After staring at the computer screen, my eyes felt as if they had pebbles in them. I turned away and realized how much time had passed by the growls from my stomach. It hates to be empty. I shut my computer down, grabbed my purse, and planned to head home for what wouldn't be a gastronomical feast. That was my aunt's territory.

The ringing of my office phone changed my plans. I answered. Probably shouldn't have.

"Claire! It's a pleasure hearing your voice again."

Feeling a bit weak-kneed from the memories the caller evoked, I plopped into the nearest chair. "Harold. How are you?" My voice sounded strained, even to me.

"Fine, just fine. I want you to know how glad I am

you're doing well after the Sanchez case."

Harold had been the attorney for one of my clients, Merle, accused of murder. Although Harold looked all of fifteen, he had the skills of a top-notch mob lawyer. I didn't trust him and definitely didn't want to stroll down Memory Lane with him. "What can I do for you?"

"I believe you were hired by my client, Iola Taylor."

My hand constricted around the phone's receiver as I imagined it was Harold's neck. "Yes. I believe, though, our business is concluded since Dixon is dead." The empty feeling in my stomach was gone; in its place was a dark cloud of dread.

"Not so. See, she hired you to protect her reputation from George Dixon. Just because he's dead doesn't mean he couldn't still ruin her reputation. Therefore, she wants to retain you to find the victim's real killer and clear her name. She admits she fled the scene of the crime. You have to believe Iola is no more guilty of killing George than the child who is angry and wishes his mother ill. Then his mother dies in an accident. A coincidence. Nothing else."

I squeezed my eyes shut, wanting to block the sight of Iola leaving Dixon's house. Experience dealing with Harold told me he already knew I was the chief witness against her.

"That was such a nice speech you just gave, I hate to have to turn you and Iola down." I took a deep breath. "If you don't know yet, you'll find out soon. I'm the one who saw her come out of Dixon's house."

"We're both aware of that, and I advised Iola on it. Nevertheless, she insists. And she'll increase your advance by another $5,000 as an incentive."

The original advance was generous. This additional

money could get me completely out of debt, with some left over. It wasn't right, though. "I can't. It's unethical."

"You've left me with no choice except to advise my client to cancel her original advance check."

Keeping my panic at bay, I responded with a bravado I didn't feel. "We all have to do what we feel is right."

He blew out a deep breath. "It's not something I relish doing. However, it's right for my client. Think it over, Claire. We'll talk tomorrow morning." With that, he hung up.

My face in my hands, I allowed myself about thirty seconds of self-pity. Forgetting all about my stomach, I flicked on my computer again in the hope I had missed something. The only way I could stay on this case would be if Iola's biggest crime was running instead of reporting Dixon's murder. Then she would be guilty of nothing more than panic and bad timing. Otherwise, not only would it be wrong, it would conflict with my sense of justice for all.

An hour hadn't produced much more information on Dixon. In a brief bio, he noted he loved Cicarelli's Pizza on Cleveland's East Side. Probably no big deal, except the place was known to be a hangout for some of the local gangsters. Regardless, they did have great pizza. It bore a closer look.

I had been to the place before on my own, trying to extract information from some of the city's most ruthless criminals. That visit had been as successful as hog wrestling at a ballet. If we uncovered something proving Iola innocent, I could keep the deposit and could actually pay Ed.

The sensible, cautious part of me took over. It hadn't been wise to visit the place the first time. Granted, Nick

Cicarelli now ran Cicarelli's instead of his shady father. I could still end up regretting going there. As in "I regret to inform you, Mr. DeNardo, your daughter is dead."

Best to deal with Cicarelli's from a distance. I found the number and called.

A woman answered and connected me to Nick's office. He picked up along with the pace of my heartbeat.

I twisted a strand of my hair and cleared my throat. "Nick? This is Claire DeNardo. You may not remember me—"

His voice was warm, friendly. "Forget you? You gotta be kidding me. What can I do for you?"

My shoulders dropped. "You're probably very busy and it's late, but I was wondering if you're acquainted with a book critic, George Dixon. He once mentioned he was a big fan of your pizza."

"Bald guy, short?"

"Yes, that sounds like the guy. I'm looking for some information. Could you help me?"

He said something, but it sounded as if he had turned his head. He was probably talking to someone else. After a moment, he returned to our conversation. "Why don't you come over? I'll make you the best pie you've ever had and we can discuss George Dixon."

Was this a trick to lure me there? Red lights flashed in my mind despite believing there was no reason not to trust Nick.

I hesitated. Was someone else there, telling him to invite me? My impulse was to decline. After all, I wasn't working the case, so why put myself in danger? A past due utility bill caught my eye. Iola's payment could take care of that. Besides, if Nick knew anything leading to someone else as the killer, justice demanded I follow through. Only not alone. Corrigan was out of the question. He thought I was off the case. Ed.

I took a deep breath and blew it out. "Sure. I can leave now." As soon as the words were out of my mouth, panic rushed in. What if Ed wasn't available?

Fortunately, Ed answered on the first ring. "Hey, kiddo. What's up?" He sounded relaxed, which meant he wasn't at work.

"How about some scrumptious, free pizza?"

He chuckled. "Hey, any pizza's good pizza. Free is even better." He paused. "What's the catch?"

I bit my lower lip. "It's at Cicarelli's."

"You gotta be kidding. What, are they giving you free pizza to make up for you almost getting killed?"

"No. This is about a different case. One that, if it pans out, I could pay you *and* give you a bonus."

"So who do I have to rough up?"

"No one. I just thought we could share some pizza while I talk to Nick Cicarelli." I held my breath, afraid he'd turn me down.

"You know you can count on me. You also know if I'm going to risk my life you need to tell me the details."

I gave him a quick rundown of the day's events. "There shouldn't be any trouble."

"Sounds like your mind is made up." Seconds ticked by. "Okay, I'll pick you up. Can't say as I agree with what you're doing, though."

"Got it. See you soon, Ed."

It was almost 11when we pulled into Cicarelli's deserted parking lot.

Ed glanced over at me. "Good thing I'm here. You're twitching like someone caught on an electric fence."

He was right. My stomach was in so many knots, a

boy scout and a sailor together wouldn't be able to untie them.

Ed asked, "Ready to rock and roll?"

I pulled my gun out and stuck it in my waistband. Ed scratched his forehead. "For God's sake, put that thing somewhere so it's out of sight. We're here for pizza and answers, not for another St. Valentine Day's massacre."

I moved my weapon so it wasn't visible. "Ready as I'll ever be."

Chapter Three

The hostess had seated Ed and me in the almost empty dining room when I heard a familiar voice.

"Claire." I swiveled in my chair.

Although I hated to admit it, my heart did a tiny flip when I saw Alex Carpenter standing there. He was as gorgeous as ever with his smoldering dark eyes rimmed with thick lashes and golden blonde hair. He was the nephew of Michael Bucanetti, a big-time mobster who ruled from New Jersey. "Hi Alex. Didn't know you'd be here."

He smiled, showing perfect white teeth. "Nick told me you were meeting him, so I invited myself. Hope you don't mind."

Trying to be coy, I raised an eyebrow and half-smiled. "Is it business or pleasure?"

"Pure pleasure." He chuckled. "I'm hoping to have another one of those interesting dates with you again."

My face grew hot. The last date we had involved hunting down a dog for illegal pooping. It was memorable, just not in a good way. "You're kidding, right?"

Nick Cicarelli chose that moment to greet me. "It's

good to see you again, Claire."

Ed spoke up for the first time since we arrived. "In case anyone's interested, I'm Ed."

"Sorry, Ed." I introduced Alex.

Ed stared into Alex's eyes. His voice a low growl. "I remember you now. It was a case me and Claire worked. Your uncle is that gangster—"

"Ed." I glared at him. "And this is Nick Cicarelli, our host."

Ed must have gotten my not-so-subtle hint and turned away from Alex. He shook Nick's hand. "Nice joint you got."

"Thanks. Place has been in the family a long time. Making pizza is our passion, I guess you could say." Nick surveyed the room with obvious pride. "In fact, I was just about to make Claire the best pizza outside of Naples. Why don't you come and check it out?"

Ed glanced over at Alex and me. To Nick, he said, "Sure. It'll be great to watch the magic happen."

Nick chuckled. "Yeah. Only one thing. You gotta wear a hairnet."

"Always wanted to be a dead ringer for my Grandma Sophie."

The two men disappeared into the kitchen, leaving Alex and me alone. Something told me it was fine with Alex.

He moved his chair so close to mine that they looked connected. "I know you wanted to talk to Nick. When he told me you'd be here, I couldn't resist." The glow of his smile was enough to make me want to put on sunscreen.

I wanted to keep some emotional and physical distance. "It's fine you're here. In fact, you may have some information I need."

He placed his elbow on the table and rested his chin in his hand. "Is that all I am to you? A source of information?" His voice turned mock-hurt. "Tell me, if my uncle wasn't Michael Bucanetti, would you even give me the time of day?"

Gazing at his take-my-breath-away face, I would not only give him the time of day; I'd give him the clock. "Alex, I'm sorry if every time we talk, it's about your uncle or some case I'm working." I shrugged. "Hey, that's my job. And unfortunately, your uncle seems to be an integral part of my clients' problems." I purposely left out Bucanetti's threat to destroy my family if I ever tipped the cops as to his goings-on. That was my secret and my burden to keep.

He ran his fingers through his hair. "Hell, I wish he had never taken me in when my parents died. If it weren't for my Aunt Carmella, I wouldn't have anything to do with him."

It never fails. I'm such a sucker for men and their angst. Placing my hand on his shoulder, I insisted, "You're not the same as him. You're a good man, and—"

He silenced me with a kiss, a real make-you-want-to-rip-your-bodice-open one. I could say my budding relationship with Corrigan made me push Alex away. It would be a lie. It wasn't until our mouths separated, that a sensible thought came to me. That steamy kiss felt wonderful and terrible. From his half-closed eyes, Alex didn't share my opinion. In fact, he zoomed in for another landing. Which I avoided, turning my head at the last moment.

Although Corrigan and I didn't have any sort of declared exclusivity, this lusty activity with Alex produced a glob of guilt in my stomach. "Alex, we can't do this."

He set his jaw. "Why not? Is it Corrigan?"

"What about Corrigan?" Ed asked, carrying a bottle of Chianti, followed by Nick who was transporting a massive pizza.

Despite that self-reproaching feeling in my gut, the pizza's aroma was enticing. In fact, if my taste buds had hands they would have been high-fiving each other with anticipation. Its presentation stopped any further action between Alex and me.

Nick set the jumbo pizza down and we admired the still bubbling mozzarella, golden crust, and generous toppings of sausage, black olives, and pepperoni.

I oohed. "It's a thing of beauty, Nick."

Nick cut the pizza with the expertise of someone who'd sliced them all his life and handed each of us a slice, then poured generous servings of the wine.

Ed's eyes darted from Alex to me and back again. "Claire, you didn't answer me. What about Corrigan?"

I took a big bite. My eyes widened and using my hand, I fanned my burning mouth.

Alex picked up a pitcher of water and poured me a glass. "Claire. Here." He placed an arm around my shoulder while I took a couple of sips. "Better?"

Ed looked on, one eyebrow cocked. He leaned back in his chair. "Hey, Buckaroo. Why don't you give the lady some breathing room?"

Alex's eyes flashed at Ed and Ed scooted to the edge of his chair. It was like the high school cafeteria fights, over which jock sat next to which cheerleader. A groan rose in my throat.

"Let's all enjoy the pizza." Nick's tranquil smile cut through the tension. "What do you want to know about that Dixon guy, Claire?"

"I'm looking into his murder."

Nick pushed his chair from the table, stretching one leg out in front of him. "The guy used to come in about twice a month. A lot of times with a woman."

"Do you know who she was?" I took another bite.

Nick rubbed his neck. "Maybe Charlotte does. One of the waitresses. Talks to everyone. Just so happens, she's on cleanup tonight. I'll get her out here."

He returned to the kitchen, leaving Alex, Ed and me. Even with keeping my head down, I could still sense the animosity Ed directed at Alex.

Nick finally returned with a woman who looked to be in her late thirties, auburn hair she could have only gotten from a bottle, and a curvy figure.

"Everyone, this is Charlotte." Nick said, "She waited on Dixon a lot. Didn't you?"

Charlotte's smile settled on Ed. "He used to come in with his sister, Felicity. Tall and skinny, like a stick. Stringy brown hair, glasses, no makeup."

She took her gaze off Ed for a moment. "There's more...Nick, my shift's almost over. Mind if I sit down?"

"Of course not." He rose to get her a chair. She had other ideas, grabbed a different seat, and squeezed in next to Ed. With a sideways glance at him, she continued. "She used to wear these clothes that fit her like potato sacks, until she met Marco Conti."

Nick interrupted. "Claire, you remember him, don't you?"

How could I forget? Marco was a strong arm for Alex's uncle, Michael Bucanetti, and for the local bosses who did the New Jersey mobster's bidding. In our short time knowing each other, Marco and I had been on opposite sides more than once.

The pizza didn't appeal to me any longer. "Do you know her relationship with him?"

"I heard Marco telling one of the guys that she looked a lot better out of those baggy clothes." She eyed Ed as if she was thinking the same thing about him. "Made me sick. Her and me hung around some." I cleared my throat to bring her attention back. "So they were seeing each other away from here. Anything else?"

"No. Except neither brother nor sister have been here for a while." She leaned toward Ed. "Great pizza, huh? You should come back and try a calzone."

Ed grinned at her. "Maybe I will."

I pounced. "Good idea, Ed. You can bring Lena with you."

He glanced around. "Yeah, she'd enjoy this place. Lena's my squeeze, hell of a woman." His eyes met mine and he was no longer talking to Charlotte. "When you find a good person, you stop sampling what's still out there."

I looked down at the table. His comments may have started with my aunt. The finale was, no doubt, about Corrigan and me.

Charlotte got the hint. "Guess I better get back to work."

"Thank you for your help, Charlotte." Not liking the woman putting the moves on Ed was no reason to be impolite.

"Don't mention it. Especially if you see Marco."

"Understood. Completely."

After Charlotte left, Nick was quick to say, "You should know, Marco and his pals don't frequent my place anymore."

Thinking out loud, I added, "Maybe Felicity and Marco are still an item. They may be meeting somewhere else."

"Yeah. Rumor has it the old gang moves around," Nick snorted, "gracing different establishments with their presence."

I turned toward Alex. "You're awfully quiet."

Alex put up both hands. "No."

My eyebrows lowered. "No, what?"

"I'm not getting involved. The less I have to do with my uncle or any of his associates, the better it is for me."

I twisted my mouth, trying to find a way to change his mind. It's a shame I'm never clever on-the-spot. No doubt some snappy comeback would pop into my head tomorrow. "Okay." My insides winced at my inadequacy.

Ed pushed his chair away from the table. "If I don't get some shut-eye, my dance moves won't win any prizes. This has been great, though. Thanks."

"Ed, we should get out so these gentlemen can go home too. Nick, the pizza was wonderful. Thank you for that and for the wine. Also, the information."

Nick smiled and stuck his hands in his pockets. "You're welcome. Consider it my way of showing appreciation for helping clean house of some undesirables. Oh, forgot to tell you. My pop is going back to Licata, in Sicily. Says he's gonna 'get in touch with his roots.' Seems real happy about it."

I smiled. "That's great." His father had owned the site of a kidnapping case I'd gotten entangled in. It hadn't ended well for the kidnappers or his father. It was good to know there were no hard feelings.

Alex insisted on walking Ed and me out. Ed jumped

inside his car and motioned for me to join him. He'd have to wait though.

"Claire, I shouldn't have turned you down so fast. I can check around, although it's doubtful even my uncle knows where his part time scum hangs out."

Guess I didn't need a snappy, snarky comeback after all. "That would be great, Alex." Ed flashed his headlights. Next, he'd be laying on his horn. "Goodnight."

Alex opened my door. "See you soon."

Ed barely waited until Alex closed my door before taking off. "I don't care for that guy."

I raised my eyebrows in mock shock. "Really?"

"What about Brian? Remember him?"

"Of course I do. And you're a fine one to talk." In a husky voice mimicking Charlotte, I added, "Did you like the pizza, big boy?"

Ed shook his head. "Okay, okay. Truce."

Silence filled the car until we reached my office. "Ed, I appreciate your going to Cicarelli's with me."

"Yeah." He patted his bump of a belly. "Pizza was good. Hope it won't slow me down in the contest."

"You and Aunt Lena will be fabulous."

"Thanks, kiddo. You going home now?"

"No. There's something I want to check on first."

He walked me to my office and wished me a goodnight. At that moment, my idea of a good night was finding all I could about Felicity Dixon.

There wasn't a lot. She was seven years younger than her brother. Went to Oberlin College in Ohio, never married. Lived in her parents' old house in Lakewood. Both parents deceased. With George gone, she appeared to be alone. Jotting down her phone number, I planned to call her at a more decent hour.

The next morning was uneventful. That is, until opening my office door and hearing the ring of the phone.

I managed to pick up the phone, despite tripping on my way to answer it and landing hard on one knee. Should have let it go into voicemail. It was Gino.

"Hey there, Claire. How ya doing? Just called to update you on my plans."

Squeezing my eyes shut and holding my breath, I hoped he'd changed his mind and was staying in Florida.

"I'll be home a week earlier than planned. Anxious to get back to my old stomping grounds."

From my voice, no one would ever know my stomach was clenched. "Oh, okay. That's great. Really." It was anything but.

"Hoped you'd say that. Could you do me a favor and let your father know?"

"Sure." I wanted to hang up and feel sorry for myself.

"My flight times will be in my email. Looking forward to seeing everyone again."

My mouth was working on automatic. "Same here, Gino."

After the call I sat down, head in hands. That gave me one week less to figure out what to do. No administrative job for me again, not if I could help it. *And I could.* I rose from the chair and got Felicity Dixon's address and phone number. A visit to her could eventually lead me to discovering Iola didn't kill anyone. The real murderer would be punished and I'd be able to start my own agency. Gino could have his back. We'd be competitors. That could be good. It could make us both better PIs. Picturing my agency's office brightened my mood quite a bit. Feeling as if I had new insoles, I practically glided to my car.

When I arrived at my destination, my mood turned darker when I spotted a familiar figure walking out of Felicity's home.

Chapter Four

It was Marco. He strolled up to my car and tapped on the window. I debated whether or not to open it. Then, hey, he could shoot me through the glass, so down went my window.

His voice was sickly sweet; maple syrup poured on frosting. "Hey, Claire. Ain't it funny how we keep running into each other?" He dropped his faux-friendly manner. "If you got any ideas of talking to Felicity, forget it. She don't need that. Understand?"

You'd think Marco would no longer intimidate me. Yeah, well, he was just as scary as ever. I swallowed hard and in a squeaky voice said, "Except I'm here to help find out who killed her brother."

He leaned against my car door and I swear the opposite side's tires lifted off the ground. "They already got the loony bitch that did it. Now get the hell out of here."

A woman with long brown hair, probably Felicity, came out and stood on the porch. "Marco, who is it?"

He turned his head toward her. "Nobody, Lissie. And she's just leaving."

I hesitated for a moment, hoping Felicity would let

me talk to her. When she did nothing more than nod, I shifted into gear and drove off. There had to be a different way to get to Dixon's sister without Marco standing guard.

Turning left, I spotted a car heading in the direction of Felicity's house. It quickly made a U-turn. I didn't realize it was an unmarked police car until the driver flashed his lights and motioned for me to pull over.

I sunk in my seat when Corrigan got out of the car's passenger side and trudged toward me. He grabbed the door handle on the passenger's side and I let him in.

Once he sat, he stared straight ahead and kept his voice low and controlled. "You told me you weren't working the Dixon case."

I kept my hands on the steering wheel so they wouldn't tremble. "I'm not."

"Come on, Claire. Tell me you haven't just been at Felicity Dixon's place."

"I didn't talk to her." That was the truth if not the intent.

His knuckles were white from clutching his thighs. "You know, you can't be on this case."

My stomach was sinking faster than a submarine. "I'm not. It's just…"

He turned toward me, his eyes full of concern and anger. "It's just, what? You can't help yourself? You've got to solve every crime? Even if it's dangerous *and* unethical?"

"Of course not." I poured out the whole story of Harold's offer and what I had learned about Dixon. The only thing I left out was why the money was so important to me. Maybe I should have explained that I needed it to start my own PI business. Corrigan might have understood. I couldn't do it. I was embarrassed for him to know I was in such dire need of the money. And what if he wanted me out of the PI business? I just couldn't tell him.

His face twisted. "So money comes before everything and everyone? What if you lose your license? Or end up in jail? I knew you took stupid risks, but, bending the law..." Stunned, I didn't argue. Instead, I watched his Adam's apple bob. A moment later, he said in a stony voice, "You're a key witness in this murder. Stay out of this case or you'll be in trouble for conflict of interest and a whole butt-load of other ethical issues." He opened the door and turned his head toward me. "Consider that your warning." He sauntered back toward the police car.

Irate tears sprang to my eyes while I thought of all the things I should have said. For instance, how much it meant to me to have my own agency. My frustration and regret morphed into fury and my fist sliced through the air. *How dare he define me as a stupid, money-hungry liar?* I mumbled under my breath, "Who needs him?"

I gunned the motor and headed back to my office to conjure up a way to talk with Felicity and perhaps find out who killed her brother. I whispered a prayer that it wasn't Iola.

On the way to my office, my dad called. "Hey, Pumpkin."

"Dad, if you're calling to continue talking about Gino, please don't. Oh, and he's coming home a week earlier than planned."

"Yeah, I just hung up with him. Said he told you, then decided to call me himself. That isn't why I called. Do you and Brian want to go to the flicks with me and Suzy? I know it's last minute. Can you make it?"

The sound of Corrigan's name stung a bit. "Sorry, Dad. He's working a case and I..." An idea slammed into my head so fast I almost got whiplash. "I'd love to come along. What are you seeing?" It didn't matter what movie we saw. The important thing was to get Suzy to be a part of my plan.

"I don't know. Suzy's choosing one. She's more up on things than me. I'm picking her up at 7:30."

Ever since Suzy moved across the street from my dad and introduced herself to him, he smiles and laughs the same way he did before Mom died. "How about I get to your house at 7?"

"That'll work." He hesitated. "I'm glad you and Suzy get along. It means a lot to me."

I had already made my peace with Dad caring for a woman who wasn't my mother. "I know, Dad. She makes you happy and that makes me happy."

"She does. See you tonight. Hey, why don't you get here a little earlier? Lena brought over some lasagna, along with her complaining that since I started seeing Suzy, I wasn't at *Cannoli's* often enough. I told her if she was nicer to Suzy we'd be there more often. You'd have thought I accused her of stoning Suzy. Got all upset and started talking about your mother." His voice got huskier. "As if I need to be reminded of Theresa." He blew out a breath. "Anyway, Suzy doesn't want any lasagna. Says she's on a diet." He chortled. "I told her she's fine the way she is. You know how women are. Anyway, there's too much for me to eat alone."

Being a third wheel wasn't the greatest for my self-esteem, still, I could drown my sorrows in the toothsome noodles, seasoned meat and gooey cheeses. "Don't have to ask me twice. I'll be there around 6. Love you, Dad.

Bye."

"Love you more, Pumpkin."

After that call, I reviewed my plan. It could help me understand the unlikely relationship between Felicity and Marco. He was a hardened thug and she was...I didn't know yet. As soon as I could figure out how to get past that small-time hood, I'd find out.

On the way to my dad's place, I fine-tuned my idea, confident it would work as long as I got Suzy's buy-in.

Chapter Five

Dad answered the door wearing a grin I could only describe as goofy. Much as he loves me, he's never been that deliriously happy to see me. "What's going on?"

"Suzy's here."

I wondered if he always wore that look when she was with him. Suzy had to know she had my father wrapped around her little finger. *I have to talk to him about that.*

"Hello, Claire." Suzy wore a purple slinky dress that provided more than a hint of her unnaturally large breasts. The dress was so short, it had no acquaintance with her knees. I must have had a scowl on my face because the woman blushed. She tugged at the hem. "It shrunk when I washed it. Doesn't matter. I like the dress and my ma used to tell me, 'flaunt it if ya got it.'"

Feeling like a nun disapproving of her student's outfit, I murmured, "It's...fine." *No wonder my father looked so tickled.*

My dad cleared his throat. "Claire, change of plans. Instead of lasagna, we're going out to eat and then see the movie. Suzy mentioned a new place near West Side Market. It's Vietnamese. You okay with that?"

"Sure." Less calories. Plus, maybe I could finagle some lasagna to take home.

I followed Suzy out the door as my dad locked up. The back view of her was as much a testament to her mother's saying as the front view. My father didn't stand a chance.

We were the only customers in the restaurant so it was easy to talk without worrying about anyone listening. After we ordered, my father beamed, "Suzy resigned at Beauty Cuts and just opened her own beauty shop."

"Congratulations. That's a big step."

Suzy laid her hand flat on her chest. "Thanks, Claire. I've been saving up a long time for this. I still need to hire a shampooer. Minor detail. I'm happy to say a few of my clients have followed me. I'm doing mailings this week to drum up more business." She squinted at my hair. "By the way, are you finally ready for your big makeover hairdo?"

I automatically smoothed down my out-of-control mane. *Do I look that bad?* "No, not yet. Wow. That's wonderful about your salon." Her new venture could make my scheme even easier to execute. "It helps me too. See, there's somebody connected with a case whose brother was killed. She really needs a haircut and style. I was going to ask if you could do her hair at Beauty Cuts. Since you're sending out notices for your own business, could you offer this person a coupon for a free cut and style? I'll pay for it. I can wash her hair and question her. She won't bolt with shampoo in her hair." I purposely left out any information about Marco. It wouldn't have helped for her to know about him and his criminal affiliates.

Dad placed a protective arm around Suzy's shoulders. "Claire, don't drag Suzy into one of your cases. Remember what happened to Lena?"

I waved my hand as if it was a windshield wiper. "Nothing even similar will happen."

Suzy's eyes widened. "Similar to what?"

My father's voice was flat. "She was kidnapped."

Suzy gulped. "Why? Who?"

I glared at my father. "It had nothing to do with me. It was some guy she got involved with." I hedged a bit. "There's no risk to you, honest."

She glanced at my dad and then returned her gaze to me. "It doesn't sound immoral, or illegal, and it'll help you. If you're totally sure nobody will get hurt, I'm in. I'll wash her hair though. You need a license to do that in Ohio." She took a sip of tea.

I grinned and then got serious. "I'll even have a hair makeover afterwards."

My dad wasn't done. "Even if this woman gets a coupon, she may not use it. I get coupons all the time and just throw them..." His eyes shot wide as he realized he had cast criticism at his beloved Suzy's marketing plan.

Suzy pressed her lips together. I sat still, afraid any movement would cause her to turn me down. She gave my father a kiss on his cheek. "It's okay, Frankie. You're right about coupons. So I plan on mailing them only to a targeted group."

She smiled at me. "Give me this woman's address and I'll send her a coupon for a free cut and style. Then I'll call her and convince her to make an appointment." Suzy blew on her nails and rubbed them on her chest. "I used to be the star salesperson at Frick's Furniture."

My dad threw me a look I could, in no way, interpret as joy. "Great. It's bad enough I have to worry about

Claire. Now you, too."

Suzy peered into my dad's disapproving eyes. "I'll be all right, Frankie. I know how to take care of myself." She grabbed his hand and squeezed it.

The waiter, with perfect timing, brought our orders. While the food tasted great, the conversation was strained.

When Suzy went to the ladies' room, I offered my dad the peace pipe. "I know you're worried about Suzy. Don't be. I'll be at her salon the whole time. Nothing bad will happen."

He shook his head and folded his arms. "It better not. I don't want to go to jail for killing anybody who hurts the two people I care the most about."

I kissed the opposite cheek Suzy had kissed. With a wicked smile I teased, "What about Aunt Lena? Don't you care about her?"

Dad laughed. "With her temper and her rolling pin, that woman could take care of anyone who gets in her way."

Suzy returned and we gabbed so enthusiastically, we missed the movie and ended up going back to Dad's house.

I stood in my father's doorway to say my goodbyes. Dad kissed me and told me to be careful. Suzy hugged me while clutching the napkin on which I had written Felicity's address and phone number.

She whispered in my ear, "The coupon goes out tonight, Claire. We don't want to waste time."

I thanked her. Then I picked up the lasagna my father donated to the cause, *my stomach*, and drove away, calculating how long it would take for Felicity to respond. *If* she responded.

Chapter Six

The next morning, I crawled out of bed after a restless night full of dreams in which Suzy shaved my head.

After a shower and a brownie for breakfast, I felt ready to take on the world. Just not ready for Harold's call on my cell.

"Good morning, Claire." He sounded much too cheerful for this time of day. "Have you thought about that proposition I presented to you yesterday? Iola is anxious to know your answer."

I frowned. "Of course I've thought about it. Unfortunately, I can't say yes until I'm sure she's innocent." Corrigan and his reprimands echoed in my mind.

It was quiet on the other end only because the wheels in his mind were so well oiled they worked silently. "Very well. You have another day. Then the offer disappears."

I envisioned those dollars blowing out of my hand and Harold catching them on his horns and pitchfork. "Understood." I knew Harold would hold me to that deadline. Savvy as he was, he'd catch on if I tried to play him and his client.

I hurried to get to my office. On the way, I realized even if Felicity got the coupon today, it could be a few days before she'd respond and maybe a few more before her appointment. If Felicity cared about her appearance at her brother's funeral, she might be anxious to have her hair styled. I needed to find out when that was.

My office phone was ringing when I opened the door. It was Ed.

"Hey, kiddo. Every time I tried to call your cell it went into voicemail. Wanna catch breakfast at the Owl? I'll spring for it."

My stomach churned as if the brownie in it didn't want any greasy company. "Thanks. Too bad I already ate."

"Come on. Gimme a break. Meet me here."

I bit my lower lip. "What's wrong?"

"Nothing." He groused. "I'm just asking you to come to the Owl. Can't you just do this one simple thing?"

My face felt hot with shame. Ed had done so much for me. I could at least consent to this. "I'll be there in fifteen minutes." I could call Suzy from my car.

I hurried out of my office without even checking for messages. Not that I expected any. Business was as slow as cold maple syrup.

Ten minutes into my drive, my phone rang. To my surprise, it was Suzy. Dad must have given her my number.

"Claire? I hope this isn't too early to call. I just had to tell you what I did."

My stomach flipped. "What's that?"

She giggled like a preteen playing Truth or Dare. "I didn't mail the coupon to Felicity Dixon. I drove to her house late last night and stuck it in her mailbox. Later today I'll call her and follow up."

I gushed, "That's fantastic! Thank you so much."

"No problem. Have to run now. I need to get my client out from under the dryer."

I was still smiling when I pulled up to the Owl, a quintessential greasy spoon with its pleather seats and other 1960's décor.

Ed waved me down. "Over here."

I made my way past a table of men in Cleveland Indians baseball caps and slid into Ed's booth. "Okay, now what's so important you had to talk to me about it in person?"

He handed me a menu. "Like I said, my treat."

"Thank you." I took the glossy thing and set it down. "Now, tell me what's so important."

He took a packet of jam from the metal holder and fidgeted with it. *Was he quitting his part time job with me?* I leaned toward him. "What is it?" I held my breath.

"How would you feel about us being related?"

My eyebrows lowered. "Related? How?"

In answer, he pulled out a small, velveteen box and opened it. Nestled inside was a gold ring with a marquee-cut single diamond.

My hand flew to my gaping mouth. "You're proposing to Aunt Lena? When?"

Ed flushed. "After the dance contest tonight. Do you think she'll accept?"

If she was as shocked by Ed's proposal as me, anything could come out of her mouth. "Is she expecting the proposal so soon?" They'd only been seeing each other for seven months.

He snapped the lid shut. "When you're our age, you don't wanna wait." Ed was 48 and my aunt was 54. "At least I know what I want. There ain't no finer lady than Lena. Present company excluded."

I must've been wearing a mushy, oh-how-romantic expression because Ed lowered his eyes to the table. "Anyway, I wanted to tell you before I popped the question."

"I know you'll make her happy." *Will I have to call him Uncle Ed?*

I wondered how this change in Aunt Lena's life would affect my dad. Since Mom died, he and Aunt Lena spent a lot of time together. Sure, much of it arguing. But in a lot of ways they had each other to help bridge the gap my mother's death left. I was relieved Suzy was in Dad's life.

I sighed. All this romance reminded me of my last words with Corrigan. We were not exactly cooing to each other. Most relationships have a beginning. Then they either progress or end. Ours started fine and seemed to progress some. Since then it has gone backward and forward a few times. It seemed like being inside a rubber band. It's possible to stretch the relationship only so far before it snaps. Not only do you end up back where you started, the sting from the rubber hurts.

"You think she'll say yes?"

"I know Aunt Lena will give you the right answer." *How was that for non-commitment?* Now that was something in which I excelled. At least in the romance department. Every time I think I'm past the horrible fear I have with relationships after my former fiancé dumped me, it rears up. A moot point though, since I wasn't sure if Corrigan ever wanted to talk to me again.

Feeling stuck in place hit me hard until Ed interrupted my reverie. "Earth to DeNardo."

"Sorry, Ed. What were you saying?"

"I asked what's going on with your latest case. That writer. Anything you need from me?"

As if waiting for its cue, my phone rang. It was Suzy, telling me Felicity had just set up a hair appointment at 3 this afternoon. Her voice dropped into a confidential tone. "She also asked for the same discount for a friend."

I swallowed hard. "The friend's name isn't Marco, is it?"

"No." Before I could feel any relief, Suzy continued, "Charlotte Pusitano. Do you know her?"

"I don't think so." The tension I'd felt a moment ago doubled. "Unless..." I cut short my thinking out loud. Could this Charlotte be the waitress at Cicarelli's? No sense worrying Suzy. "Never mind. I'll be there at 2, okay?" I added, "Afterwards, let me know what I owe you." Maybe I could pay her back by sweeping her salon floor. Or borrow money from Dad. Heck, maybe I could even eliminate myself as the middleman and have Dad pay her directly. I snorted in disgust at my dire financial situation. Ed was staring at me.

"Either a case has you in knots or the smell in here doesn't appeal to you."

"A case. That critic's murder. Dixon."

"I read one of his reviews. Tore the writer apart. On a book I liked. I wanted to murder the guy myself."

When I blinked hard he asked, "What? You think I don't read?"

"I'm just surprised you knew who Dixon was."

The waitress showing up prevented me from offending Ed any further. When she left again, I changed the subject back to his proposal.

Although we spent the rest of the time discussing that

and the related dance contest, my mind whirled, thinking how to pull off this caper at Suzy's salon without anyone being the wiser. Corrigan would have me shipped to a deserted island if he knew. And if Marco found out what I was up to, I wouldn't have to worry about a new hairstyle. He would give me a crew cut starting at my neck.

When the check came, Ed reached for it. He pulled out a worn leather wallet and counted out the dollars. Looking down at the bill, he asked, "So what the hell's going on with you and Corrigan?"

My spine straightened. "What do you mean?"

Ed's eyes found mine. "You two are playing tug of war. One day one of you is gonna get tired of the game and let go. The other'll fall on their face, wondering what happened."

I folded my arms across my chest. "My relationship with Corrigan is not your concern." Realizing how rude my comment sounded, I back-pedaled. "I understand you're trying to help. The truth is, we're like chocolate cake and olives. Both are fine on their own, just not when they're together. We'll figure it out on our own."

Ed opened his mouth and raised his index finger to make a point, when a text came through for me.

It was Corrigan, asking if I could meet him at 10 for coffee at The Cup, a café in Gordon Square, a revitalized area of Cleveland. "Speak of the devil." I didn't answer right away. Was it business? An apology? Or had he discovered the fine line I was walking with this current case?

Ed was watching me with the stillness of a hawk. "Don't screw it up, kiddo."

Maybe Ed was right. Maybe I needed to give a little in my on-again, off-again relationship with Corrigan. I shook my head slightly to stop myself from focusing on him now. I'd think about him later.

"Thank you for breakfast, Ed." I lightly touched his hand. "My aunt's a lucky woman."

It could have been the bad lighting in the place, but I prefer to think he blushed.

Once outside the Owl, I patted Ed's arm. "Good luck with the dance contest. Hope you have even better luck with the proposal."

Ed patted the pocket into which he had slipped the ring. "Thanks. I got a feeling the evening will go as smooth as Kentucky Bourbon."

I smiled at that, and then again as I thought about my meeting with Corrigan. Last time we talked, it ended badly. I wondered if this one would too. Like drinking cheap whiskey, burns going down.

Chapter Seven

I got in my car and stared at my phone. After taking a deep breath, I replied to Corrigan. I had just enough time to get to The Cup before going to Suzy's salon.

All the way over to the coffee shop I rehearsed what to say. *Who was I kidding?* As soon as we started talking, all my neutral words would evaporate. Giving myself a pep talk, I lifted my chin and resolved to stay cool.

Entering The Cup, I spotted Corrigan sitting at a back table. I commanded myself to stay unruffled no matter what Corrigan said to goad me. I fixed a grin on my face and joined him.

"Glad you could make it, Claire." His tone was even.

"No problem. I *do* have to make it quick. I have a hair appointment." I sounded stiff, on guard.

"This won't take long." He would have been a great Sphinx. His face betrayed nothing, although he seemed relaxed enough.

I, on the other hand, was suddenly aware of how cold my hands were. "What is it?"

He played with the handle of his coffee cup. "We can't keep doing this."

I placed my hands between my knees to warm them. "What's that?"

"Fighting." He scooted his chair closer to me. "Every time you're involved in one of my cases, we tear down whatever we've built up. I'm not doing it anymore."

Did he mean we were totally done? I bit my lower lip so I wouldn't blurt out something nonsensical. Or worse, beg him to reconsider.

He continued, "I'm through lecturing you and trying to stop you from doing stupid things. I've decided—"

"What stupid things? Solving cases? That's my job, you know. And if you didn't act so high and mighty—"

He interrupted my tirade by leaning over, taking my face in his hands, and kissing me. Not a hard, smashed lips way, nor in a shut-me-up way. Rather, it was sweet and succinct. It made me hope we were going to be okay. His eyes remained closed for an instant after he released my lips.

The earthier side of me wanted to plant my mouth onto his once more. Thank God my self-control hadn't checked out. In fact, it stood on guard, wanting immediate clarification. I couldn't meet his eyes. "Was that a kiss goodbye?" Inside my head was a voice whispering, "No. Say no."

"No, not at all." He ran his fingers through his thick hair. "I care about you, so I may be too hard on you. Once in a while, that is."

Once in a while? "Go on." It was hard to breathe.

He hesitated a moment longer. "From now on, you do your job and I'll do mine. No interference from me. It can't be any other way if we want our relationship to work. We stay out of each other's way."

He leaned back in his chair as if he'd just solved the

Israeli-Palestinian conflict.

I wasn't sure how to respond. Admit I had feelings for him as well? What if this relationship ended up like my engagement to that cheating so-and-so, Justin? Left for a dental hygienist. Me crying on the floor of my bedroom closet. Memories of the hurt I felt when my fiancé jilted me flooded back and I went for flippancy. "You show you care by making my job harder?" *Stick with the topic, my investigations.*

He put his hands on my shoulders. "That's not my purpose. Even when I don't know what you're up to, I worry about you. So I guess you'll have to get used to it."

His touch warmed me. Still, I had doubts and my mind frantically slapped up roadblocks. "We'll always be at odds, like with the Adler and the Corozza cases."

"Yeah. You have to admit, though, both of those turned out fine."

I closed my eyes, trying to shut my mind down too. Another kiss might move the heat from my head to other areas. Too bad we weren't alone. My lips must have curled into a smile.

"Are we good?" The excitement on his face reminded me of a kid getting a puppy.

I nodded. "Do you want to meet me tonight at that dance contest Ed and Aunt Lena are in?"

He smirked. "Wouldn't miss it."

I checked the time then gathered my sweater and my purse. "I've got to go. See you around 7?"

"Yeah." A hint of doubt darkened his face. I knew what he wanted to ask.

Offhandedly I explained, "It really is a hair appointment." I didn't include anything about Felicity so maybe

I just skirted around the truth. Either way, I brushed my lips against his cheek and left him with the glass of soda I'd barely touched and a half-smile on his lips.

***

It took me a while to find Suzy's salon. It was located in a tiny detached former house near St. Emeric Hungarian Church in Cleveland. Parking was a challenge since doing the parallel kind wasn't one of my talents. I finally nabbed a spot three blocks away. Afraid Felicity would beat me there, I ran all the way. Inside the place, I almost plowed into the front counter.

"Whoa, girl." Suzy held up her hands. "You've got plenty of time."

I leaned against the Formica counter, covered with hair products for sale. Catching my breath, I glanced around the room. There were three hairdressing stations, each with a chair, mirror and storage space. Two shampoo bowls stood in the back of the room, where there was another doorway. Across from the stations were two giant chrome hairdryers, a restroom, and another counter with a coffeemaker and water cooler. With all this equipment in such a small room, it would only take a few steps to get from one part to another. In these close quarters, it would be easy to strike up a conversation with Felicity.

"Are you ready?" Suzy asked, whipping out a black nylon cape and slipping it over my shoulders.

I crossed my fingers. "Let's hope this works. Not all my ideas are good ones." I thought back to the dog-stalking case I'd been on earlier in my career.

"You're too hard on yourself." Suzy led me to the shampoo bowl. "Sit and lean back. We've got some time before your 'mark' comes in."

I sat straight. "She's not a 'mark'. She's a potential witness."

Suzy waved her hand. "Sorry. Your *witness*. I'll seat her at the station closest to the dryer."

"Then I'll sit in the dryer chair right by Felicity, like I'm waiting for you to work on my hair."

"Yeah. While I'm coloring Felicity's hair, I'll tell her I need to shampoo her friend. That'll give you some time alone with Felicity." Suzy's voice dropped into a conspiratorial tone. "See? I know the drill." Her smile revealed her pride in setting this up. She might have even been looking forward to the excitement.

Not me. My insides were trembling like a trailer in a tornado.

I leaned my head back so my neck rested on the black porcelain sink. Suzy wet my hair and doused it with vanilla-smelling shampoo. She had just begun massaging it in, when her fingers stopped. Her words were clipped. "Felicity and her friend are early."

I strained my neck and saw Felicity come in first. I gasped, horrified, upon seeing the woman who came with Felicity. Charlotte, the waitress from Cicarelli's. My plans to question Felicity were about to be washed away. I should have strategized better. Instead, in a loud whisper I said, "Quick, cover my face with something."

Suzy didn't miss a beat. First, she stepped in to block the view of both women. "Welcome, ladies. I'm Suzy and I'll be with you in a sec." She reached for a white jar, and plopped this viscous green stuff on my face and finished washing my hair. Barely moving her lips, she whispered, "Don't move until this facial mask dries." She wrapped a towel around my head. With a wink, she added in a normal voice, "There, now. Just relax."

Suzy directed Felicity to take a seat. Still tilted back, I couldn't see what was happening. So I ignored Suzy's instructions and lifted my head enough to see. Despite shifting this way and that, Charlotte blocked my view.

Suzy, smooth as mousse, slid a chair over next to Felicity and addressed Charlotte. "Have a seat. It's more comfortable than standing."

I had to give Suzy credit for thinking so well on her feet. Knowing she was trying this hard to help me made me warm to her a bit more.

Now I had a straight view of Felicity. She was unusual looking with her pale skin and angled grey, wolf-like eyes. Dark shadows under those eyes and frown marks in the corners of her mouth betrayed the stress she was no doubt under. She was fashion-model thin and slouched in the styling chair as if she didn't have enough energy to hold her spine straight.

While thus occupied, I felt Charlotte's gaze settle on me. I grabbed a magazine from a stack next to the sink and stared down at it as if committing to memory the article comparing methods of dusting furniture. The room turned quiet except for the soft strains of classical music. I never would have taken Suzy for a Mozart fan.

Suzy cleared her throat and in a just-making-conversation tone, began, "I'm glad you both came in. Felicity, I know you got one of my coupons. Is there some particular reason you came in today? A special occasion? Maybe some family function?"

Oh dear God. Suzy was starting the investigation without me. I popped out of my chair, my mouth open, ready to speak. To my dismay and discomfort, a clump of the drying mask dropped from the tip of my nose into my mouth. Surprised, I inhaled sharply and the piece lodged in my throat. I couldn't breathe. I began wheezing, unable to get any air. Close to hysteria, my hands flew to my neck.

My gasping for breath must have caught Charlotte's attention because she leaped from her chair. "I know the Heimlich maneuver." She spun me around so my back was to her and she wrapped her arms around me, digging into me with her fists.

Suzy cried, "I'll call an ambulance."

Before Suzy could do so, Charlotte pulled her fists into my abdomen and the offending piece of mask flew out of my mouth with so much force it landed on the back of the sink. I took a welcomed, ragged breath and turned, forgetting myself, to thank my rescuer. I didn't realize that during my coughing spasms and Charlotte's fist thrusting, much of the remaining mask had fallen off. Charlotte's sour, angry expression told me, loud and clear. My face was bare and the game was over. Maybe I did need that ambulance after all.

Charlotte's lips thinned and she poked me in the chest. "I know you. You're that woman asking all those questions at Cicarelli's." She stuck her face so close to mine I could tell where her liquid makeup ended. "What do you want with Lissie?"

Out of the corner of my eye, I could see Suzy grab a broom and take a warrior pose. "Okay, you two, walk away from each other or I'll use this."

I stepped back and hoped Charlotte would follow suit.

Instead she ripped off her nylon cape and threw it on a chair. "Lissie, we've been played. I told you nothing's ever free. Let's get the hell out of here."

Panic was about to loosen my tongue. Before I could do something undignified, like pleading, Felicity raised a limp hand. It reminded me of a Roman Emperor giving a half-hearted signal for life or death. "I need to look decent for my brother's funeral so I'm staying." Her eyes focused on me. "Why can't you people leave me alone?" Her voice broke and Charlotte, her arms opened to embrace Felicity, moved toward her friend. A shake of Felicity's head stopped her.

Her comfort and support rejected, Charlotte dropped her arms and turned on me. She hissed, "This is your fault. Poor Lissie has enough to deal with without you sticking your nose in her business."

Suzy spoke in a soft tone someone would use on a child who had scraped her knee. "Charlotte, let's wash your hair while Felicity's color sets."

They say music sooths the savage beast. Suzy's voice must have done the same to Charlotte because she followed Suzy to the sink. Being no fool, I gave Charlotte a wide path. I rubbed the front of my neck as if that would sooth my scratched and sore throat. "I'm just trying to find out who killed your brother, George."

Felicity, her eyes closed and her voice weary, asked, "What do you want?"

She looked so fragile that for a moment I was afraid if I questioned her she'd break. Against all PI rules of investigation, I asked, "Are you sure you're up to it?"

She rubbed her forehead. "If it'll stop you from bothering me, yes."

I perched on the edge of the chair Charlotte had used and began with an easy question. "Were you close with your brother?"

"He insisted we be." Her voice was controlled and

even. "If you're wondering, the police already have my whereabouts at the time of George's...murder."

So the police had questioned her. Not that I was surprised. Nor was I shocked Corrigan hadn't mentioned it to me. "Did George ever talk about Iola Taylor? Or did you know her?"

Twisting her mouth she said, "He thought she wrote slop. Which means nothing. My brother thought a lot of people were dreadful writers, including me."

"As an author that must have hurt."

She looked away. "I'm not, I mean, I'm not an author." She grabbed her handbag from the ledge, pulled out a wrapped mint, and slipped it into her mouth. "I wanted to be." Her cheeks sunk in even more as she sucked on the candy. "But *big brother* didn't think I had the talent."

No affection in her voice. Understandable. It followed, though, that if George was that big of a jerk to his sister, he was probably even nastier to other people.

Felicity continued. "Not surprisingly, I couldn't find an agent who disagreed with him." Her lips thinned. "So I accepted it. Iola, on the other hand, had a good reason to kill him. She had a career and he was ruining it." As if to herself she added, "Of course looking at it that way, there were lots of other people who'd want him hurt too."

She sat back as if she was done. I couldn't let that happen and leaned in toward her. "Like who?"

Biting down on her mint she confided, "Brother dear enjoyed gambling. Unfortunately, he lost more than he won, and he owed lots of people money."

Right away I thought of Marco and his boss, Michael Bucanetti. Two dangerous men to owe.

"It wasn't Marco if that's what you're thinking. In

fact, he tried to help George."

"How?"

"He negotiated to get my brother more time to pay up. Marco even gave him tips when George refused to stop gambling. Not that he took them. My brother always thought he knew better." She frowned. "He never accepted that all he really knew how to do better was rack up debts."

"Who did he owe?"

She dismissed my question with a wave. "Marco's real protective of me. He's making sure nobody comes after me for George's debts."

Nothing in my experience could paint Marco as a good guy, so I had to ask, "Why is he doing that?"

"We're in love. In fact, we're getting married next week. Marco doesn't want to wait."

I managed to choke out, "Congratulations."

"Thank you. Suzy, isn't it time to shampoo me?" Our conversation was obviously over.

While Suzy checked Felicity's hair, Charlotte followed carrying a towel and a chip on her shoulder as big as the shampoo bowl. She stared me down. "You oughta be ashamed of yourself, taking advantage of Lissie like this." She curled her upper lip. "If I was her, I'd have told you to go—"

Felicity's sigh halted Charlotte's tirade. "It's all good, Charlotte. Now, can we finish up the hair styling so I can go home? I have to get ready for the onslaught of visitors at the wake tomorrow. People who'll lie and say they liked George."

Once Felicity and her self-proclaimed protector, Charlotte, had their new hairdos, they departed but not before Charlotte threw me a look that cursed me and all my future children and pets. I put up a 'you-can't-scare-me' front, all the while wondering if my aunt knew how to cast off the *malocchio,* or evil eye. Not that I believed it in, but just to be safe.

No sooner had the two women closed the door behind them when Suzy turned to me. "Did you get what you needed?" She looked as hopeful and eager as a girl scout selling cookies.

That enthusiasm and her calm resourcefulness chipped away at my last bit of reservations about her. She did her best to help me, beyond just allowing me to use her salon. I gave her a quick hug. "I think so." I still needed time to process the information. At least now, though, I had something to chew on besides my nails.

Suzy returned my hug then sat me down in her styling chair. I was ready for a trim. Except once Suzy snipped off a long tress of my hair, I couldn't stop myself from grimacing. She either didn't notice or ignored it. "Are you going to that dance contest Ed and your aunt are in? Me and Frankie will be there, a front table."

"Brian and I are going." *If I'm not bald.* A few minutes went by and she was still snipping. Terrified of the result, I asked, "Are you almost done chopping? I mean, I've got some investigating to do."

"I bet. Look, I'm shaping, not chopping your hair. And yes, I'm almost done. A blow dry and you're ready. You and Brian should sit with us. You know, we can be like Ed and Lena's cheering section."

"Good idea. We will." I shifted in the chair. "It's okay if you don't blow dry it." I started to rise.

She applied gentle pressure on my shoulders. "Five more minutes. Honest-to-God."

What if at this moment Iola was languishing in jail

and George's real killer was wandering the streets? *While I was getting my hair done.* I crossed my left leg over my right and shook my foot. Then quickly reversed the position.

Suzy turned off the dryer. "*Voilà*, as they say."

I glanced at myself with my new extremely short, straight bob. My eyebrows shot up and still barely hid underneath my bangs. "Suzy! What did you do?" My hair barely covered my ears.

Suzy threw her shoulders back and defended her work. "It's a great cut and it looks good on you. It shows off those huge eyes of yours." She turned away from me and made a big show of cleaning her station.

Afraid I wounded her pride, I backtracked. "I only meant my hair is shorter than I've ever worn it." I tugged on the ends, as if that would make it longer. When she didn't respond, my regret over my outburst grew. "It'll just take me a little time to adjust. I mean, thanks, you did a nice job." After what she'd done to help me, I had no right to be upset about my hair. Despite never having been a good enough actor to sell bananas to a monkey, I hoped she bought what I said.

"And thank you for letting me use your place. You helped me so much. What do I owe you?" I wondered if she'd take a post-dated check.

Suzy finally looked at me again. "Nothing. I got to have an interesting day. Besides, Felicity gave me a good tip. Look." She pulled a $100 bill from her pocket. "Now go. I'll see you tonight." She fluffed my hair a bit and tsk'd, "And remember, your hair will always grow."

Chapter Eight

I sat in my car fiddling with my bangs, wondering if they *did* bring out my eyes.

A text came in from Corrigan, interrupting my hairdo inspection. He wondered if we could meet at the VFW Hall to watch Ed and Aunt Lena a little later. Remembering our agreement, I squelched the urge to ask him why. At the next light, I responded that it was okay. We'd meet at 7:15 at the front entrance.

This would give me more time to dig into George's gambling history. The learning process would start with a phone call I didn't want to make. In fact, I put off calling until I was in my office.

My nose wrinkled like it had detected something rotten as soon as my cousin, Anthony, answered his phone. We were related on my father's side, but rarely saw each other. He lived in the city of Gates Mills, in a neighborhood too ritzy to invite his less successful relatives. Fine with me, since he had made his money defending scum who drove fancy cars and wore expensive suits. Even after he became a corporate lawyer, he still associated with those unsavory characters he had managed to get declared innocent of nefarious acts of which they were, no doubt, guilty.

"Anthony, it's your cousin Claire."

"Claire." He nearly growled. "I swear to God if you weren't family I'd hang up on you."

I squeezed my eyes shut. "You heard about the Joey Corozza case?" Anthony had given me advice on that murder, all the while insisting his name be left out. I gathered that didn't happen.

"Hell yeah, I heard about it. Still catching flak."

My voice turned scared-kittenish. "I'm sorry. Nobody got it from me."

"Yeah, okay. I guess we're good."

I released a breath. "I'm glad to hear that because I just need a bit of information. Please."

"What kind of information?"

My words fell over each other. "George Dixon. Who did he owe?" Silence on the other end so long I thought Anthony had hung up. "Hello?"

"I'm still here. Oh, what the hell. For Uncle Frank's sake. Go talk to Tommy Columbo at the Beef and Brew. It's downtown, on 12th and Superior."

So relieved he decided to help me again, my words flooded forth. "Thank you! Thank you so much! I'll leave your name out of it, I promise."

"It doesn't matter this time. In fact, tell him I sent you. Tommy owes me plenty of favors."

I shuddered, thinking what my cousin did to earn those favors. "Great. Thank you again, Anthony."

"You're welcome. Make sure you tell your dad I said hello."

"I will. He'd love to see you." I almost bit my tongue off. My father called Anthony *pomposo,* pompous and self-important.

"Yeah, I'll set something up."

The vagueness in his voice told me he would do no such thing.

I realized I had enough time to either go home and change or to get to the Beef and Brew, then go from there to the VFW Hall. I opted for the Beef and Brew. I would be less than fresh, but maybe armed with more information on who killed George Dixon.

Aunt Lena, always with impeccable timing, called while I was driving down Interstate 90.

"Claire? Is that you?"

"Yes, Aunt Lena. You called me."

"Sorry, I'm just nervous about tonight. Ed is such a good dancer and I'm not. I almost wish he had another partner. Then again, I don't like the idea of any other woman with her arms around him."

I didn't want to picture that either. "You'll do fine." A big Buick cut in front of me and I hit the brakes. This wasn't the time to talk on the phone. I hated driving anyway, afraid of a flat tire, a breakdown, an accident. You name it. "I really can't talk now. I'm on I-90."

"You're always somewhere. I called to remind you about coming over and helping me get ready a little earlier. This is going to be a big night. I can just feel it."

My mouth formed an 'O.' Did she know Ed was going to propose? "What time?" With a sinking feeling I wondered if I'd have to put off seeing Tommy until tomorrow.

"The contest starts at 7:30, so…about 5:30?"

I didn't want to disappoint her. If I got my questions answered, I could scoot over to Aunt Lena's with enough time. "Okay. I'll be there. And please don't worry. You'll be the dancer everyone wants as their partner. See you soon."

Ten minutes later, I was cruising for a parking spot by Beef and Brew. After several times, I parallel parked, crookedly of course, and entered the pub.

A guy in the lounge waved and shouted. "Lunch is over. You're still welcome to sit in here."

I smiled and approached the dark wood-and-brass bar and lifted myself onto a stool. "I'm looking for Tommy Columbo. Is he here?"

"You're talking to him." The bartender smiled, showing teeth too perfect to be real. The grin disappeared. "Who sent you?" His hand reached below the bar and I was sure he was going for a weapon.

My words shot from my mouth like bullets from a machine gun. "Anthony DeNardo. I'm his cousin, Claire. He said to talk to you. He said you'd talk to me. Will you talk to me?" I stopped myself realizing I sounded like one of those old-fashioned dolls where you pulled the string and they recited phrases.

"Yeah, okay. What's your pleasure?" It turned out he'd been reaching for a drink menu.

"Diet soda, please. And some information."

"Diet soda coming up. Info, it depends."

If I had to grease his palm, I was out of luck. The closest thing I had was some lip balm. "On what?"

"On what you want to know."

"George Dixon. Who did he owe money to?"

Tommy filled a glass with ice and poured the soda into that same glass. "Dixon? That ain't the question to ask. The one to ask is who *didn't* he owe? Word was he couldn't get a loan if he put up his soul for collateral. And trust me, lots of guys around here needing a soul."

I took a sip of my diet soda to mask my frustration.

"All right, but who was the biggest debt holder?"

Tommy picked up a swizzle stick and rolled it between his fingers. Likely, he was a smoker or a recent former smoker. "Sorry, that's all I know." He handed me my bill. "Give my regards to Anthony."

$12.00 for a diet soda. I almost fell off my seat. No wonder I'd never been to this place before. I gave him my credit card, hoping I was enough under my limit to cover the drink and a tip.

He stepped away to run my card and then handed it back to me, along with the receipt, on which he'd written, "Thanks for coming."

I jammed my credit card and the receipt into my purse, nodded a farewell, and left. I stuck out my lower lip and exhaled deeply. I still didn't have enough information to show if Iola was innocent, and Harold would be calling me in the morning to discuss my decision. I kicked a piece of gravel and instantly looked around, feeling foolish.

It was time to get to Aunt Lena's house, but my keys weren't in my purse's side pocket, their usual place. I rested against my car digging around for them. In so doing, the Beef and Brew receipt fell out. On the back, Tommy had scrawled the name, Martin Beckman. He must not have felt safe saying the name aloud. Was I brave enough to find this guy by myself?

Probably not. I could mull it over while I drove to Aunt Lena's.

I located the keys at the bottom of my purse, jumped inside the car, and stepped on the gas.

Chapter Nine

Aunt Lena was waiting for me, her hair in rollers. I suppressed a grin. I didn't think anybody still used those things. She had her dress on but it was open in the back.

She was fanning herself. "It's like an oven in here." She wiped her forehead. "Zip me up."

"Okay, just first take a couple of deep breaths. It's just nerves."

She inhaled and I pulled the zipper closed. "Now turn around and let me see how you look."

Aunt Lena spun around. "Well?" Her dress was *where-are-my-sunglasses* pink with a fitted bodice. It ended in a full, multilayered flared skirt landing mid-calf. The see-through half-sleeves hid her plump upper arms.

I beamed like a parent watching their kid go to the prom. "You look wonderful."

She dismissed my compliment with a wave of her hand. "No I don't. I look like a baked ham. All I need is a glaze."

I stifled a chuckle. "Let's fix your hair. And smile. You've got a big night ahead of you." I could have slapped myself for that last comment. I didn't want my aunt to figure out there was more to tonight than a contest. Luckily she was too wrapped up in her stage fright to notice.

"I should've gone to the beauty parlor." She started ripping the curlers from her hair.

I tsk'd. "Here, let me do that before you tear out your hair." My phone rang just then.

"Go ahead, answer it. Maybe it's Ed wanting you to tell me he's cancelling." She sounded almost hopeful.

It wasn't Ed. "Hello, Claire. It's Harold. Iola's out on bail. And I wanted to remind you tomorrow morning we need your decision. Will you assist Iola in finding the real killer or not?"

My mind was happy she was no longer in jail, but my gut refused to join in the celebration. "I'm busy right now. We'll talk tomorrow." It looked like I would be doing some investigating after the contest.

"Excellent. I'll contact you in the morning. Have a pleasant evening."

Aunt Lena was studying me. "What answer? Are you gonna do something you shouldn't?"

I looked up at the ceiling and exhaled. "Don't you have enough to worry about? It's nothing, just business."

"Oh, sure. Like with those hoodlums from the East side? That kind of business?" She was referring to a previous investigation and not, I hoped this one.

I didn't want to tell her this case would probably feature more than one hoodlum, maybe a whole bunch of them. No need to worry her or for me to think about it. Tonight was going to be about family and perhaps a new addition to ours. Ed.

"No, not at all. It's a case concerning an author."

My aunt turned toward me. "The one charged with

killing that critic? That one?" She lowered her voice. "That woman writes smut. Naked people beating each other. With a mind like that, who knows what she's capable of?"

"Aunt Lena, those stories are fiction. Anyway, how do you know about them?"

"Angie brought one into the bakery." She pointed her finger at me. "If your Uncle Tommy ever tried to smack me he'd have learned a rolling pin isn't just for pie crust."

I shook my head. "Fine. Now you wanted me to come over. Let me fix your hair. Then while you're putting on your makeup I'll pick earrings to go with your outfit. We better hurry or we'll be late." She fanned herself. "Even that name, Iowa is—"

"Her name is Iola, not Iowa. Can we drop it?"

Aunt Lena harrumphed.

I put eyeliner on her as a final touch and she was ready. All the way to the VFW Hall, she stared out the window not saying a word. I'd never seen my aunt so quiet. We pulled into the hall's parking lot. "Are you okay?"

She didn't have a chance to answer because Ed had his hand on the passenger side door and almost pulled it off its hinge. "I got worried you wouldn't show." He helped my aunt out of the car and whistled. "There oughta be a law against a woman looking as good as you, Lena."

She giggled and squeezed his hand. "You're not so bad yourself." Ed had on a grey sports jacket. His shirt was the same color as Aunt Lena's dress.

I smiled. *Such a cute couple.* "You two go ahead. I'll find Dad and Suzy."

I didn't get far when Corrigan called to me and I ambled over to him. To my surprise and delight, he kissed me. And not one of those 'Nice-to-see-you' pecks where the emotion is almost expected and then disappears immediately after lips part. It was more like an 'I-wanna-be-with-you' kiss. If a heart could grin, mine would have.

He cleared his throat. "Sorry I couldn't pick you up. Police business." I caught myself before I asked him if it was about George Dixon's murder or Iola getting out on bail.

I squeezed his hand. "That's okay. You're here now."

"And you, looking great with your new style." *Maybe my haircut wasn't so bad.* He twirled me around. I felt like a little girl and wondered if he'd pat me on the head. Instead, he kissed me once more and we entered the VFW Hall side-by-side.

We found Dad and Suzy at a table toward the front of the dance floor. My father was handsome in what appeared to be a new charcoal-colored suit. It fit well so Suzy must have picked it out. Left to himself, Dad's clothes would be one size too big. He claimed that's what made them comfortable. When I tried to compliment him on his appearance, he smoothed his shirt and looked down. "Save the praise for Suzy. She's the whiz with style. Not to mention looks."

Suzy wore a strapless black number and looked ready for the Academy Awards' red carpet or to play hostess at a Las Vegas casino. It certainly showed off curves I only thought possible in comic books. Even Corrigan did a double-take. Of course, he coughed into his hand to cover his stare. He didn't fool me. I couldn't blame him, though. She did look eye-catching.

Dad took Suzy's hand and lifted it as if she had won a boxing match. The affection on his face for her was mutual. I realized at that moment, how important Suzy had become to both of us. She had helped me and gone out of her way to be my friend. All unnecessary, but appreciated. My dad had not been this happy since my mom died. Suzy would never replace my mother. I didn't think she wanted that anyway.

Corrigan saved me from getting all misty-eyed by asking me what I wanted to drink.

As soon as he sat down with the cocktails, the contest commenced. Ed and Aunt Lena were third in a field of five. The first couple waltzed and jitterbugged as if they had been doing so all their lives. The second two was just as good, and I worried about Aunt Lena's lack of confidence.

At last, Ed and my aunt burst upon the dance floor. I held my breath and even crossed my fingers under the table. I needn't have worried. Ed's moves were as smooth as melted Gouda and he spun Aunt Lena around so that together they moved with the coordination and grace of a butterfly's wings...until their dance number ended in a step in which my aunt threw herself into Ed's arms. I don't know exactly what happened. All I could say is that at first, Ed caught her and even managed to lift her up. But he lost his footing and stumbled backwards. Both of them crashed into the fourth couple, knocking them over as if this was a bowling tournament.

Audience members, including my dad and Corrigan rushed to help. Thus began the melee, with a few supporters of couple number four yanking Ed off the woman. I couldn't tell who threw the first punch. Not that it mattered. Soon fists were meeting faces and bellies. Corrigan, his shirt torn and a scratch on his face, extracted himself, then pulled Dad, Ed, and Aunt Lena out. While she had no injuries, Dad's new jacket was torn, and Ed had the beginnings of a great shiner. Without the four of them, the fight seemed to lose its energy. The sound of sirens got the remaining brawlers' attention and the fighting petered out until those who still had intact chairs and tables sat, while the others leaned against the walls.

The manager, who had rushed to call the police, backed down when they arrived, claiming he'd called them in error. When they left, he rubbed his face hard and snarled, "Thanks to me, you's guys won't be hauled off to jail, but," his arm swept across the area, "somebody's gotta pay for this mess."

To my surprise and relief, the man from dance couple number five agreed to pay the damage, claiming, as he rubbed his jaw, that he'd had a great time.

It seemed everyone else was also relieved. That is, everyone except my aunt. Her hair, stiff with hairspray stuck out in every direction and her eye makeup ran down her face and almost met the lipstick smear on her cheek. All of this giving her the appearance of an escapee from a horror movie. "Aunt Lena, are you okay?"

"No, I'm not." Her voice raw. "Claire, would you take me home? *Now?*"

Ed, holding a glass of ice to his eye, said, "Lena, I'll take you."

My aunt stiffened, "No thank you. Claire?"

I guessed there'd be no marriage proposal that night. "Of course."

Ed's eyes darted from Aunt Lena to me and back. He reached for my aunt's arm to no avail. She had drawn herself in.

My dad and Suzy stayed with Ed while Corrigan walked my aunt and me to my car. *So much for romance, Aunt Lena's or mine.* I gave Corrigan a wistful smile.

On the way home, my aunt stared out her window. Besides the motor, the only noise in my car was my aunt sniffling. I wanted to reassure her, but I had no clue as to the issue. "Are you upset because of the fight? Nobody got really hurt. Or arrested."

"That's not it." Aunt Lena didn't even look my way.

I was stumped. "What is it then? It might help to talk about it."

She gestured like a frustrated conductor. "I'm just a fat, old woman. I made Ed collapse. And I don't want to talk about it." Once we reached her house, she declined my company and rushed to her door, closing it quickly behind her.

I slapped the steering wheel as if I was responsible for my aunt's love life. I shifted in my seat and stepped on the gas, feeling restless and distraught. Going home would only make it worse. I needed to do something worthwhile. I headed to my office. Maybe I could find something on that loan shark, Martin Beckman. At least I could help Iola and if she wasn't involved in Dixon's murder, my malnourished bank account.

Chapter Ten

An insistent knock at my office door woke me. I must have fallen asleep searching for the elusive Mr. Beckman. I needed more than the few pieces of information I'd found and wondered if another visit to Tommy Colombo was in order.

Corrigan stood at my door when I unlocked and opened it. His half-smile was pure smart aleck. "I see you've been sleeping with your keyboard again."

"At least I'm monogamous."

He stifled a laugh. "I wanted to make sure you were all right."

I tilted my head. "Why wouldn't I be? Do you mean because of last night?" I caught myself before I exhaled deeply. My tongue felt like it was wearing a wool coat. I needed to brush my teeth, but settled for covering my mouth. "I wish it hadn't happened, and I'm glad nobody was hurt. At least physically. I better go see my aunt today. I wonder if she's at *Cannoli's* this morning. What are you smiling at?"

"You look cute all messy like that."

Cute? "I'd prefer to be mesmerizing or fascinating."

He leered at me. "Wish I could stick around to learn *how* fascinating. Unfortunately, I have a wake to go to."

The light in my head turned on. "Dixon? Ohmygod, I forgot."

Corrigan's contented look disappeared. "You were thinking of going?"

My hands on my hips, I asked, "Why not?"

As if our recent talk just popped into his head, he held up his hands like he was surrendering. "Nothing. I better go or I'll be late." Without another word, he left.

This agreement we'd made to stay out of each other's way wouldn't be as easy as it sounded. Still, I liked it. Not arguing made for a much more pleasant day.

I calculated how much time I had and hurried out the door. I hoped to make it to the internment long before the minister said amen.

I arrived at the cemetery just as someone was standing at the head of Dixon's grave, reciting a poem. Charlotte, standing at the foot of the grave spotted me and frowned. To my relief she made no move toward me. Corrigan, his hands folded in front stood a respectful distance behind the grievers. He nodded a greeting but made no effort to join me.

Dixon's sister leaned into Marco, her head buried in his chest. His eyes narrowed when he spotted me. He whispered something in Felicity's ear and she straightened. Her face, puffy from crying turned wary.

Another speaker moved to the head of the grave while Marco stared at me and ground his fist into the palm of his other hand. Although I was sure he imagined his palm was my head, I stayed put. He would not kill me in front of Corrigan. I tried to tell that to my heart, which was beating so hard it sounded like the rhythm section of a band.

Corrigan took note of Marco's gestures then crooked his finger, beckoning me to follow him. He stopped when we reached the drive. Believing he was going to lecture me, I jumped in, mouth first, brain second. "You don't need to worry. I can handle Marco."

The vein in his forehead made like a worm. "He looked ready to put you to rest."

I licked my lips. "I'm not always the damsel in distress. I don't need you to sweep in and rescue me."

"My mistake." I thought he'd stop there remembering our agreement. He didn't. "I'm just telling you that guy means to hurt you."

I didn't want to fight and hoped he didn't. "Okay. Let's get back there."

We both returned, with Corrigan on one side of the mourners and me on the other. The ceremony ended soon after without further incident. The crowd began to disperse, except for Marco and Felicity, who lingered close to the grave.

I stayed put in case Corrigan wanted to talk, but he was staring at his phone, texting. I hesitantly took a couple of steps closer to the couple for a better view. Felicity was leaning over the grave, touching the coffin for the last time. Marco was looking down at her when two loud bangs in quick succession cracked the silence. Marco twitched and fell.

Chapter Eleven

I froze until Felicity's agonized scream pushed me into action. Crouching down, I began to move toward her. Corrigan pulled his gun, yelled at me to stay down, and dove at Felicity to shield her with his body.

The second the shooting stopped, Corrigan took off in search of the killer. I made my way on trembling legs to Felicity to offer what reassurances I could. Charlotte, who had left along with the rest of the mourners, came out of nowhere and flew to Felicity and me. Felicity resisted both of us, dropped to her knees and cradled Marco's body. None of us moved until the police and ambulance arrived.

Although the authorities lost no time getting to the scene, Marco was dead before he touched the ground. Despite the police talking to everyone at the burial, nobody admitted to seeing anything or anyone unusual. It took Charlotte and an EMT to separate Felicity from Marco's body. Despite my knowledge of Marco as a murdering scumbag, sympathy tears sprang to my eyes as I watched them tear her from the man she loved.

Felicity was taken to the hospital for an ankle injury,

probably sustained when Corrigan pushed her down so she wouldn't be shot. Charlotte insisted on going with her. Just as well. Felicity's emotional injury, to my way of thinking, would be harder to treat than her ankle.

Once the ambulances sped away, I sat on the curb, with my chin resting on my chest, my arms wrapped around my middle. Corrigan joined me and placed his hand on my back.

"How are you doing?"

I pushed my bangs from my forehead. "I've been better, but I'll live. Too bad Marco won't." A twinge of guilt for being so flippant about a death vanished when I realized Marco could no longer make good on his threats to my family's wellbeing should I go public with information on him and Michael Bucanetti. Maybe it was this realization or trauma from what had just happened. I don't know. I broke out in giddy laughter and could not stop.

Corrigan enveloped me in his arms and rocked me as if I was a child awakening from a bad dream. I clung to him for a moment, ignoring the idea that a hardcore PI doesn't fall apart at a shooting that wasn't even directed at her.

I slowly pulled away and wiped my face. "Thanks. I'm a big girl. I've seen worse."

Corrigan's voice was tender. "Sometimes it's the ones you think won't bother you that do."

Before I could respond, a uniformed cop approached and informed Corrigan they had found a shell casing next to one of the mausoleums. Corrigan squeezed my hand, then stood, brushed off his trousers and left with the other policeman.

Since I had already given my statement, I was free to

go and made my way to my car, thinking of returning to my office. The truth was I was too shaken to think straight so I headed to *Cannoli's* instead. My nerves screamed out for one of my aunt's rich chocolate éclairs to help me clear my head. At least, that's what I told myself. In reality, what I really wanted was not to be alone.

On my way there, I remembered something I should not have forgotten. *Iola was out on bail.* Could she have been lurking around at the gravesite, waiting for a clear shot? Of whom? Was that bullet meant for Felicity instead of Marco? If so, why? Another thought popped into my head. Did Martin Beckman, the loan shark, or any other debt collector want Marco killed for interfering in Dixon's gambling?

With each spin of these thoughts, my head throbbed. With a sigh, I realized I didn't have time to be comforted by my aunt and her éclairs.

When my phone rang, I half-way hoped it was Corrigan, checking up on me again. It was Ed, who was more concerned with Aunt Lena than in discussing my case.

Although he had sworn off smoking a while ago, he sounded like he could use a cigarette. "Lena won't see me. Will you talk some sense into her? I know she's embarrassed about the contest, but hell, that was my mistake, not hers."

My heavy heart got heavier." Just a minute, Ed. I'm pulling off the road to talk."

I turned into a fast food parking lot, and closed my eyes. Relationships were so fragile it was frightening. I thought of Marco and Felicity, of Corrigan and me and now Ed and Aunt Lena. "I want you both to be happy, so I'll try. Just not this minute. I have to…I've got to find somebody."

"Who?"

"A loan shark named, Martin Beckman. Once I learn where he hangs out, I'll need you to come with me." In truth, I needed his courage since I had none.

"You want to talk to Marty Beckman? Are you serious? You don't have the money to be playing the ponies."

"Come with me. Afterwards, I'll talk to Aunt Lena."

"Kiddo, I've been pushed down stairs, hit in the head and now maybe getting my heart broken. Before I do anything, I need the lowdown here. Beckman is not, I repeat, not the guy you want to just drop in on. I had a buddy who owed him. Beckman smashed his nose, then his hand. The guy breaks bones like other people say hello."

I took in a deep breath and exhaled. "A client, well sort of client, is charged with a murder. Beckman..." My next words caught in my throat and my cheeks were wet. I lowered the phone from my ear and sobbed, first softly then louder until I heard Ed yelling over the phone if I was okay. I swallowed hard. "Yeah, I have to go, Ed." I hung up before he could protest. My sobs began anew.

I sat in my car for another fifteen minutes hoping to pull myself together. My phone rang again.

"Listen kiddo," Ed's voice was stern. "I'll help you find Beckman. Just don't cry anymore. Deal?"

"I wasn't crying because..." I waved my unengaged hand in the air. "Never mind. Deal. You seem to know a lot about Beckman. Where do we find him?"

"You sure you want to do this?"

"Yes, I'm sure." I sounded as eager as a prisoner asking the hangman if he knew how to tie a knot.

He paused then exclaimed, "Hey, Lena's on the line.

I'll get back to you."

This time, he hung up on me. Maybe I wouldn't get to meet Beckman today, but there was someone else I needed to talk with. Iola.

I called the numbers she had provided when she hired me. Even though her voicemail was full, there was still another way to reach her.

"Harold, it's Claire. Where's Iola? I need to talk with her."

No matter what the situation, Harold, in his barely post-pubescent boy's voice, always seemed to have it under control. "Why? Are you ready to work for her again?"

"First, hear me out." I described the general picture of what had happened at George Dixon's burial.

"Um, hm." *Why didn't he seem surprised?*

"I appreciate your telling me, Claire. And it just so happens, I'm on my way to the police station. They brought Iola in for questioning about that aforementioned event. Of course, she's innocent of that crime. Just as she's innocent in Mr. Dixon's unfortunate demise."

"Spoken like a true lawyer."

He chuckled. "A leopard doesn't change its spots and I don't profess to be anything except an attorney who wants justice for his client. You can be part of this. Iola still wants you on her side."

"Why is she so interested in my help? There're plenty of good private investigators out there."

"She liked your sincerity."

I would as soon trust a man selling snake oil as believe Harold.

"We still need your answer. Yes or no."

I acknowledged my gut's instinct to steer away from

this case, while still recognizing that my brain's argument was more convincing. I liked having my own PI business, and I didn't want to turn it back over to Gino. Giving up on Iola meant giving up on my independence.

"I promise you'll get my answer tomorrow. Bye, Harold." I ended the call, hoping Iola was cleared of Marco's murder. If they had enough to charge her, I would have to give up any possibility of working for her. Just like, I would give up the idea of my own PI firm. Gino's return to take back the business was the root of this conflict. Whenever I pictured myself saying 'my *boss*, Gino' my jaw clenched.

I pounded on the dashboard in frustration, knowing I couldn't depend on what the police determined. That could take days, weeks even. On the other hand, talking to Martin Beckman could turn up something. Thinking about what Ed had said about the guy, I checked my nose in the rearview mirror, hoping when my visit was over I wouldn't look like a boxer who'd lost the match.

Back at my office, I realized I couldn't very well find Beckman without knowing what he looked like. I returned to what little information I'd found. One of the pieces included small photos. *How did I miss these?* One had Beckman standing alongside Michael Bucanetti, Marco's boss. For living in New Jersey, this mobster seemed to spend a lot of time in Cleveland. Another photo had Beckman at Whistledown racetrack. I had gone to the track a couple of times just to watch the horses and the people. Never to bet. Gambling on horses wasn't my thing. I gambled every day that I would have enough money to pay the rent. That was enough for me. I recognized the area where the picture was taken. I clasped and unclasped my hands, wondering if I should wait for Ed to call back.

After ten minutes, I grabbed my purse, threw in three chocolate cashew clusters for fortitude, and sped over to Whistledown. I wasn't sure if Beckman would be there, or what to say to him, but I had to do something. I bit into one of the chocolates for inspiration.

***

Being Saturday and with the adjacent casino going full steam, Whistledown was busier than ever. After trolling for ten minutes looking for a parking spot, I hiked to the front gate along with at least twenty other people hoping not to lose their shirts. Me, I was hoping not to lose my life.

Once inside the gates, I headed toward the area I recognized in the photo. Chances weren't great Beckman would be in that spot, but I had to start somewhere.

Luck did not favor me. Beckman was nowhere to be seen. I slouched against a pole and chomped down on the second chocolate piece. Now thirsty, I pulled out my wallet, which contained $1.32 and a button. Swallowing my pride, I found the least busy concession stand and bargained with the guy for half a cup of a diet cola. As I crumpled the empty cup to toss out, I felt someone's eyes on me. It was Martin Beckman.

Surprised, I busied myself with the racing schedule I picked up. Had he been watching me all this time? If so, like a not-too-bright finalist in a spelling bee, I couldn't understand how I'd gotten this far. My plan had been to locate and observe him, not the other way around. After I was sure I wouldn't be interrupting him in the middle of committing a crime, my plan was to question him.

Beckman's companion, who was big enough to double as a door, approached me. Sounding like he'd had his nose broken more than once, he said, "Mr. Beckman over there wants to know if you'd like to join him in his box seats."

Surprise gave way to fear and I stalled. "Are you sure he meant me?" My voice came out Mickey Mouse squeaky.

"You wanna come or not?" The glint in his eyes told me turning Beckman down would be unwise.

"If you put it that way, I'd love to join your friend." I followed him to where his boss was standing.

Beckman held out his delicate hand. His long fingers wrapped around mine. "Hello. I'm Martin Beckman. You wanted to meet me?"

Chapter Twelve

My eyes opened wide and without thinking, I stepped back. "How did you know?"

He wore a predatory smile. I could almost swear he sharpened his teeth into points. "Let's discuss it in more comfortable surroundings." He nodded at his goon to help me find my way to his box seats.

"Please, sit down." Beckman motioned to a folding chair and I collapsed into it before my shaky legs could give out. He primly lowered himself into the seat next to me and crossed his legs. "Now, why are you here?"

Sometimes words shoot out of my mouth like cannon balls. This wasn't one of those times. My throat turned dry and my words stuck in my gullet. All I managed was a croaking noise.

"Dennis, go down and get the lady some water."

Beckman's muscleman, growling under his breath, left on his errand. My heart beat to the sound of his footsteps. Despite the usual noises of a racetrack, the silence between Beckman and me was ear splitting.

Dennis returned and thrust the cup of water at me, his dark eyes daring me to refuse. Since I'm neither brave nor crazy, I took the water and drank to the last drop.

If a snake could smile, it'd look like Beckman. "Let's start again. Why are you here? Please don't insult me by saying it's to gamble."

"I don't know..."

"Ms. DeNardo. Can I call you Claire?" Without waiting for an answer, he continued in a light tone, as if we were discussing the lunch menu. "A certain restaurant's bartender learned it's not wise to keep secrets."

Dennis cracked his knuckles. I wondered if he'd cracked Tommy Columbo's head, the bartender from Beef and Brew.

Beckman continued, "You want some information on George Dixon? Here it is. He owed me money...A lot of money. But a dead man don't pay his debts. End of story."

I nodded like a bobble head version of myself. "But Marco Conti was killed too and—"

His face clouded and his voice turned to ice. "Dennis, help this lady out of here."

Dennis grabbed my arm. When I hesitated, he twisted it and I winced.

A familiar voice came from an adjacent box. "Drop her arm or I'll drop you." It was Ed. He'd been there for I don't know how long, with his head buried in a racing form.

Through clenched teeth, Beckman asked, "Who the hell are you?"

Dennis snarled and didn't let go. He cast his eyes toward his boss.

Another person announced, "He's with me." That voice I would have known in my sleep. Corrigan. I hadn't noticed him leaning against a nearby pole. Like

Ed, he'd hidden his face behind a racing form. He flashed his badge. "Now, let's all play nice."

Beckman nodded at Dennis and the thug dropped my arm. I rubbed the feeling back into it, wondering if the ache in my shoulder would ever go away.

Ed joined me. "Come on, Claire. Let's go to the ground floor."

Staying there for the final act would have been futile. Neither Corrigan nor Beckman said another word. They both seemed to be waiting for my departure.

On our way down I asked Ed, "How did you know where I'd be?"

He held his explanation until we were almost to the concession stands. "You told me you wanted to find Beckman. I said I'd help. Folks in the know, know where Beckman hangs out. Simple." He glanced at my bruising arm and hung his head. "I should've paid more attention so you wouldn't have come here by yourself. As you found out, I wasn't lying. The guy's dangerous, and that hood with him looks like a loose cannon, a mountainous loose cannon."

"Don't feel bad, Ed. I was taking care of myself." My ego was just as bruised and it stopped me short of thanking Ed.

"Sure you were."

I crossed my arms, but the left one still ached, so I dropped them both to my side. "Did you call Corrigan?"

He brightened. "Funny how that worked. He claimed he was already on his way over here to question Marty Beckman about some guy who got assaulted."

My stomach dropped. "Was it Tommy Columbo?"

"I don't know." He peered at my face. "You know, you don't look so hot. Let's find you a bench."

We located one by the entrance and I sat down, lowering my head into my hands. *What if Dennis beat my name out of Tommy?* Ed offered to get me some water. I declined, craving a chocolate martini instead.

Less than ten minutes later, Corrigan spotted us and hurried over. As soon as he was within hearing distance, I asked, "Did Dennis beat up a bartender named Tommy Columbo?"

"Not that I've heard. I'm here investigating an assault on the owner of a bowling alley. Beckman claims he and that gorilla who works for him are peace-loving guys and the victim just had an 'accident.' He paused. "Now, please, tell me. What made you think you could handle Beckman alone?"

While I was relieved Tommy didn't receive a beating because of me, I was still angry at his betrayal. *And I even tipped him.* "I wasn't here to 'handle' him. I could have though." I didn't tell Corrigan I had my gun with me but forgot to load it. "I wanted to know more about Dixon's gambling debts."

Corrigan looked up at the ceiling beams. Then he pulled out his old reliable notepad. "Let's see." He ran his index finger down a page. "Here. Both Beckman and his pal were attending a preview at the Playhouse when Dixon was killed. Dozens of witnesses." His eyes narrowed. "We've got Dixon's murderer. You even saw Iola Taylor leave the scene of the crime."

I stuck out my lower lip far enough to blow air into my super-short bangs. "What about Marco's murder?"

Corrigan shut his notepad and in slow motion, stuck it back into his suit pocket. "Don't tell me you think it was a coincidence Marco was shot while Iola was out on bail." I started to protest. He just talked over me. "Let me finish. To be thorough, I did get the whereabouts of Beckman's ape at Marco's time of death. Says he was at his mother's house. We'll check it out. Satisfied?"

I slouched on the bench, my arms around my middle as if all the stuffing in me had been pulled out. Then a thought occurred to me. If Corrigan was so convinced Iola committed both murders, why was he coming here to question Beckman instead of trying to get a confession from Iola? Didn't that take precedence over an assault case? I massaged my temples. It didn't make sense. Yet.

Ed, who had been listening to Corrigan and me, said, "You two can finish hashing it out. I told Lena I'd be over at *Cannoli's* in..." He checked his watch. "Twenty minutes. If I leave now, I might only be five minutes late."

Just as he turned away, I remembered my manners. "Thanks, Ed. And good luck."

He twisted around, saluted me, and continued on his way.

Corrigan and I, tired of sparring, sat on the bench in silence. Despite acting as if I didn't need help, I was happy to see him. When he covered my hand with his and intertwined his fingers with mine, I got a nice warm feeling and could not keep a smile from my face. It must have been contagious, because he could not stop it from taking over his visage either. We remained like that for several minutes.

We couldn't stay like that forever. Sure enough, questions I needed answers to spoiled the moment. "What if Dixon's murder wasn't related to Marco's? I mean, Iola had a motive for killing Dixon. But what would be her motive for killing Marco? "

"Maybe she was aiming for Felicity Dixon. You

know, dispose of the whole family.''

I disengaged my hand from his. "Come on, if you believed that you wouldn't have asked about Dennis's whereabouts. Marco must have had plenty of enemies.''

Corrigan didn't disagree, so I pushed harder. "You just brought Iola in as a formality. You think someone else killed Marco.''

He placed both hands on the tops of his thighs. "Remember our agreement. I stay out of your business and you stay out of mine. It's time for me to get back to work. Come on. I'll walk you to your car.''

We made our way across the parking lot without talking. Every time I thought to break the silence, I stopped myself, reluctant to start the tug of war at which we were so good. When we arrived at my car, he kissed me as if he wanted his lips to linger on mine all day. Not a bad idea.

I turned the ignition without putting my car in gear. Instead, I let my thoughts go where they might. They returned to Dixon's murder. He may have owed a lot of people, but Beckman's comment about a dead man's inability to pay made sense. Unless, Dixon's actual death was a mistake, an error in estimating how much punishment the man could take. Someone inexperienced in the fine art of killing probably wouldn't be able to gauge that. So then, it most likely was not Beckman or another of his ilk who killed Dixon.

If nonpayment of a debt wasn't the reason for Dixon's death, what was? Why would somebody kill a critic if not for money? The clouds in my brain cleared. Maybe Dixon was killed because he seemed to specialize in tearing people down, even his own sister. The killer most likely had suffered a blow to his or her ego and that affected their income. That could mean the killer stood to suffer a loss of income if Dixon was allowed to destroy their reputation.

I needed to read more of Dixon's reviews. If he tried to destroy Iola, maybe he did the same to others. I pushed the uneasy feeling I had about her presence at Dixon's house to the back of my mind. It refused to stay there and rested atop my stiff shoulders.

***

Two hours later, I had read enough of Dixon's venomous critiques to wonder why the man lived as long as he had. Of the many he had skewed with the tip of his pen, one author besides Iola stood out. Jon Willemy wrote a series of unauthorized biographies. Like Iola, he was local. Maybe he was worth looking into.

My stomach let out a growl so loud it could have startled the tenants downstairs. All I had eaten was three pieces of chocolate. I needed something more. Maybe an éclair from *Cannoli's*. I wondered how Ed was faring with Aunt Lena. My first impulse was to stay out of it, but these were two people I cared about. Funny, when I first encountered Ed, I had been terrified of him, but now was thrilled he would be part of our family. *Or would he?* I hadn't heard from him since he'd left the racetrack. Was that a good or bad sign?

No sooner had that question flashed in my mind than I was on my way to *Cannoli's*. If there was a problem, I hoped it could be resolved in the hour I had before darting off to see Willemy at his book signing.

When I arrived at my aunt's bakery, the only two customers were on their way out. I didn't see Ed's car in the parking lot, nor did I see my aunt hustling about, bringing in trays of bursting-with-cream éclairs, slices of tiramisu and other goodies. My stomach roiled so that an éclair no longer appealed to me. Angie, Aunt Lena's longtime friend and employee, moaned when she strolled into the dining area and saw me, "Thank God you're here. Talk some sense into your aunt. She's back there moping and we're running out of everything."

I closed my eyes and took a deep breath. My hope had been that Aunt Lena and Ed had patched things up. I gave the door to the kitchen a timid push and entered. As Angie claimed, my aunt sat on a stool, recipes in front of her. She was staring straight ahead, though.

I greeted her with a hardy, "Hi, Aunt Lena. How's it going?"

"Oh. Hi, Claire. What are you doing here?"

"Are you still upset about last night?"

"No." Her eyes said otherwise, as did the red splotches on her cheeks.

Keeping my voice casual, I asked, "Has Ed been here?"

She nodded and her tears fell. I put my arms around her, feeling helpless. "Tell me what happened."

She blew her nose and sniffled. "He proposed."

I grabbed her hand. "What did you say?"

"I said no." She pulled her hand away. "Last night at the dance contest, I realized I'm not some spring chicken. I'm almost 55. Ed's just a baby."

"Aunt Lena!" I wanted to shake her. "He's 48. You two are so good together. Plus he loves you." I pulled up a seat. "How did you two leave it?"

She brushed tears away. "He said he wouldn't take no for an answer."

Smart man. "Think it over, Aunt Lena. Imagine your

life without Ed."

She grabbed a bunch of tissues and wadded them up in her hands. "If I marry him, he'll expect to have, you know…"

They hadn't slept together yet? I coughed to cover my amazement. "Sex?"

Aunt Lena's face turned red. "I know. Nowadays everyone falls into bed on the first date. But we didn't. He's a real gentleman."

I shifted from one foot to the other. "So you don't want to have…relations?" I refused to allow any images to inhabit my mind.

She looked down at her blouse and brushed off a non-existent piece of lint. "It's not that. It's just, he'd see me naked."

We hadn't just entered uncomfortable territory for me, we'd set up camp. Still, I asked, "Does he know that's what you're afraid of?"

She nodded. "He said love makes the other person beautiful." She shredded the tissues. "But he hasn't seen me."

Angie chose that minute to come through the swinging door. "So that's why you been walking around here like you lost your family. For God's sake, Lena. You've got a great figure. You just have a lot of it. Marry that man, or I swear, I'll make sure I'm his new partner, and not just to dance, either."

I sucked in a breath, not knowing how Aunt Lena would react.

She harrumphed and placed her hands on her hips. "Angie, I always knew you were fast. But Ed wouldn't look twice at a scrawny woman like you."

Angie outlined her torso with her hands. "Scrawny?

The men at Immaculate Conception's dance last week couldn't keep their eyes off me." She leaned over and grabbed the phone. "Call Ed and tell him yes. Don't be an idiot."

Aunt Lena's eyes darted from Angie to the phone. Then to me. "Claire, do you think I'm crazy to turn Ed down? You know him."

I got the same squirrelly feeling as when my father asked me if he was too old for Suzy. As then, I went for answering with a question. "How do you feel about Ed?"

Angie answered for her. "She's nuts about him. It's always " 'Ed this' and 'Ed that.' Admit it, Lena. Call him."

"Angie's right, Aunt Lena."

She sniffled once more and took the phone from Angie just as my phone rang.

It was Iola Taylor.

"Claire, I'm sorry to call you before you've made your decision about working for me, but we need to talk. Without Harold. Can you meet me at The Winery in Tremont tonight at 6:30?"

My aunt's and Angie's escalating voices became background noise to me as I imagined Corrigan walking into the Winery just as I sat at Iola's table. My voice turned bird-chirp high like it always does when I'm anxious. "I don't think—"

"Please. I promise you, it'll be worthwhile."

"Can't you tell me what it is over the phone?"

When she didn't answer, my fear of passing up valuable information knocked my good sense aside. "Okay. I'll see you there." I wondered how late Willemy would be signing at the bookstore. I didn't want to miss talking to him because I was waylaid by Iola.

When I got off the phone, Aunt Lena was standing there, silent. Then a smile started at the corners of her mouth, and soon her whole face joined in.

"Well, what happened, Lena?" Angie looked ready to shake my aunt.

Aunt Lena's voice trembled. "Ed's coming over." She clapped her hands together. "He's going to ask me again. This time I'm saying yes."

Angie and I hugged the bride-to-be and jumped up and down with joy and excitement. Angie broke free and grabbed the last three éclairs on a nearby tray. She passed a pastry to my aunt and one to me. "This calls for a toast." We lifted our éclairs and wished my aunt the best. We hugged again and my affection for her and my soon-to-be Uncle Ed glowed inside me.

He'd be at *Cannoli's* in twenty minutes but I couldn't wait around. "I'll call you later. I'm so happy for you."

The only way I could make it to The Winery on time was to speed. Unfortunately, one lane was closed on the highway so I got there late and was afraid Iola had left. I hate being late. What if she was going to confess, but talked herself out of it and left? I needn't have worried. Iola was sitting at a small table in the back of the room.

She wore the same broad brimmed hat and had her oversized sunglasses on. It was warming up outside, yet she had a heavy black turtleneck sweater on. Despite all the cover-up, I could tell the last few days had worn on her. As I sat down, she clutched my hand as if it was a life jacket. "Thank God you came."

I managed a weak smile and withdrew my hand. "What did you want to tell me, Iola?"

She leaned forward and whispered with stale breath, "I know who killed George Dixon."

The waitress appeared at our table. "Can I get you both something to drink?"

We quickly ordered two cups of tea and waited for the woman to leave. "Okay, Iola. Tell me." I must have sounded skeptical.

She glanced from side to side then removed her sunglasses. Her eyes were red and the area around them so dark it looked like she was wearing a mask. "Have you ever heard of Jon Willemy?"

I sat back in my chair while the waitress set the tea in front of us and I let out a long breath. "Yes, I have. Why do you think it was him?"

"He hated Dixon. That worm of a critic tried to singlehandedly sink Jon's career. When I saw Jon Willemy last month, he told me he'd like to kill Dixon."

My eyes narrowed. "Did you tell the police this?"

"Of course. But I believe Jon gave them an alibi. Said he was with his paramour, Philip." She snorted. "Philip would sell his soul to protect Jon."

I pushed my untouched tea away. Corrigan had not said a word about Willemy. Not that he was obliged to. I tried to keep any impatience from my voice. "Okay, but is there more to this? If not, Harold could have just told me this over the phone. Or you could have."

She wiped the corners of her mouth with a napkin. "I wanted to tell you in person. There's more." She pulled out her phone and scanned her photos. "A while ago I snapped these pictures." She stopped at one. "Take a look at this."

It was a photo of George Dixon cuddling with an exceedingly good-looking young man. Dixon's expression was akin to a piranha's spotting a filet mignon in the water.

"Okay, so Dixon liked younger men. What of it?"

"The sweet young thing in Dixon's claws is Philip Somebody-Or-Other, who happens to be Willemy's boy toy or love of his life, depending on who's telling the tale. And, so you know, Jon Willemy doesn't like to share." She pointed at someone else in the background. "That's him there."

I peered at the picture again and enlarged it. Willemy didn't look like he was having as good a time as Dixon. "You think Willemy killed Dixon because Dixon was moving in on his lover?"

She grabbed her phone out of my hand. "Willemy already hated Dixon for what that weasel did to his career. Dixon trying to take Jon's new love could have been the final straw."

"Did you show this to the police?"

She leaned over and hissed, "Fat lot of good it did me. Don't forget, that pretty boy gave Willemy an alibi."

"Then I'm not sure what you want from me." That was not entirely true but this murder case filled my head with so many questions they fell on top of each other. I picked up my teaspoon and played with it, waiting her out.

When I added nothing further, she sniffed and straightened in her seat. "I see Jon's got a new book out. He'll no doubt be successful with Dixon gone." She motioned for the check, and folded her hands on top of her napkin. "In fact, he's doing a book signing at the Wise Owl bookstore tonight."

She believed she'd hooked me and was trying to reel me in. I squirmed in my seat. There were ethical issues with me working for Iola. But wouldn't it also be unethical for me to ignore evidence in a murder case that might prove her innocence?

I planned to see Willemy tonight, but I didn't want Iola to know that. I could not get her hopes up that I'd be on her team. Or that I'd get anything from him other than a book. Besides, I still didn't trust her. "Thanks for the tea, Iola. I'll think about what you said. I really need to go now."

I stood to leave, but Iola clutched my forearm and squeezed. "I didn't kill George Dixon. I swear. You must help me." She released me and with shaky hands, put her sunglasses back on. "You'll look into Willemy, won't you?"

I wanted to tell her everything would be all right, but I doubted platitudes would help. Besides, if she was Dixon's killer, nothing would be okay. At least, not for her.

***

On my way to Willemy's book signing, I called Corrigan to check on Iola's story. Corrigan would be upset I had agreed to see Iola, but I told myself I could deal with that. When it went into his voicemail, I didn't leave a message.

By the time I made it to the bookstore, there was a long line of people waiting to meet Willemy and buy his autographed books. I joined them and watched the author interact with his fans.

A deep baritone voice behind me in a pure West Virginia drawl asked, "Have you read Jon's other books?"

I turned and realized the young, slightly built man with longish blond hair and green eyes, was talking to me. "No. Have you?"

"All of them." He smiled, showing large, straight teeth. "You should too. You'll like them."

I smiled back and then it hit me. This blond cutie was the guy in the photo Iola showed me, Philip. I suppressed the urge to squeal with delight at this opportunity. "Sounds like you're a fan."

"Oh, I *am* a fan. A huge one. He's a real artist."

I kept an eye on the line. It was moving faster than I expected and I didn't have much time to question Philip. "Sounds like you know him well."

"Yeah, better than most people."

My hand flew to my heart and I feigned excitement. "Tell me all about him."

He beamed like a 4-H member over a prize cow. "He's one of the best writers I know. Very passionate. I noticed that about him when we met."

"So tell me more about his passion. Does that also mean he has a bad temper?" There were only two people ahead of me and we were almost at the signing table. "I remember reading that critic, George Dixon. He cut Willemy's work down. I'd have been furious if someone said what Dixon said about me."

Philip's face, open and friendly earlier, closed. "I don't know about that."

Before I could probe more, it was my turn at Willemy's table. With a weary, plastered-on smile, the author, who closer up looked to be in his mid-forties, picked up his pen and opened one of his books. "Hello, dear. Can you spell your name for me?" While he waited, pen poised he addressed Philip. "I'll be ready to leave soon."

My mind blanked and by rote I began, "Claire De-Nardo, C-l...No, wait. I'm a private investigator and I'd like to talk with you when you're done here."

"What about?" He looked as if he wanted to duck

under the signing table.

"I just have some questions. It won't take long."

His eyes bulged and he hunched down. "If this is about Dixon's death, I've already talked to the police and have nothing more to say to you or anyone else."

I wasn't going to get anything from Willemy at this rate. I changed tactics. "I'm not investigating the murder. No. I'm...well, I'm writing a book about it. Yes, and I need your help." I wouldn't have blamed him if he'd laughed in my face over my stupid, lame lie.

Instead, he raised one eyebrow. "Go on."

I could feel my face getting hotter as my fibs piled up. "I've already talked to his sister, Felicity. And Iola Taylor. You were my next interview."

"What makes you think you can write a book?" He waved his hands around, his voice full of condemnation. "Oh, I know. Everybody's an author nowadays. What garbage!"

Chastised for a make-believe attempt at writing, I said, "I have a masters in Mass Communications and I was editor on my high school newspaper."

"Ah ha, just as I thought." He pointed his finger at me. "You have no real experience. However, as it turns out, I am between projects, this current book being the last of the series. Perhaps my co-writing could lend the book some gravitas." I could almost see him counting his royalties. He lowered his voice. "Believe me, if half of what I've heard about Dixon's life is true, a book about him could be a best seller. Think about it. I'll write while you investigate his activities." He sat back in his chair with a self-satisfied look.

I pretended to consider his proposition, even while my mind screamed there was no such book. But as long as I was in the pool, I might as well splash around. I set the scene, now I was going to play it to my advantage. "That's tempting, but I'll need more than just your ability to write. I'll need to know about your relationship to Dixon."

Willemy cleared his throat. "I have, shall I say, intimate knowledge of the man. Now I won't say another word here. If you're interested, call me at this number." He jotted his contact information on a promotional bookmark and thrust it at me. "Now, please go away. Shoo." He turned to Philip. "Would you get the car for me?"

I slipped the bookmark into my purse and left the store. At least I was pretty sure Willemy had a bad temper. I wondered if it was bad enough to kill Dixon.

I walked to my car wondering how I could talk to Philip again. As if my wish commanded him, Philip came up behind me. "I heard you say you're a private investigator."

"Yes. And?"

"Seems to me you know more about Jon and George Dixon than you let on." He blurted out, "I need your help, but Jon cannot know."

I rubbed my eyes. This was turning out to be an excruciatingly confusing day. "What exactly do you need my help with?"

He stuffed his hands in his pockets, glanced around the parking lot, and swallowed hard. "First, I better introduce myself. I'm Philip Reeves and I think Jon killed George Dixon."

Chapter Thirteen

I stiffened. "What did you say?"

He repeated his statement, this time enunciating each word as if English was my second language.

I tried to keep my voice low and even. "How do you know?" I should have asked right then why he was telling this to me instead of to the police. And why he had provided Willemy with an alibi. But I didn't want to risk him bolting on me.

He ran his fingers through his hair. "I found one of his shirts in the trash. He'd worn it that same day Dixon was killed. It had blood on it."

My head was pounding so hard with this new information, I could hardly think straight. "What did he say when you asked him about it?"

He looked away. "I didn't ask. Didn't want to rile him." He shrugged. "I thought maybe he'd gotten into a fight. Jon's temper sometimes can get the best of him. It wasn't until later I found out about George."

"But when the police asked, you supplied Jon with an alibi."

"You know about that, huh? Well, I shouldn'ta done

that, but I didn't think, except to protect him."

"I understand." I didn't, but I wanted him to keep talking. "You just said Jon has a temper. Has he ever been violent toward you? If he has, the cops—"

His hand sliced through the air to stop me. "No, he's never hit me. And please don't go to the cops. I mean, not yet. Maybe never. See, first I want to hire you to find out if Jon did kill George."

I squinted at him. "And if he did? You know, there's a photo of you and Dixon. Looked like you two were really cozy. Was Jon jealous?"

He looked away. "There was nothing between George and me, not that he would've turned me down. But I know how it looks. If Jon did it, it'll near break my heart but I'll go to the police."

I put my hand over my mouth and blew out a big breath. While I felt bad for Philip, I couldn't help him. The only bright spot with this new twist was that it might prove Iola innocent. "I'm sorry, Philip, but the best advice I can give you is, if you have evidence, go to the police with it now. Let them sort it out."

"I can't. See, Jon is everything to me."

He could also be a killer. "Where is the shirt now?"

He didn't even look at me. "I hid it."

My lips were forming to ask where, when we were interrupted.

"Philip, I was waiting for you to bring the car around." It was Jon Willemy. "I need some help with the unsold books." As if just noticing me, he added, "Hello again, Claire. I didn't realize you and Philip had things to talk about outside the bookstore." This last comment was tinged with suspicion.

Before Philip could reply, I jumped in. "I dropped my

car keys and Jon saw me searching for them. He was nice enough to stop and help me."

Jon placed his hand on the small of Philip's back, directing his comment more to him than to me. "How very gallant." His sentence was riddled with sarcasm.

"Yes, I have them now." I jiggled my keys to make my point.

Jon chuckled, but it seemed forced. "Then we'll be on our way."

I thanked Philip, got in my car and drove off. If my car went as fast as my mind, I'd have been pulled over for speeding.

It was about 10. and, although I wasn't tired, I decided to go home. Maybe I would get a brilliant idea on how to get Willemy's bloody shirt without spilling any of my blood. Chewing on my lip, I debated the best way to do so.

I just walked through my apartment door when Corrigan rang me. Through a yawn he said, "You called earlier, but you didn't leave a message. Either you were doing something you really didn't want me to know about, or you missed me so much you just wanted to hear my voice." He tsk'd. "Much as I'd like to think it's the latter, I'd put my money on the former. Come clean. What is it?"

My words came out hesitantly. "Did Iola Taylor, um, tell you about, um, someone named Jon Willemy?"

I heard him draw in a sharp breath. "I thought you said you'd stay out of this. Claire. You're a witness! You can get in deep trouble. You should know better."

I felt like a toddler scolded for sticking my finger in the cake frosting. "I know it and I'm not doing anything wrong. Iola contacted me. I'm merely wondering if she was telling the truth."

"Okay. Yeah, she gave us Willemy's name, even showed me a photo of Dixon's arm around some pretty boy she said was Willemy's partner. So, okay. Possible motive, but the guy has an alibi."

"Why didn't you tell me?" I flinched at the whiny character of my question.

Either he didn't notice or didn't want to notice. "I didn't think it was important."

"Well, what if there was more—"

I was interrupted by a knock at my door. Not a good thing this late at night. I asked Corrigan to hold on and, under my breath, cursed the building owner for not replacing the current ineffective security system.

I shouted, "Who is it?"

"Thank God you're home! It's Felicity Dixon. Can I come in?"

"Brian, I'll call you back." I ended the call before he could protest. Then took a deep breath to steady myself and let Felicity in.

My face must have registered my shock because she began by apologizing. "I hate to drop in on you like this. I'm sorry. I know it's late. I should've called first, but…" Her voice trailed off. "I had to talk to you before I go crazy. With Marco gone, I…" She tore at her hair, obliterating the style Suzy had worked on.

I fingered my collar. "No, no it's fine." I ushered her to my sofa while trying to keep my voice from rising to the level only dogs hear.

"Can I get you some tea?" I wanted her relaxed. Heck, I wanted to relax. Once again, my phone rang. Corrigan calling back. I didn't answer and it went into voicemail. I'd return his call later. Talking to Felicity couldn't wait.

"No, thank you. I'm here to talk about Marco. I want to know who killed him." Her fist flew to her mouth to stop a sob.

I'd like to know who did it too and thank them. "Aren't the police looking into his death?"

She blinked back tears and folded her hands in her lap. "You knew Marco. The cops are probably happy he's dead. You know, one less street hood to deal with."

"I'm sure that's not true." How awful she must have felt, especially since I had no doubt it was accurate.

The look she gave me told me she knew I was lying. "Nobody knew him like I did. Especially that horrible man, Michael Bucanetti."

My chest tightened at the sound of the familiar name. "Have you had any dealings with Michael Bucanetti?" My phone rang once more. Corrigan again. This time I picked up. "Call-you-back-later. Bye."

Felicity stared at her hands. She had bitten her nails down to the quick. "Not directly, but I'm aware that he's a mob boss from New Jersey and Marco worked for him. I also know he's got his hands in all sorts of things here in Cleveland. I take it you know him?"

"We're acquainted." I didn't mention the cases in which Bucanetti played a big part. Or that I'd even had occasion to talk with the man. Although Marco was dead, I didn't know if Bucanetti would hire someone to continue with the threat to my family I'd incurred while working on another case.

"Then you know why I don't want his help. Marco didn't talk much about his job, but I think even he was afraid of Mr. Bucanetti."

"What help did Bucanetti offer?" I held my breath.

"He said he wants whoever killed Marco to be punished. I do too, but not by him." She opened her purse, took out a hard candy and stuck it in her mouth. Then she wrapped her long, thin arms around herself. "First my brother, George, then Marco. Now I've got this gangster…"

"And you wanted to talk to me about…?"

"Like I said, I know the police won't try very hard to find Marco's killer but," her voice hardened, "I want whoever did it to be sorry they were ever born. I'm sure that would happen if Mr. Bucanetti found the killer. Then I'd owe him and I've seen what happens to the lives of people he considers in his debt." She shuddered. "Remember, I cooperated with you when you had questions for me, despite Charlotte's advice. Please hear me out."

She watched me with her red-rimmed eyes. Curiosity battled with fear, keeping me mute. She continued, "I want to hire you to find the killer first. I'll pay whatever you ask."

I sucked in a shaky breath. This would mean going against Bucanetti, a terrifying thing. That led to my biggest objection.

I could get killed.

On the other hand, if I survived, I might have enough money to open my own business and give Gino this one back. My phone rang again and again. I ignored it.

I thought back to the time at Suzy's salon. "What about Charlotte?"

"She'd be furious if she knew I was even here without her. She's a good friend, but sometimes a bit overprotective. I'll keep her away from your investigation."

Someone pounded at my door. "Police. Open up."

Recognizing the voice, I hustled to the door and flung

it open. Corrigan stood there, gun drawn, in attack stance. He holstered his weapon. His jaw was tight enough to snap. "What the hell's going on? Are you okay?"

I stepped back and he spotted Felicity. To stop him from saying anything I pressed my hands against his chest and explained, "We were discussing her deceased fiancé when you interrupted."

He lifted his chin toward my visitor. "Evening, Ms. Dixon." He crooked his finger at me to follow him into the hallway.

"I'll be back in a minute, Felicity." I ducked out the door ready to give Corrigan a piece of my mind. Before I could do so, he closed the door, grabbed me and planted a kiss on my lips that had me reeling. As soon as he let go, he muttered, "That's because I'm glad you're okay." A scowl crossed his face. "Now that that's established, I'm telling you don't get involved with Felicity Dixon."

I crossed my arms. "I didn't ask her to come over."

He mused, "There was no love lost between Dixon and his sister, so she's not here because of that. My hunch is she wants you to find Marco's killer. And that means you could get yourself hurt. Even killed."

"I'm not admitting to anything, but didn't we agree not to get into each other's business?"

He rubbed his jaw. "Yeah, but this is different."

"No, it's not. I'm just doing what a private investigator does. Talking to a possible client. Gathering information. Nobody's pointing a gun at me or waving explosives." *Yet.* I held my breath, hoping Corrigan would give up without a fight.

He scowled. "Okay. For now. But don't say I didn't warn you. And next time, don't hang up on an officer of the law."

I released my breath. "I won't."

"If you get any information that could lead to the arrest of Marco's killer—"

"I know. Report it. But I don't have anything. Now about Dixon's murder…"

He peered at me with suspicion. "What about it? If you know something, better tell me."

I gave him the rundown of my conversation with Philip, ending with, "Jon Willemy could very well be the killer and that shirt could prove it."

Corrigan made a quick call. When he finished, he ran his hand through his hair. "Why didn't you tell me this earlier? That shirt could be long gone, if it even existed."

"It does. And I tried, but—"

He made a chopping gesture I took to mean stop talking. I hoped it was that, instead of him wanting to lop off my head. "Anything else you *tried* to tell me?"

I jutted my chin forward. "It's not like this happened a week ago. I found out tonight."

"Yeah, after you met with Iola Taylor, which you were fully aware you weren't supposed to do. I swear, sometimes I wonder if you even use your head."

It was as if he had snapped the rubber band holding my emotions back. "Use my head! I always do, except when I go along with you saying you'd keep your end of our agreement."

"Wait a minute! You're the one—"

I didn't let him finish. I turned the doorknob, stepped inside my apartment, and slammed the door. Not my most mature moment. Instantly regretting my reaction, I opened the door wide enough to stick my head out and watched him stomp away. I swallowed my desire to run after him and ignored the miserable feeling welling up inside me. Heartsick, I turned my focus back to Felicity.

She stood, favoring her non-injured ankle. Her face was blank. "First, I didn't hear what you two were arguing about." I started to protest, but she stopped me. "It's your business. In any case, thank you for not letting Detective Corrigan know about Mr. Bucanetti contacting me. Even if he understood I don't want that mobster's help, it would have complicated things." She clenched her fists. "And I definitely don't want anything to get in the way of finding Marco's killer."

I wouldn't want Bucanetti's help either. Last time he 'helped', two people died. I also understood Felicity's pain and anger, but she sounded like she could rip the killer apart with her teeth. It was scary. "If I find the killer, what's to prevent you from taking justice into your own hands?"

She twisted the engagement ring on her finger. "If it'd bring Marco back, I'd skin the killer alive. But it won't so, yeah, the cops can have him." Deathly calm she added, "Mr. Bucanetti can just as easily have the bastard beaten to death in jail as outside."

The hairs on the back of my neck and my arms stood up. Bucanetti was already looking for Marco's killer. If I found the murderer first, Bucanetti might be happy. Unless it turned out the assassin was one of his own men. Regardless, I didn't want to delve back into gangsterland. It was frightening and I didn't belong there.

My brain called me a coward. It was right. And Felicity was probably right about the police and Marco's murder. Corrigan was probably right that I should stay away from this case. Why did I feel so wrong in turning the job down, then?

I looked at Felicity and put myself in her place. My empathy brain cells wanted to bring her a casserole. My accounting brain cells realized if I couldn't work for Iola, I would need Felicity's job just to pay the bills.

While all this was going through my mind, Felicity returned to the sofa, perching motionless, like a lioness waiting for an opportunity to get what she wanted. When I didn't speak, she sighed, "I'll pay you whatever you ask. I have quite a bit of money now."

I gripped the arm of the sofa. Her offer of money made the job sound better. As long as the killer was not one of Bucanetti's men. If it were, Felicity's money would be used strictly for my funeral.

"Just so you know, Mr. Bucanetti believes it's an outside job."

Next she'd offer me a bite of the red, juicy poison apple. Still, relief, excitement, and caution made the rounds inside me.

I wondered fleetingly if Ed could break away from his fiancé, Aunt Lena, long enough to protect me.

Felicity and I discussed the contract that she would sign at my office the next day. With a melancholy smile, she thanked me and made her way to the door.

Alone again, I thought about Marco and any enemies he would have had and who would've wanted him dead? *Everyone.*

I started putting the puzzle of Marco's murder together, but I didn't have many pieces. The ones I possessed came with questions. Did Martin Beckman, the loan shark, have a problem with Marco? What, if anything, did Bucanetti have to do with Marco's death? Was there another person involved?

I was stumped, so out of frustration, I added what I

knew about the Dixon case. The more I moved the pieces around the more it seemed as if there weren't two puzzles, but one huge one. Besides Felicity, other people were part of both men's lives. In addition, both victims were involved in gambling.

Too bad so many other puzzle pieces weren't available. Dread flowed through me, thinking of how I had to go about getting them.

I drummed my fingers on the table trying to come up with a plan. It was impossible. I managed to mentally sidestep thinking of Corrigan as I assembled the puzzle, but the memory of our argument tumbled back into my head.

I picked up my cell phone to call him. Set it back on the table. Self-righteousness blanketed me. He should be the first to apologize. Then the pretend-nothing-is-wrong part of me pushed ahead, insisting the whole argument was inconsequential. As I ruminated over what to do, my phone rang and I grabbed it, hoping it was Corrigan.

It was Philip. *How did he get my number?*

He rasped, "The police were here looking for a bloody shirt." He followed the statement with a string of hurtful obscenities.

Once he ran dry I said, "Philip, I was trying to do the right thing."

"The right thing for who?" His soft voice wavered. "Jon's furious. He may even kick me out, thanks to you. You stay away from us."

"Let's talk about this." I felt like I was falling into a pit, unable to pull myself out. "Philip, don't hang up." My plea fell into emptiness. He was already gone.

Chapter Fourteen

I called back the number on my phone, but it went directly into voicemail. I didn't leave a message.

Feeling as two-faced as a queen in a deck of cards, I recited to myself all the reasons why telling Corrigan about the shirt were justified. It didn't make me feel better. I didn't even know if the police had found anything. Calling Corrigan to ask didn't strike me as a good idea. I flopped onto the sofa and brooded. Next, I got worried, recalling what Philip had said about Jon's temper.

I tried Philip's number once more. Again, it rolled into voicemail. I told myself he just wasn't picking up. Besides, he told me to leave him alone. I chided myself for worrying and forced myself back to the table full of clues that left me clueless.

By 1in the morning, I'd gotten no further than before Philip's call and decided to try for some sleep.

Three hours later, my eyes popped open. As if through some sixth sense, I was positive some harm had come to Philip. Feeling colder than the room's temperature warranted, I dressed as fast as my numb, fumbling fingers allowed.

I looked up Willemy's address, assumed Philip also lived there, grabbed my gun and rushed from the apartment. As soon as I turned my car's ignition, common sense and my fear of what could happen flooded in.

Despite wanting to slice my hand off because it called Corrigan, I was relieved when he answered.

"What is it, Claire?" I could hear his anger loud and clear.

"I'm worried about Philip Reeves. Willemy's partner."

His voice dropped its hostile tone. "Are you still at home? I'm only five minutes away. We need to talk."

"Can't you tell me over the phone?" But like Philip had done to me, Corrigan hung up before I got my last words out.

I returned to my apartment, pacing back and forth as I waited for Corrigan.

When he finally arrived, I bombarded him with questions. "Did you talk to Philip Reeves? What happened? Why couldn't you tell me over the phone?"

Corrigan unbuttoned his jacket and took his time answering me. "We didn't find Reeves or the bloody shirt."

My head jerked back. "What do you mean you didn't find him? I talked to him about three hours ago and he said you'd been at Willemy's house."

His voice was terse. "Yes, but only Willemy was there. He claimed there was no such shirt and that Philip Reeves wasn't there. Then he told us if we wanted to come in, we'd need a search warrant."

My hopes rose. "Are you getting one?"

"You're kidding, aren't you? I've already stuck my neck out. Outside of you, Philip Reeves is the only one who claims Dixon's blood is on Willemy's shirt."

His implication was clear. I could hardly hear him for the buzzing in my ears. "I didn't make this up. You need to find Philip. Get a search warrant or put out an APB on him."

Corrigan spoke in a tone meant to calm me. "I don't think you made it up. I think, maybe, Iola and her one-step-away-from-being-a-criminal lawyer Harold might have set you up so you would help them. Even if I'm wrong, there's no way I could do either of the things you're suggesting. Unless there's a missing person's report or a corpse, I can't do anything more. Without Reeves and that shirt, there's no case against Willemy."

I felt as if I had just run a marathon and was gasping for breath. "Then what are you suggesting? We do nothing? What if Willemy hurt Philip?" My voice rose. "Even killed him?"

Corrigan gently grasped my arm. "Not likely."

I pulled away, clenched my teeth and stewed.

My silence didn't fool him. "Claire, now don't go doing anything dangerous. Or illegal. I'll inquire about Reeves's whereabouts informally. Okay? Are we good?"

I nodded, but it wouldn't be okay until I knew Willemy hadn't hurt Philip. My jaw relaxed enough for a yawn to escape and spread to Corrigan. It was 4:30.

Through his yawn he said, "I'm going home to catch an hour or two of sleep. You should do the same."

"Good idea." Except a quick kiss turned into a longer one and showed some real promise. That is, until a text came on his phone.

He broke away and cursed when he read the message. "I've got to get back to the station."

I strained my neck, trying to read the words. "Something about Willemy?"

He shoved his phone in his pocket without responding.

Call it woman's intuition or a PI's instinct, but I was convinced that text concerned Willemy. *What if they'd found Philip's bloody body in a shallow ditch?* A finger of dread wrapped around my heart. "Is Philip alive?"

"This doesn't concern Philip. Gotta go." Corrigan's lips brushed against my cheek and he exited through the door.

I thought of running after him, but knew it would do no good. If Philip had been truthful about the bloody shirt, where was it and where was he?

I supposed this was where the 'I' in PI came in. Except 'I' didn't relish snooping around Willemy's home by myself. Or confronting him about Philip's whereabouts and wellbeing.

Even if I had the nerve to do it, it would be light outside in another hour. I'd be caught and arrested for trespassing. A drive-by was a possibility. I knew it was like trying to grasp a cloud but I had to do something.

I grabbed a breakfast pastry to sooth my grumbling stomach and perk me up. I headed out the door. If it were later, I'd have called Ed to see if he was willing to help. I yawned and stretched and wondered if he would be as available to hunt criminals after he married my aunt.

That early in the morning, there wasn't much traffic so I made it to the suburb of Westlake in less than thirty minutes. The houses along Willemy's street were mid-twentieth-century homes situated on Lake Erie and had lovely views. They didn't have much in the way of backyards to hide things or people.

A light was on in what was most likely the living room. Somebody must have been home. I hoped it was

Philip, unharmed.

I made a U-turn and parked two houses away from Willemy's and waited about five minutes. I was hoping to summon some courage to go up and ring the doorbell. Courage never showed up, but I decided to go to the door without it. Before I could get out of my car, the light in the house flicked off. A car barreled out of the garage and down the driveway. The driver was alone. I couldn't be sure who it was, but if I'd had more than $1.24 in my pocket, I'd have bet it was Jon Willemy. Wherever he was going, it looked like he was in a hurry. I hoped Philip's body wasn't stuffed in the trunk.

Chapter Fifteen

I took off after Willemy. One thing Gino had taught me well was how to follow someone. At 5:30 in the morning., it was more challenging because there wasn't much traffic on the road to blend in with. At least full daylight had yet to assert itself. I stayed at a safe distance as the driver headed toward Lakewood.

Finally, he parked in a familiar parking lot and I realized I'd done the right thing by following him. To keep him off-guard, I drove past him and parked in a nearby area. I'd no sooner turned off the ignition when the mystery man left his car. I watched, amazed, as Philip snuck up to my office building and tried the door.

I bolted from my car, gun in hand, and got to him as he tried the door again. "Philip. What are you doing here?"

He turned toward me and even in the dim light, I could see his split lip and discolored eye. "I left Jon." He pointed to his face. "This was his going-away gift. Only he doesn't realize it."

I lowered my gun. I felt as bad as if I'd been the one who hit him instead of the one who told Corrigan about the shirt. "I'm sorry."

He waved away my apology. "It's not your fault. When the cops came over, Jon figured out I had his shirt."

A worm of fear wiggled into me. "Did you give it back to Jon?"

"Maybe I should've, but I kept telling him I didn't have it. He went crazy, accusing me of setting him up for blackmail." He sniffed. "I denied it, of course. I never would have done that. He didn't believe me and I couldn't convince him. I told you he has a temper and he'd been drinking."

My voice was a whisper. "What happened then? Does he know you're here?" I was glad I had my gun.

"He passed out. I grabbed my stuff and took off. I can't take another scene like that." Despite his towering height, he looked like a child who just learned the Easter Bunny doesn't color eggs and leave baskets of chocolate.

Anyways," he pulled a small brown bag out of his jacket and thrust it at me. "Here's the shirt. I don't want to go anywhere near a police station, but figured someone oughta have this. I trust you'll do what's right with it."

My arms were shaking as I took the parcel. This shirt could clear Iola and put the real killer behind bars. "Philip, if this has George Dixon's blood on it, the police will need to talk to you. And you did lie when you gave Jon his alibi."

He looked away. "They might not find me."

I raised my head so my eyes could meet his. "What are you planning to do once you leave here?" I did not see happy times ahead for him.

"I'm going away. Not sure exactly where yet. Not go-

116

ing to hurt myself if that's what you're thinking." He touched his eye with his fingertips. "I know now Jon's not worth it."

Despite his assurance, I wanted to keep an eye on him. "Why don't you come up to my office and we can put some ice on your eye. I could even make some tea."

"Can't. I'm taking off. If it is George's blood on this shirt and it turns out Jon killed George, I don't want to be here to find out.

I had so many questions that might never get answered if Philip left. In desperation I said, "The swelling around your eye is going to get worse without some ice. It could even impair your vision. That won't help you."

He scanned the parking lot, probably wondering if Willemy had found him. He must have decided it was worth the risk. "You have a point."

When I unlocked the building's entrance, he added, "Can't stay long, but ice and some tea would be nice."

Philip sat while I placed a couple cubes from my small refrigerator into paper towels. Then I pulled two cups from the cupboard under the sink and dropped a teabag in each. I returned to my outer office and handed him the cold packet. "Do you think Jon might have killed George Dixon over you?"

Philip flinched as the cold hit his face. "Jon's possessive, but I think it had more to do with money."

I nearly dropped the cups. "You mean revenue he lost because of Dixon's reviews?"

He shook his head. "Forget I said anything."

"Did Dixon owe Jon money? Or was it the other way around?" Keeping my voice level I asked, "By any chance, is Jon a big gambler?"

Philip blew on the tea and took a sip. "I've been flappin' my jaw too much. I better go. Thanks for the ice and the tea." He set his cup down and stood.

I slipped between him and the office door. "It must have been a lot of money." When he didn't say anything, I added, "I'll find out, but it'd look better for you if you told me."

He lowered his head. "I'll take my chances."

Since I'd left my gun by the refrigerator, I used the only weapon available to get him talking. Threats. "You know as soon as you leave, I'll be right behind you, taking this shirt to the police."

"Do whatever you need. But I'm asking you to give me a two-hour head start."

I couldn't commit to his request. It was wrong. The right thing to do would have been to draw my gun on him and force him to stay while I called the police. Except by the time I retrieved my weapon, Philip could be out the door with me chasing him, a man with legs as long as my entire torso. I did have the shirt, after all. I pressed my lips together and said nothing.

With a curt nod, he strode out the door as a man determined to ruin his life.

The moment Philip left, I called Corrigan. "Philip Reeves just left my office. He gave me Willemy's shirt." I didn't want to tell him about leaving myself unarmed. Instead, I rushed my words and gave him the make and model of Philip's car and license plate number, happy I at least had the presence of mind to note that bit of information.

Corrigan didn't exactly erupt with praise for me. "I'll put out an APB on him. I sure hope you're on your way to the station with the evidence." After a moment's hesitation he murmured, "Good work, Claire."

I was in my car and on the road less than a minute later. The bag containing the shirt lay next to me. For the first time since Iola's arrest, I allowed myself to fantasize. If the blood on Willemy's shirt was Dixon's and the police caught up with Philip to substantiate the evidence, the murder charges against Iola would be dropped, and I'd get my fee and new PI business. I suppressed my vision of unlocking the door to my new office. As Gino used to tell me, "Don't count your chickens until they get to the other side of the road."

Imagining all that made it feel like I'd flown to the police station. Corrigan was waiting for me. Donning gloves, he removed the shirt from the paper bag.

I sucked in a breath. As Philip had claimed, there were blood spatters down the front of the shirt and one of the sleeves.

Corrigan bagged it and handed it to another cop. "This goes to the lab. We'll see if it really is Dixon's blood." The other cop disappeared with the parcel.

I frowned. "Of course it is. Why else would Willemy have stonewalled you when you went to his house?"

Sarcasm filled his words. "For all we know, it's Reeves's blood. He's not exactly been Mr. Honesty, has he? Or are you going to go all Dorothy on me?"

"Dorothy who?" This wasn't exactly the reception I thought this evidence warranted.

"Wizard of Oz." He gave a backward wave of his hand. "Forget it. Guess I'm getting punchy." He motioned for me to follow him to his desk.

It was obvious he needed sleep but I was too tired and short-tempered to cut him any slack. Furious, dagger-sharp words tumbled from my brain into my mouth. Pressing my lips together was the only thing stopping them from coming out.

He rubbed his face hard as if trying to wipe away his obvious need for sleep. The dark under eye circles I noticed earlier this morning seemed to have grown and deepened. He looked past exhausted and on his way to collapse.

My anger dissipated. "Have you gotten any sleep in the past 48 hours?"

He gave me a wry smile. "Yeah, when I leaned against the coffee maker waiting for it to brew." He collapsed into his chair. "Dixon's autopsy report came in while we were at your apartment."

Back to business. "Were there any surprises?" Even as I asked the question, my hands clenched into fists.

"Report says cause of death was from massive blood loss, like we thought. We're still checking the folders and newspaper."

I waited but he didn't add anything more. "Why do you think the killer used more than one folder?"

His response was a shrug. Maybe I could get more information using my feminine wiles. I tilted my head to one side and cast my stare at him through my eyelashes. "You must have a theory about those cuts." In a throaty whisper, I suggested we discuss it, man to woman.

While Corrigan's expression turned to wary amusement, something, probably an eyelash, lodged in my left eye. I began blinking furiously to get it out.

Corrigan handed me a tissue as tears rolled down from my affected eye. Lucky for me, his phone rang and diverted his attention.

"Corrigan speaking. Hey Johnson. What's up?" Corrigan's mouth went from a neutral position to a frown. "Okay. Thanks for the heads-up."

Corrigan's eyebrows furrowed. He looked straight at me. "That was Dan Johnson from the Canton police. One of their cops gave Reeves a ticket for speeding but he hadn't gotten the APB at that point."

The offending speck in my eye had washed out by itself but now I felt the sting of my own ineptitude. I was the one who let Philip get away. I wrapped my arms around my stomach and bent over. Corrigan sat silent for a moment then grabbed his jacket and stood. "Come on." He hooked his arm through mine and pulled me up.

"Where are we going?" I stumbled against the desk leg.

"I've been off-duty for so long I'll be back on duty soon. And not to be disrespectful of the deceased, but Dixon will still be dead after I get some sleep. So I'm taking you home then going to bed."

"But my car's here." I licked my dry lips. *Did he mean we'd go to bed together?*

He didn't hesitate. "We'll pick it up in the morning."

My thoughts raced and I tried to remember which underwear I had on.

Chapter Sixteen

Corrigan didn't say much during the ride to my apartment. I kept quiet too, my emotions bouncing all over. Although Philip slipping through my fingers embarrassed me, Corrigan's proposition made me nervous and excited at the same time. When we finally arrived at my place, my nerves were firing so furiously, I wouldn't have been surprised to see sparks flying from my head.

He placed his arm around me and led me inside my building. Up the stairs we went, my knees ready to buckle like a cheap bed frame. I unlocked my door and stood still, afraid of spoiling the mood. He cradled my chin in his hand and kissed me with more tenderness than I'd ever experienced.

There was a hint of him pulling away then he returned, now pressing himself harder against me. He was humming the tune and I knew all the words.

Until he broke away and the song ended. His voice was shaky and his eyes heavy-lidded. "God, any other time! But I've got to get some sleep. Can't do my job without it. You could use some too."

It felt as if he had just tossed me in an ice bath. I bit

my tongue rather than try to convince him to stay. If we were ever to have a 'first time,' I did not want it to be because I talked him into it.

I took a step back. Incapable of putting a complex sentence together, I tripped over my words. "Right. Of course. Need our rest."

He flung open my door. "Get inside and close the door before I stop using my brain."

I stumbled into my apartment and watched, dumbfounded as he took off down the hallway. My mind registered what had just happened, but my body remained ready for action.

I was still standing by the door when my phone rang. The fire Corrigan lit inside me was already flickering. But hearing my aunt's voice doused it with cold water.

"Claire honey, I hope you were already awake. I couldn't wait any longer." My aunt's voice was light and carefree. Getting engaged was good for her.

"I was up."

"Can you come to *Cannoli's* now? It's important."

I glanced at the time. "I've only had two hours of sleep. Unless it's a matter of life or death, can I come over this afternoon? I don't want to be on the road this exhausted."

"You shouldn't keep such late hours. But nobody died, so get some rest."

"I will. Thanks, Aunt Lena." I leaned against the wall and kicked off my shoes. That's when I remembered my car was still at the police station. My clothes still on, I crawled into bed, Getting a ride to my car could wait until after I slept.

By the time I woke up, it was noon. I swung my legs over the side of the bed and sat there, groggy. My mind slowly focused and I thought of two things. Philip getting away and retrieving my car. Well, three things. The chocolate cranberry and cashew caramels I had in the freezer. I kept them there so I'd have to wait for them to defrost before I could devour one. Today was a good day to take out two.

That gave me the immediate motivation to slip out of bed. While shuffling to the kitchen I remembered Aunt Lena's request. I checked my messages to see if she had called. She had. Three times. There was one from Harold, demanding I notify him ASAP with my decision on helping Iola. *What a self-important jerk!* With a steel grin, I deleted his message. The final, best message was from Corrigan. In a sleep-tinged voice, he asked when it'd be best to come get me. *After that last kiss, he could get me anytime.* I giggled and was ready to phone him when I heard a firm knock at my door.

"Claire, it's your aunt. Open up. I know you're in there. Brian told me."

Oh Dear God! She probably woke the poor guy up. No wonder Corrigan sounded half-asleep when he called. I smoothed my slept-in clothes with my hands and flung open the door.

"Aunt Lena, come in. I was sleeping and had my phone off. You shouldn't have called Brian."

She stepped inside. "I didn't. He called me with congratulations. Ed asked Brian to be a groomsman." She looked me up and down. "I hope you're not going anywhere looking like you just rolled out of bed."

My eyes turned toward heaven. "I *did* just roll out of bed." A smile then spread across my face. "When's the wedding?"

"May 22. It'll be in Las Vegas."

I hoped Elvis wasn't marrying them. "Vegas? How did you decide that?"

"Ed's cousin owns a wedding chapel. First, we'll do it right by having Father Joe marry us in a private ceremony at Incarnation. Then it's off to the Chapel of Wedded Bliss." She paused and grabbed my hands. "I couldn't wait until you came to *Cannoli's*. I've got to know. Will you be my maid of honor?" She watched my face carefully.

If she was searching for any sign of reluctance, she didn't find it. "I'd love to." I threw my arms around her and hugged her. For a fleeting moment, I missed my mother. She would have joined in with this celebratory embrace.

My aunt must have been on my wavelength. "I wonder what Theresa would think."

In a husky whisper I replied, "She'd approve."

Aunt Lena stepped out of the hug and wiped her eyes. With a melancholy smile she said, "Got to get back to *Cannoli's*. Angie's holding down the fort and probably cursing up a storm that I'm not back yet." She turned to leave then looked over her shoulder. "I already asked Angie to be my bridesmaid. She's such an old friend, I couldn't leave her out."

My phone rang just as Aunt Lena left. Harold. Unsure if I was ready for this, I steeled myself and said, " hello."

"Claire. Harold. I believe you owe me a decision."

My thoughts flashed from Iola to Willemy and then to Marco's death. The words I needed to say stuck in my mouth as if they had been rolled around in honey and peanut butter. "I'm going to have to turn Iola and you down. I have another client whose case doesn't involve a conflict of interest. I'm sorry."

He huffed into the phone as if I had called him an ob-scene name. "Very well. I perhaps shouldn't say this, but I believe you'll regret your decision. Goodbye."

I regretted it already, watching my dream of a new office sail by. Maybe if Willemy's shirt showed Dixon's blood, I could squeeze back into Iola's case. If not, I had better get working on solving Marco's murder. At least that case I could dig into without worrying about cross-ing the line into unethical behavior.

With that in mind, I texted Corrigan to come pick me up. The sooner I was back to work, the faster I could conclude the job for Felicity. Among the many problems with Marco's case was Bucanetti. He and I were running a race to see who could find Marco's killer first. If I didn't do it, Felicity's payment would join Iola's. I wouldn't even be able to pay my bills, let alone start my own business.

The chocolates were defrosted by now and I gobbled them down, feeling better with each bite. I finished them and was using my forefinger to pick up the slivers of chocolate that had fallen when Corrigan texted back. He would be over in fifteen minutes.

I scrambled to the shower and was throwing on fresh clothes when he knocked on my door.

I opened it hoping for at least an impassioned em-brace. I settled for a quick brush of the lips and, "The blood on Willemy's shirt is Dixon's."

Chapter Seventeen

My jaw clenched. *I just turned Harold down and Iola was innocent.* I sunk into that corner of Hell called Regrets. Corrigan's next words yanked me back up to earth.

"Don't get too excited." He pulled out his notepad. "According to the bartender at Beef and Brew downtown, the victim and Willemy got into a yelling match that turned into a fistfight. Willemy socked Dixon in the nose. Blood everywhere. Two other people witnessed the fight."

I felt as deflated as a beach ball with a bad leak. I grabbed Corrigan's arm. "Was the bartender's name Tommy Columbo?" I waved my hand. Did it even matter? "Isn't there some way to tell when the blood got on the shirt?"

He shook his head. "Sorry Claire. I know you wanted Willemy to be Dixon's killer, but Iola Taylor's still our number one suspect." He placed his arm around my shoulder. "Come on. Let's get your car."

On the way, Corrigan brought up my aunt's wedding. "I was pretty surprised when Ed asked me to be his groomsman. But I didn't hesitate. Ed and Lena are great people."

"They are. Funny to think a murder brought them together. Speaking of which, have you gotten anywhere with Marco's murder?"

He glanced at me, an eyebrow raised. "I know you and Felicity weren't just idly chatting. Did you take her case?"

"What if I did? There's no conflict of interest." I bit my lip. I hadn't meant to sound so defensive. I just didn't want my taking the case to start an argument.

Corrigan seemed to be trying his best not to fall into the fight trap either. He twisted his mouth like a patient avoiding his medicine, but finally offered, "We know the make and model of the gun used. That's it. No leads so far."

"Me either."

By then we arrived at my car. He leaned over and kissed me. "Next time, I won't leave you at your apartment door."

I kissed him back. "That a promise?" I slipped out of his car and back into mine.

Once Corrigan drove off, I blew out a deep breath. It was time to find out who killed Marco Conti. This wasn't going to be easy.

Back at my office there was a message from Felicity, asking if I'd made any progress yet on her fiancé's murder. I drummed my fingers on my desk, deciding how to answer her. While I was rehearsing how to tell her, somebody knocked at my door, then let himself in.

"You Claire DeNardo?" The man was stocky, with a swarthy complexion, and dark hair.

"Yes I am. Can I help you?" Something about this

guy set me on edge. I slipped my hand into my desk drawer for my pepper spray.

"I'm here with a message from Mr. Bucanetti. He wants you should be available to converse with him at 3today. It's 2so that's an hour from now."

Aside from the fact that he didn't believe I could tell time, I had no argument.

"He also wants me to tell you not to let anyone else know yous two are talking. Or what you talk about. Bad things could happen if you do. Got it?"

I nodded again, hoping my voice would return. Too bad it didn't come back until Bucanetti's messenger had vanished. The hairs on the back of my neck finally laid down again and I tried to keep my mind off the imminent phone call.

A cup of tea would calm me. Of course, a chocolate martini or two would really take the edge off, but I needed my wits about me. I made the tea and returned to my desk with it. Instead of sitting, I paced, took a sip then returned to pacing. Despite telling myself Bucanetti merely wanted to find out what I knew about Marco's murder, I trembled inside. I knew nothing and I was pretty sure Bucanetti wouldn't want to hear that. Making this worse, if that were possible, was knowing Felicity didn't want Bucanetti's help. There was no way I could tell the mobster that. Not if I liked inhaling air through my nose rather than through a hole in my chest.

I forced myself to sit down and take some deep breaths. That's when I remembered a feeling I got when I first met Charlotte. She didn't like Marco, or at least didn't think he was good for Felicity. I wished I had thought to ask her why. Maybe it was for a reason other than he was a hired killer.

My phone rang at exactly 3. Bucanetti was punctual, probably his only admirable quality.

In a husky, too-many-cigars-and-liquor voice he said, "Claire DeNardo. Ya know, I've done business in Cleveland for thirty years. No problem. Now it's like you show up at everything. You're like what'dya-call-'em, herpes. Think you got rid of them, but they come back. How the hell do you always turn up in my business?" He didn't wait for my answer. "Never mind. Business is business. Tell me what you got on the sonofabitch who killed my boy, Marco."

I cleared my throat. "Well, you see..."

He sneered, "You got nothing. I understand. He was like a thorn in your side. You don't care who shot him." His voice turned calm, reminding me of how it feels before a bad storm comes through.

I thought fast. "That's not true. Marco and I could never be friends, but I want Felicity to have closure. That means I need to find whoever murdered Marco."

I squeezed my eyes shut and held my breath, glad bullets didn't go through phones.

"Another thing I remember about you. You got balls. Too bad it didn't work with you and my nephew, Alex." We'd dated a few times and there was definitely chemistry. If only Bucanetti hadn't raised him and treated him like a son. Of course, I have to admit the biggest reason it didn't work was my feelings for Corrigan.

Bucanetti continued, "That's not important. Ya know, me and Marco went way back. His old man worked for me before Marco took his first communion. You remember what he did for you, too, when your aunt got involved with that *lecchino,* Corroza. So, when you find out who killed Marco, you tell me. I trust you kept my business number from before. "

Alarms going off in my head were so loud I couldn't hear myself speak. I think I said, "Yeah, but what'll you do if I don't have any information?"

"Let's just say if you find the killer before me, I'll forget about that deal we made back when Joey Corrozza ate a bullet. You know, it'd be nice for your aunt to be safe. I mean, considering she's getting married soon."

"How do you know…" There was no use continuing the question. He'd hung up. I sat motionless, the phone still to my ear. As I lowered my arm, panic rose in my chest. How was I going to find the killer without having any clues?

I talked my panic down enough so I could function. The first person I needed to question was Felicity. It seemed in my limited experience, that people often knew more than they realized.

I massaged my neck while waiting for Felicity to answer her phone, but it went into voicemail. Maybe she finally crashed and slept. I left a message asking her to call me back right away.

Funny, I had been acquainted with Marco over one thing or another for a few months, but knew next to nothing about him. I was depending on Felicity to fill me in.

My phone rang about five minutes later, but it wasn't Felicity.

"Hey kiddo, what's happening?"

"Ed. Hello and congratulations." Much as I would have enjoyed talking to my future uncle, I couldn't help but be disappointed it wasn't Felicity. Then I felt guilty. "I hear the wedding is in Vegas."

"Yeah. My cousin's chapel." He sounded almost embarrassed. "But I drew the line at being married by some guy dressed like Cupid."

I giggled in spite of my problems and myself.

"I didn't call about that, though. I want to make sure you don't get any ideas about me quitting working for you."

"That's good to hear, Ed, although I'm not sure my aunt would agree."

"We had a good heart-to-heart about a lot of things. I gave. She gave. It's all okay."

That must have been an interesting conversation. "As long as she's all right with it, I am too. In fact, I need your help with—"

"Got it covered."

"What? You don't know what I'm going to ask."

"True, but if it's about Marco Conti, he was quite the ladies' man. Maybe one of those damsels heard he was getting hitched and killed him."

The neck ache I had been resisting disappeared. "I'm not even going to ask you where you got your information, but do you have any names?"

Pride came through in his voice. "Only his latest conquest besides Felicity. That Dixon girl has bad luck with men. A creep for a brother and a scumbag for a lover. Anyway, her name is Wisteria Flowers. Hell of a name. Works at a doughnut shop on W. 130th, Donut Heaven.

"Have you told Corrigan about Wisteria?"

"Had to. The guy's in the wedding party."

I couldn't fault Ed's reasoning. "Okay. I guess I'll go visit her. Or have you talked to her already?"

"No, not yet. If you want, I can do it after my shift."

"No, I'll do it. By the way, how did you find out about her?"

"I know people who know people."

I assumed that was all the explanation he was going to give. "Thanks, Ed."

After we hung up, I looked up Donut Heaven's exact location and headed out. I reasoned there were worse places to go than a doughnut shop. I idly wondered if they had any of those chocolate-frosted, crème-filled delights. Pushing my sweet tooth's desire aside, I went over in my mind my line of questioning. Now if only Wisteria was at work.

There was one other car in the small parking lot, with a couple of teenage boys eating doughnuts at a table and sneaking glances at the woman behind the counter. I couldn't blame them. She looked about my age, but that's where the similarity ended. Her auburn hair was tied in a ponytail that fell between her shoulder blades. With her tiny waist, curvy hips and flat stomach, it was obvious she didn't eat the product. The buttons on her uniform strained with the effort of keeping her breasts from breaking free. Doughnuts and a woman who looked like her. Every man's fantasy.

"Can I help you?" Her voice was soft, almost lyrical.

"I'll have a chocolate-covered, crème stick and are you Wisteria?"

She puckered her full lips. "Yeah, I'm Wisteria. Do you want the doughnut for here or to go?"

"To go." I didn't want to have to choose between taking a bite of the crème stick or asking questions. "I'm Private Investigator Claire DeNardo. Did you know Marco Conti?"

Over her shoulder, she called out to a fellow worker. "Betty, could you take over here for a second?"

A large, older woman came out and huffed, "Sure.

Just coming off my break anyway." The smell of cigarettes clung to Betty and I had to stop myself from wrinkling my nose.

"Thanks. I'll be right back." Wisteria came around the counter. "Let's talk outside." I followed her through the door. She turned so fast, I almost bumped into her. "Like I told that cute cop, Marco and me had a thing going for a while. Until I started getting calls, telling me to leave him alone. At first I ignored them, even laughed about them. Then I came out of my apartment one day and somebody had slashed all my tires."

"How did Marco respond?"

"He wasn't happy. Said he'd find out who did it and make them sorry."

"Did he?"

She bit her lower lip. "Somebody killed him before he had a chance. But he did replace my tires."

A real gentleman. "Did you still see each other after that?"

She dusted powdered sugar from her bosom. "Nah. But a guy like that is never faithful. He probably found another bed to lay in."

"Do you have any idea who threatened you?" Names flashed through my mind.

"Just that it was a woman. Couldn't have been that little mouse Marco was marrying. He was probably the first guy who gave her more than a sneer."

The spinning in my mind stopped and picked a name. "Did you ever meet or talk to the fiancé's friend, Charlotte?"

"That's who Marco thought was threatening me." She looked into the store window. "I gotta get back."

"One more question. Was the cute cop's name Corrigan?"

A knowing smile spread across Wisteria's face. "Yeah. A real hottie. He could set my sheets on fire anytime."

I held my temper in check. "Thank you for your help."

Back in my car, I thought about how cops and doughnuts go together. Add Wisteria to the mix and how could Corrigan resist? Then my common sense took over. Wisteria was gorgeous, but I was... cute. I frowned. Cute only wins if the word describes a bunny. I ripped off a piece of the doughnut with my teeth, and pushed Wisteria and her seductive curves from my mind.

My next move was to talk to Corrigan. In person. My bet was on Charlotte as the source of threats to Wisteria. Still, I had no intention of confronting her on my own.

When I learned Corrigan wasn't at the police station, I had a hunch where he was. I made it to Felicity's home in half the time it would have taken me if I had obeyed the traffic laws.

Sure enough, Corrigan was there. I parked behind him. Spotting me, he got out of his car and rapped on my window. When I lowered it, he said, "Something tells me you went to see Wisteria Flowers." A smile began to form when he said her name, but he squelched it almost too fast for me to notice.

As tempted as I was to ask him what he thought of her, I decided I probably didn't really want to know. "Ed told me about Marco having a girlfriend on the side, and I went to question her."

His voice didn't betray anything. "What'd she tell you?"

I related Wisteria's story to Corrigan, omitting her

comment about him.

"Interesting. Ms. Dixon claimed she didn't have any idea about Marco's side action."

"She knows now, doesn't she?" Having been cheated on by my former fiancé when I was in graduate school, a wave of empathy surprised me with its force. "Poor Felicity. To be grieving over Marco and then finding out what a weasel he really was." Afraid of making it sound too personal if I said more, I shifted gears. "Charlotte has to be the one who made those threats."

Corrigan's eyebrows shot up. "You mean Charlotte Pusitano? I'm on my way to her place now. This time don't follow me. It could get ugly."

"I've already experienced Charlotte's wrath."

"Maybe you have, but you still can't tag along. This is strictly a police matter. Sorry, Claire."

He was treating me like a kid sister who always made a pest of herself. He wasn't sorry at all. I tapped on my steering wheel with my fisted hand. "Fine."

He ran his hand through his hair. "Claire, listen—" I raised my window and stared straight ahead. He pounded on the glass to no avail.

I felt stupid for doing something so childish and lowered the window again. Too late. He was heading back to his car. Without hesitating, he sped away, probably saying some choice words about me. I debated trying to catch him. But a woman's scream drowned out my thoughts. The sound came from Felicity's home.

Chapter Eighteen

I grabbed my phone and my gun and flung open my car door. My mind told me to move it, but my body was inert matter. The sound of a gunshot acted like an electric shock, and I was jolted out of my car. I was halfway to Felicity's house when she burst through her front door, her face the color of plaster. She screeched to a halt, almost slamming into me. Despite a blood smear on her chest, she didn't appear to have any injuries.

She stared past me. "Charlotte knew about Marco's cheating." Her voice broke and she lowered her head until her chin touched her chest. "I didn't mean to hurt her."

The crème stick I'd eaten earlier churned in my stomach. "Where is Charlotte now?"

She didn't look up. "The kitchen."

I was torn between staying with her or seeing if I could help Charlotte. Felicity decided for me when she tottered and passed out onto the grass. Since she was breathing, I reasoned she wasn't going anywhere. I punched 911 into my phone, which was what I should have done when I first heard the scream. Wishing my legs could pump as fast as my heart, I darted into Felicity's home and straight into the kitchen.

A gun lay on the floor, probably where Felicity had dropped it. A streak of fresh blood snaked through the room and ended by the patio door at the back of the house. A siren sounded as I stepped out into the backyard. Charlotte was lying, unconscious, where she must have fallen, too weak from blood loss to go on. Despite a bullet wound to her chest, she had a pulse.

Corrigan appeared at almost the same time as the ambulance. Once the EMT attended to Charlotte, I returned to the front yard where Corrigan stepped around that EMT and began questioning a now-conscious Felicity. Despite his efforts, the only answer he received from her was a blank stare.

The EMT pronounced Felicity to be in shock and they whisked both her and Charlotte to the hospital. Once treated, Felicity would be charged with aggravated assault and, if deemed fit, would be jailed.

After the ambulance took off, Corrigan stood in front of me, arms crossed like a genie in a suit. "How is it wherever you go, bodies are found? It doesn't matter if I'd been in the same place as you a minute before. You're like a one-woman, high-crime area." He scratched his head. "You know, you could have gotten yourself hurt."

I nodded, wishing he would wrap me in his arms and give me a piece of chocolate. I quickly reminded myself this was real life, not a fairy tale. "It's looking more and more to me like Charlotte killed Marco."

Corrigan made no comment and I continued. "According to Wisteria some woman told her to stay away from Marco. And Felicity just claimed Charlotte knew about Marco's infidelity. I've seen Charlotte's protectiveness in action, and I think she would be very capable of getting rid of Marco. I'll bet she even rationalized her motives, telling herself she did it to help Felicity."

He rubbed his chin. "That accounts for a motive, but at Dixon's burial, did you notice the direction Charlotte came from to comfort Felicity? Even if she'd been in the general area of the shot, she'd have had to move with superhuman speed to get to Felicity. Plus, what did she do with the gun? We still haven't found it."

My lower lip pushed itself out. "I don't know."

Corrigan's phone buzzed with a text, so he didn't pursue my lack of explanation for those pesky details. After he read it, he stuck his phone back in his pocket. "They transferred Ms. Dixon to jail. She told the officer transporting her she wanted to talk."

I puffed out my chest. "Since I'm the one that saved the day, I should be allowed to hear her statement."

Corrigan looked at me as if I'd said I believed in unicorns. "Why don't I just make you a junior police officer, with a badge and everything? Claire, I can't let you in on this. Right now I've got two murder investigations that may or may not be related, an assault that is probably related to one or both of the murders, a missing witness and another witness who keeps getting involved where she shouldn't." He took a breath and his eyes narrowed. "How many clients do you have now as a result of all of this?"

"Only Felicity." I wondered if I'd have to withdraw from her employ too now that she would probably be charged with assault with a deadly weapon. I had the bad luck to once again be a witness. I didn't have to wonder long.

"You know you can't keep—"

"Don't say it." My voice was as sullen as a teen that had her cell phone confiscated. That dream of a new office aided by Felicity's payment vanished like a mirage.

Chapter Nineteen

Corrigan headed back to the station while I returned to my office. On the way there, it hit me. If Charlotte was charged, how long it would take Bucanetti to find out? Then how long before Charlotte joined Marco and George Dixon in the morgue?

I stared at the traffic light, waiting for it to turn green and wondered, not for the first time, which dots were connected. Did Charlotte kill Marco to protect Felicity? Could she have also killed George Dixon for the same reason? Questions spun in my mind like tires stuck in mud. They whirled round and round getting nowhere.

After a bit, my stomach grumbled, feeling neglected. I had a taste for pizza. Cicarelli's pizza to be exact. Nick Cicarelli was the one who first brought Charlotte to my attention. Maybe he could provide me with some insight into the woman.

If not, I could still enjoy some great pizza.

Before I started to head to the East Side, my father called. "Claire, you're going to hear from Suzy later on today. She's throwing a shin-dig. Tell her yes."

My brows knit. "A party? Is it a special occasion?"

My brain began running through birthdays, anniversaries, and obscure holidays.

"It's a surprise engagement party for Lena and Ed, and Suzy's going to ask you to bring them over to her house without letting them know."

"How am I supposed to do that?" *Use a cattle prod?* Suzy was not exactly Aunt Lena's favorite person. In fact, my aunt still referred to Suzy as 'that woman.'

He sucked in a breath. "I know, but Suzy wanted to throw them an engagement party, so could you—"

I thought back to Suzy's help with Felicity and interrupted my dad. "Sure, I'll do it. Suzy's a good person."

"To God's ears. Now if Lena can get past the notion I'm cheating on your mother. I'll always love Theresa, but Suzy...she makes me happy."

My heart warmed hearing that. "Aunt Lena will come around. After all, Uncle Tommy died and she's taking a new husband. Dad, I've got another call coming in. I love you and I'll make sure they're at Suzy's."

I took the incoming call and wished I hadn't.

That hoarse voice began, "Claire. How come you didn't tell me Marco's killer is in the hospital? I had to find out on my own." It was Bucanetti.

Any lingering warmth froze. How did Bucanetti know about Charlotte and why did he think she killed Marco? In a voice sounding more assured than I felt I responded, "I'm not completely sure she killed Marco. No sense bothering you until there is some proof." I held my breath hoping he'd buy my answer.

"You got until tomorrow this time to find out if she did it." He ended the call without reminding me of the consequences of failing. Just as well. I knew what they were and what I had to do.

Pizza would have to wait. I sped to the police station, rehearsing in my mind how to get access to Felicity. I had to find out if Charlotte had confessed to Marco's murder. Pronto.

A lump the size of a giant meatball settled in my stomach. If Charlotte was guilty, how could I turn that information over to Bucanetti knowing he'd have her killed as retribution?

I sat in my car for a few minutes, taking measured breaths hoping to lower my heartbeat. But all it did was make me dizzy.

Once inside the police station, I asked for Corrigan.

He approached me and took hold of my arm. "Why are you here?" From his tone, I could tell he didn't think this was a social visit.

"I have to speak with Felicity now. Please." I must have looked pathetic, because his expression softened.

He led me back to his desk and swung a chair around for me. "Have a seat. Tell me what's going on."

I wanted to spill it all, Bucanetti's calls and his intentions toward Charlotte. But to tell him the whole truth could hurt people I loved. Knowing I couldn't do that made me feel like I was trying to hold a crumbling building together against an earthquake.

With my options few, I reminded Corrigan that, until or if Felicity was charged with a crime, I still worked for her. I added that, if Charlotte was Marco's murderer, I could lay claim to the rest of Felicity's fee. That in turn would allow me to fund my new PI business. It was sort of the truth. Still, I hated him thinking my motives were strictly mercenary. If I hadn't needed to protect my family and Charlotte from Bucanetti, I would have wholeheartedly spilled my guts.

Corrigan wore his cop face and I couldn't tell if he bought my money-grubbing act. Without giving me a clue as to his thoughts, he said, "She already made bail. I assume she'll see you."

I released the breath I held, even thanking him twice.

As I turned to leave, he grabbed my hands. "Hold on. See if the story she tells you matches her statement. She claims she was so distraught after the police told her Marco was cheating on her that she attempted suicide. Charlotte somehow showed up and tried to stop her. They struggled and the gun went off." The smirk on his face told me he didn't believe her.

I mumbled, "It could be true."

He tightened the grip on my hands. "You can't possibly buy that."

It didn't matter what I thought, as long as Bucanetti bought it. "Felicity adored Marco and she was under a lot of stress…" I couldn't meet Corrigan's eyes.

His phone rang and he dropped my hands.

When Corrigan spoke Philip's name to the caller, I leaned in closer to hear more, but miscalculated and tipped my chair too far. The seat went out from under me. Reflexively, my hands shot out onto Corrigan's desk to catch myself from falling face first. I scrambled to regain my balance and scraped together any dignity I had left.

Corrigan's eyes widened as he stared at me. He ended his call with, "Yeah, I owe you." Then turned to me. "Are you done with your acrobatics?" He shook his head and that tiny blood vessel in his temple shimmied a bit.

I ignored my clumsiness and his irritation. "What about Philip Reeves?"

Corrigan looked toward heaven. "Still no sign of him,

but he'll turn up."

I narrowed my eyes to slits and stared at Corrigan, trying to read his thoughts.

"Come on, I'll walk you out." He stood and motioned for me to rise. We were practically to the station door. "Are you going to be okay?"

"Of course." I kissed his cheek and did my best to stride confidently away like one of those women in a deodorant commercial. It was an act. With two deaths and Philip MIA, I felt as if I was drowning and Bucanetti was holding my head under.

Chapter Twenty

I was so lost in thought I couldn't recall how I made it to Felicity's home without causing an accident. I turned off the ignition and sat in my car, trying to collect my thoughts. Giving up that lofty ambition, I got out of my car and rang her doorbell. Twice. I was about to leave when she yelled through the door, "Go away."

"Felicity, It's Claire. I'm here to help. Can I come in?"

She cracked open the door. "My brother and fiancé are dead, and my best friend is in the hospital because of me. How could you possibly help?"

I had to talk fast before she shut me out completely. "At least let's talk, before Bucanetti gets to Charlotte."

Her eyebrows shot up. "Did he tell you he was going to hurt her?"

I rubbed my forehead, hoping to ward off the headache I felt coming on. "Not exactly. But he thinks she killed Marco, so he might."

Felicity's face paled and she gripped the doorknob.

That's when my hunch turned solid.

Felicity gave Bucanetti the information that Charlotte

was involved in Marco's murder. But why? Had Charlotte confessed to Felicity before Felicity shot her? As soothing as a nurse before she gives you an injection, I said, "If you let me inside, we can sit down and talk."

She stepped back and I cautiously walked into her foyer, relieved she hadn't slammed the door on my foot.

She collapsed onto a loveseat in the living room. I sat on the edge of the chair directly across from her and blurted out the $1,000,000 question. "Did Charlotte kill Marco?"

She rested her head in her hands for a moment. Then taking care with her words, she replied, "I never said that."

"Do you have any reason to think she did?"

She wrapped her arms around herself. "No, of course not."

"She never hid the fact she didn't like Marco."

"A person doesn't kill someone just because they don't like him."

"Don't they?"

She dropped her chin. "I don't know."

I bit my lower lip, debating whether to keep pressing her. "If you insist on staying quiet, you could be sealing Charlotte's fate." Not that I was so sure I could save anyone from Bucanetti.

Her eyes blazed. "I told you, I don't know."

I made a half-hearted attempt to stand. "I'm not accusing you of anything, but I can't help if I don't know what's going on."

"How do I know you won't run to the police if I tell you anything different from my statement?"

Fibbing to her was not an option. I am not the greatest of liars, unless I'm telling someone they look nice when they really look terrible. "You don't. Heck, I don't know what I'll do. But if you want Charlotte to live, we've only got today. Bucanetti's calling me tomorrow and if I don't have a good reason for him not to bump off Charlotte, she doesn't stand a chance."

Felicity didn't say anything for a moment. Then, in a restrained voice, she said, "I knew Marco wasn't what most women would think of as good husband material. But he was the only man who ever treated me with any kindness. He was sweet and gentle with me. I loved him." Her lower lip wobbled and she stopped, took a deep breath and continued. "Charlotte never liked Marco. She told me not to trust him, but I thought she was just jealous. I didn't listen, so she must have started spying on him for proof."

I didn't move, afraid I'd shatter the atmosphere. The air seemed heavy with words unspoken. Felicity was leaving out some chunks of information, but I chose not to say anything.

"When Mr. Bucanetti first called me, I was crazy with grief. I'm not sure exactly what I told him." She pulled on a loose sweater thread.

Feeling as if I was swimming in a bathtub, getting nowhere, I took a different tack. "Where was Charlotte when Detective Corrigan came here?"

"In the garage. What does that have to do with Mr. Bucanetti?"

I tried to keep my impatience at bay. "Do you want to keep Charlotte safe or not?"

Her jaw set. "Of course I do. I didn't tell the police she was here and they didn't ask."

"What happened when the detective left?" I put up my hand like a school-crossing guard. "I know. You told them you attempted suicide and Charlotte stopped you. But what happened between the time Detective Corrigan left and Charlotte came inside?"

"All right." She straightened, took in a shaky breath and exhaled. "As soon as he left, I grabbed Marco's gun. I was so out of my mind with grief and anger, I wasn't sure what I was going to do with it. Before I even decided, Mr. Bucanetti called. I don't remember my exact words, but I babbled on about Marco, and Charlotte knowing Marco had betrayed me."

"Charlotte came inside and I dropped the phone. I was waving the gun around, screaming at her. She admitted she'd known Marco was cheating on me but said she took care of it. For me. She begged me to put the gun down. Instead, I threatened to kill her if she didn't tell me what she did."

Felicity began to hiccup and took a sip of water from a glass next to her. "She didn't explain. She just reached for the gun and it went off."

I perched on the edge of my seat. "Do you think by taking care of it, she meant she was responsible for Marco's death?"

Her chin quivered. "I don't know. And now I may never know." She dropped her face into her hands and began to cry.

I waited until her sobs abated. "She'll pull through." I didn't have a ticket into the future, but hoped I was right. "The best thing we can do for Charlotte right now is to keep Bucanetti from thinking she killed Marco."

Even if she did.

Felicity nodded, grabbed a tissue from a nearby box and blew her nose. "Should I call Mr. Bucanetti? Tell him I wasn't thinking straight and to ignore what I said?"

"Please." I wasn't sure that, even if she reached him in time, he'd call off the dogs. It didn't matter if Charlotte had a part in Marco's death or not, she needed protection. But since she was still unable to confess, I hadn't moved beyond the *Start* square on this board game called *Murder*.

*** *** ***

Back at my office, I went ahead with my plans to talk with Nick Cicarelli, Charlotte's employer. But this time, rather than spend precious minutes driving over to Mayfield Heights on the other side of town, I called him. I hadn't had much luck in my current case, but at least I was fortunate enough to get hold of Nick. Too bad that, besides telling me about Charlotte's tough upbringing, with a father who ran off and an alcoholic mother, the only other bit of information he had was about a guy who had seemed interested in Charlotte.

"The guy's first name is Dennis. He's a petty hood wanting to be in the big time. I don't know his last name. Anyway, today he shows up asking for Charlotte. Soon as he found out what happened to her he took off."

I recalled Martin Beckman's muscleman. "Could you describe him?" I held my breath. The late George Dixon owed Beckman a lot of money and Marco was getting in the way of Dixon racking up gambling debts he couldn't pay. If I were a gambler, I would bet Dennis was linked to both Marco and George Dixon's deaths.

"Big guy. Nose looks like somebody used it as a punching bag. You know him?"

"I think I do." Another possible piece of the puzzle. "Okay, thanks." After we chatted a bit more and I promised to return and try his latest pizza creation, we ended the conversation.

I checked the time, wondering if Felicity got through to Bucanetti and if she knew anything about this guy, Dennis. I called her. When she didn't answer, I left a message to get back to me as soon as possible.

I drummed my fingers on my desk, reassuring myself Felicity was probably on the phone with Bucanetti. Fifteen headache-inducing minutes went by and still no return call.

I couldn't wait any longer. Maybe Felicity had cooled Bucanetti's desire for Charlotte's blood, but I didn't want to take the chance. Charlotte needed protection. I grabbed my phone to do what I should have done to begin with.

Warn Corrigan about Bucanetti.

Chapter Twenty-One

I didn't go through with contacting Corrigan. My cold feet affected my brain and I ended the call before he answered. I didn't know if I was up to taking that chance. What if Bucanetti learned I squealed on him? I had my family's safety to consider. In that flash of stupidity, I decided I'd have to protect Charlotte from that New Jersey hood.

I was almost out the door to go to the hospital when my phone rang. Corrigan. My first thought was not to answer. My second one was to realize he knew I called so I'd have to talk to him sooner or later. Thinking I'd just tell him I called him by mistake, I got only as far as uttering the first syllable of my false explanation before he interrupted.

"Did you talk to Felicity Dixon?" rushed from his mouth.

I nervously peeled off what was left of my fingernail polish. "Yes."

"What was her story? Was it any different from her statement to the police?"

Feeling as if quicksand was one step in front of me

and a mountain cliff's edge right behind me, I decided to trust Corrigan to pull me out before I sank. I exhaled a shaky breath. "No, but that's not why I called. You need to—"

"Hold on just a sec, Claire."

I heard muffled conversation and Corrigan returned to the phone. "Gotta go." With no further explanation, he hung up.

I sagged against my office doorframe. My family was, for the time being, safe from Bucanetti's far-reaching grip.

The minute I felt calm enough to form words, I tried to reach Felicity again. Again, my call rolled into her voicemail. I could only hope she was still on the phone with Bucanetti.

I inhaled deeply and made my way to the hospital, telling myself there was nothing to worry about. After all, the police had posted a guard at Charlotte's hospital room door. I stiffened. *Since when would that stop Bucanetti?*

I blew through two red lights on my way, finally pulling into the parking garage when my phone rang. Felicity.

"Mr. Bucanetti had me picked up. I just got home." Her voice was unsteady. "Charlotte's safe. For now." She swallowed audibly.

My pulse went from a gallop down to a trot. "What about you?"

"I don't know if I'll ever be back to normal, but I'm hanging in there."

"Good. Oh, by the way, did Charlotte ever mention a guy named Dennis?" I congratulated myself on sounding casual.

Her voice crackled with disgust. "That creep. He worked for the vulture my brother owed. Charlotte told me she dumped him. Why?"

I didn't want to play all my cards so gave her a non-committal, "Just heard his name mentioned a while ago. No biggie."

I ended the call as I pulled into the hospital's multi-level garage. No spaces on the ground floor so I began the slow ascent to find a parking spot. "Come on, come on." I tapped my hand against the steering wheel, grumbling at the creeping vehicles in front of me.

I took the stairs to Charlotte's room and spotted Corrigan talking with the uniformed cop guarding her. Corrigan strode over to me. "Why are you always in the places you shouldn't be?"

I bit my lower lip, and dove in. "I was afraid Charlotte was in danger. If she's involved in Marco's murder, Michael Bucanetti could want her dead."

Corrigan peered at me through eyes like slits. His voice was controlled fury. "If you knew Bucanetti and his gang of miscreants were after Charlotte, why didn't you tell me earlier?"

I felt my temper rise like lava in a volcano. "I tried. But you kept interrupting me, too busy to give me a chance—"

"Excuse me. Is either of you Detective Corrigan?" When Corrigan raised his hand, she continued, "Dr. Woldcraff would like to speak to you right away about Ms. Pusitano."

Corrigan spun on his heels, but then looked over his shoulder at me. "Don't go anywhere. We need to talk some more."

I swung my purse over my shoulder and marched into

a nearby restroom. I should have known Corrigan would get mad. Even though I tried to tell him about Bucanetti earlier. I splashed some cold water on my face and slunk back to the hallway near Charlotte's room.

The doctor and Corrigan came around the corner. I didn't want to spar with Corrigan any more today, but I stuck around. I caught his eye and must have looked so contrite, he just nodded his head toward the exit. I didn't hesitate to take that as meaning I wasn't on the hot seat any longer.

I gladly walked toward the elevator and told myself Corrigan already knew about Bucanetti. Plus, since Bucanetti had been signaled not to execute Charlotte, there was no reason for me to be concerned for her safety. I admit, I was taking a coward's way out, but there really wasn't anything I could do. Besides, I needed to see if this Dennis fit into the equation. And how.

My stomach growled in agreement. It also told me I needed to eat. Thinking about what was in my fridge depressed me, so I called my dad. His leftovers were better than anything I could buy prepared.

When he didn't answer his phone, I wilted, thinking of a trip to the grocery store. That depressed me so much I settled for picking up a burger, fries, and diet soda and driving back to my office where I planned to eat the greasy meal. Even worse, I had to charge it since I was broke.

I'd just ripped open the to-go bag when I got a call from my aunt.

"Claire, honey, I need a tiny favor."

Hearing her pull-one-over-on-you tone of voice, I steeled myself for a whopper of a request. "What is it?"

"I just made manicotti with sausage, but it's more

than I can eat. I'd love to share it with you. That is, if you're hungry."

I was salivating onto my phone. "It so happens, I'm famished."

"Okay, it's ready now so hurry up and get here."

"I'll be there in fifteen minutes." I tossed the oily bag and its contents into the trash.

Floating toward the heavenly scent of my aunt's cooking, I made it to her home in no time and gave her a cheek kiss.

"You don't look so good." She squeezed my chin. "When was the last time you had a decent meal?"

I gently pulled my face away. "Stop. Check out these thighs." I slapped the tops of my legs. "Do they look like they belong to a starving person?"

***

I patted my extended abdomen and reflected on the scrumptiousness of my aunt's pasta, buried in cheese, fat with sausage, and redolent with basil-infused tomato sauce. While I seriously contemplated a nap, Aunt Lena grabbed her purse. She had softened me with the promise of food, then lowered the spatula. "Now that you're full, you can come with me to look at wedding dresses."

Too late to back out. "It's already 8. You won't have much time."

She snorted, "When you have a body like mine, you don't have that much to look at. Come on. There's a dress out there with my name on it."

I heaved myself from the chair and pulled out my car keys. "Where to?"

"Simon's on Center Ridge has nice clothes. If they don't have anything, we'll call it a night."

The parking lot for the store was almost empty. We were the only customers and the clerk was bearing down on us.

"Are you ladies looking for something in particular?"

My aunt, who had already started browsing through the formal gowns, nodded. "I need a dress for a wedding."

The clerk smiled and clapped her hands together softly. "We have some lovely mother-of-the bride gowns." She turned to me. "What are your wedding colors, dear?"

Before I could answer, Aunt Lena set the woman straight. "The mother of this bride's been dead for twenty years."

The woman's fingertips flew to her open mouth and she stammered, "I'm so sorry. I mean, not just for the loss of your mother, but mistaking who—"

My aunt waved away the apology. "It's okay. I'd like a dress that isn't slutty, but lets the groom know what he's getting. You know what I mean?"

I squirmed. "Aunt Lena!"

"What? You don't think Ed's—"

"I don't want to think about Ed's anything."

My aunt shook her head. "You kids think you're the only ones with urges."

Thankfully, the salesperson cleared her throat and held up a demure pastel green dress. "This would go nicely with your complexion, ma'am. Don't you think so?"

"That looks pretty, Aunt Lena. Try it on."

Aunt Lena wrinkled her nose as if the dress was made of overripe cheese. "I don't think so. I want more, you know, va-va-voom." She wandered to another section of dresses and scooped up a couple. At last, she glanced around and disappeared into the dressing room.

In no time at all, she returned, sweeping in front of me. "What do you think?"

She twirled around in a cream-colored chiffon dress devoid of any decoration save one oversized, hot pink taffeta rose that appeared to blossom between her breasts.

I merely blinked, almost speechless. "Are you going to try the others on?"

She pressed her hands against the dress's pleated skirt and looked hard at herself in the triple mirror. "Nope. This is the one" She examined herself from all angles. "You and Angie can get bridesmaid's dresses to match this rose." She looked down at her cleavage. "It's not too much, is it?"

The flower was so huge it looked like it was about to devour her breasts and then start on the rest of her, but I swallowed any words of criticism. It was clear from the look on my aunt's face she loved the dress. I chose my words like a true diplomat. "If you adore it, get it. Show it to Angie and see what she thinks." It was my cowardly way of avoiding negativity.

She played with one of the dress' petals. "It's not like I couldn't wear it again."

Make sure it's far away from a swarm of bees.

"But you're right. It's a good idea for Angie to see it. I don't want to have it where I like something so much I can't see if there's a problem with it."

"Whatever you decide, Aunt Lena."

She twirled in front of the mirror again. "I'm taking it."

While the clerk was ringing up the sale, Aunt Lena leaned toward me. "Next, we'll go shopping for your maid of honor dress. We'll pick one that might inspire

Brian to start thinking. You know, being part of a wedding gets people in the mood."

When I snorted in response, she lightly slapped my arm. "You don't think it could happen?"

"Sure I believe in miracles, but if I only get one, I'd pray for being able to afford my own PI business."

She shrugged. "Who says you can't have a husband and a business?"

Yeah, all I have to do is solve a murder while looking alluring. Nothing to it.

By the time I got my aunt home, it was 9:30. I headed to the office to pick up my notes and go through them once more before going to bed. Maybe I would get an inspiration just as I was dropping off to sleep.

I made it as far as my apartment door when my phone rang. Gino. I groaned, worried he would be coming back to reclaim his business even sooner.

"Hey Claire, I know it's late, but I figured a youngster like you wouldn't be asleep. I need you to do me a favor."

Two favors in one night! "What is it?" My polite, co-operative side scolded me for not outright agreeing to do the favor. My more sensible side realized with Gino, that favor could be anything from contacting a buddy of his to placing a bet on a pony.

My reluctance didn't seem to register, because he didn't skip a beat. "I knew I could count on you. Frank raised you right. All I need is you to make up a letter, an announcement, saying I'll be back in business the end of this month. I'll send you the list of who it goes to. Shouldn't take you long. What'dya say?"

I squeezed the phone until my knuckles turned white. He wasn't even home yet and was already giving me administrative work. I wanted to scream. Instead, I swallowed my anger, deciding this wasn't the battle to fight. "Sure, Gino. It'll take a couple of days, but I can do it."

"Great. I've gotta split now, got some people waiting for me."

I grabbed my notes and a pen and marched into my bedroom.

Chapter Twenty-Two

The roar of the garbage trucks outside my window woke me. I sat up and heard a rustling noise. I'd gone over my notes all right. In fact, I rolled over them in my sleep. I groaned and fell back onto my pillow. Someone was pounding at my door as if their life depended on it. I obviously wasn't meant to stay in bed.

I grabbed my robe. "Who is it?"

"Brian. You weren't still sleeping, were you?"

"No, no. I'll be right there."

I ran my fingers through my hair and gulped down some mouthwash on my way to the door. "What's up?" I leaned against the doorframe.

He took one look at me and smiled. "Yeah, I can tell you've been up for hours."

"Is that why you're here? To check on my hours of sleep?" In spite of myself, I yawned.

"No, I wanted to say I know I came down hard on you yesterday. You should've told me about Bucanetti before, but, well, I'm sorry."

I'm a sucker for a man wearing an apology. "It's okay." I couldn't help myself. "You know, I did try to tell you." I tilted my head. "Wait. You came all the way here for that?"

"If you decided to hold a grudge, I was going to try to soften you up with breakfast."

"Food and an apology?" I put my arms around his neck. "This is sounding better and better."

He nuzzled my cheek. "Don't get too excited. It's breakfast at the hospital." He pulled back. "Before we eat, I want to talk to Charlotte Pusitano. On the way over here, I got the notice she's awake. We need to get moving."

Once we were on our way to the hospital, I recounted my recent conversation with Nick Cicarelli about Dennis Rudkowsky, Beckman's enforcer.

"Interesting. You have a theory about this Rudkowsky guy?"

I debated not telling him for fear he'd call me insane, but I didn't want to risk withholding the information just to have it blow up in my face. "A while back, Felicity told me Marco had put himself between her brother, George, and his gambling debts. Maybe Dennis and Marco had a confrontation and rather than duke it out, Dennis killed Marco. Maybe, unwittingly or not, Charlotte let it drop that Marco would be at George's funeral."

"Pretty fancy thinking." Corrigan reached for his phone. "A guy like Rudkowsky is sure to be in our data base. We'll bring him in for questioning."

As we drew closer to the hospital and Charlotte, I made Corrigan laugh regaling him with the story of my aunt and the wedding gown. It relaxed me to hear him laugh and to see those adorable dimples.

That mellow state dissipated as soon as we reached

Charlotte's floor. Corrigan murmured, "Wait here." He flashed his badge at the guard and took a step into Charlotte's room.

I was miffed. He enticed me down here. Now he expected me to stand around listening to my foot tapping on the floor. I snapped, "I'm within my rights to hear Charlotte's answers."

He gave me a pained look but didn't say anything. I followed him as closely as a stamp on a letter. Charlotte's eyes darted from Corrigan to me. She didn't look happy to see either of us.

"Ms. Pusitano, in case you don't recall, I'm Detective Corrigan with the Cleveland PD. I'm here to talk to you about the events leading up to you being shot."

"And you remember me, Charlotte. Claire DeNardo. I'm—"

"Just about to leave." Corrigan finished my sentence.

Charlotte closed her eyes. "I don't remember what happened." Her voice was scratchy and her words thick.

Taking a huge chance, I inched toward Charlotte's bed and quickly said, "Maybe Detective Corrigan's absence might nudge your memory." I motioned toward the door with my chin.

She gave a short nod.

I sidled up even closer and waited, holding my breath, praying Corrigan would play along.

I imagined his eyes shooting daggers at me, but I held my ground.

He didn't move and I doubted he planned to, but good fortune smiled at me. His phone rang. He glanced down at it and muttered, "You're lucky I have to take this." I wasn't sure if that comment was for me or Charlotte. Anyway, he left the room.

The moment he did, Charlotte looked at me, her eyes wide. "Didn't want Felicity to know about us."

My stomach twisted into a pretzel. "You and Marco?" My voice must have registered my shock.

She shook her head hard. "Dennis."

I wanted to make this piece fit into the puzzle so I pounded it in place. "He killed Marco, didn't he?"

She turned her head toward the wall. I gripped the guardrail. "Michael Bucanetti is looking for whoever killed Marco and it's not to shake their hand." Her body tensed. "I can help if you'd just tell me—"

Before I could finish my pitch, a nurse bustled into the room. "I'm sorry, but you'll have to come back later. Charlotte needs to rest."

Corrigan stepped in behind the nurse. "No, *I'm* sorry. This is a murder investigation. Once Ms. Pusitano answers our questions, we'll let her rest." He stood at the foot of Charlotte's bed and peered down at her. "We need an answer, Charlotte. Did Dennis kill Marco?"

For a moment, all I could hear was the humming of the medical machinery that measured Charlotte's life force.

Her voice wasn't much louder. "I don't know." She clutched her thin hospital blanket and pulled it up to her chin.

Ignoring Corrigan and me, the nurse checked Charlotte's blood pressure monitor. "BP is way up. You two have to leave *now*." She shooed us out.

He held up his index finger. "Just a second. Charlotte, I'll be back later. I hope you think about what Ms. DeNardo said. If you want to help yourself and Dennis, be ready to talk."

Corrigan grabbed my arm and dragged me away.

I looked at him as if he had just waved a white flag before the battle even commenced. "We can't leave it like this." I tried to shake loose and return to Charlotte's bedside, but he held tight.

"We can't endanger her life, either. Let's give it a rest for now and get something to eat. She's not going anywhere." By the set of his jaw, I knew not to argue.

Once we located the cafeteria and set our food trays down, Corrigan pulled out his notepad. "Got this from our data base. Dennis Rudkowsky, aka Dennis Rudd, currently works for Martin Beckman. He has a record going back ten years with charges including assault with a deadly weapon, assault and battery, and just good ole assault. A real sweetheart. With a little bit of luck, we'll have a chance to chat with him soon."

Before I could form my question, Corrigan added, "No, you can't be there."

I slammed down my pastry. "You wouldn't even know about him if it weren't for me."

"Maybe so, but best I can do is fill you in later."

"Sure you will, next week when it's convenient. I'll bet you leave out the most important stuff, too."

He held up his hands in mock surprise. "How could you not trust me? I'll answer whatever questions you have. Promise." He chucked me under the chin as if I was a little girl.

I dropped my napkin onto the table. "I'm finished. You can take me home now." He glanced at me sideways but didn't say anything.

Our stilted conversation on the way to my apartment didn't break the ice that had formed between us. His dry lips merely brushed mine before he turned to go. But re-calling honey gets more information than vinegar, I pulled him back and gave him a kiss hot enough to keep his lower regions wondering where the fire was.

"You can expect more of that once you tell me what happens with Dennis."

In a husky voice he replied, "For more of that, I'll even get you his mother's pet names for him."

"I'll be waiting." I pushed him from my doorway, stepped inside, and closed the door. I waited on the other side until the sound of his footsteps faded.

I still wasn't convinced Corrigan would tell me everything. I grabbed my notes and picked up my car keys. With a bit of luck, I could find Dennis Rudkowsky before the police did.

I planned to head to the racetrack where I first encountered Beckman and Dennis, but there was no way I was going near that small-time hood without my gun. Frustrated at myself, I sucked the air through my teeth. My gun was at the office. I hadn't wanted to carry it into my aunt's home. Cursing, I got in my car to go back to the office to retrieve the weapon.

The office elevator wasn't working. Again. I took the stairs two at a time until reaching my floor. I unlocked the door and hurried into my waiting room and toward my office to grab my gun.

A quick glance toward my desk was all it took for me to realize I didn't have to rush to the racetrack. Dennis Rudkowsky was slumped backward in my chair, three bullet holes in his chest.

Chapter Twenty-Three

My skimpy breakfast threatened to make a curtain call, but I swallowed hard and confirmed Rudkowsky and I were alone. Then I pressed my fingers against his neck, hoping to feel a pulse. Nothing. He was as dead as the stuffed squirrel my father kept on his mantle. My hand shook as I dialed 911.

I paced, waiting for the police to arrive when my eye spotted the butt of my gun lying on the credenza at the other end of the room. I jerked to a stop, feeling cold and hot at the same time. Someone had moved my gun. Had the killer used his own gun on Dennis, or improvised and used mine?

A single set of footsteps heading to my office interrupted those ruminations. It couldn't be the police. The pace was too leisurely. Already jumpy, the sound echoed in my ears. My first thought was to grab my gun. Would doing so smudge the murderer's prints? Thank heaven I didn't have to decide.

"Hello, Claire." It was Harold. He jerked to a stop when he spied Dennis's body. "Oh, dear. I'm sorry to burst in on you in at such an inopportune time."

I found my voice. "He was dead when I got here." Irritated because I was offering an explanation to somebody who had no business visiting me, I practically spit, "What are you doing here?"

Harold ambled over to the credenza and leaned against it. "While I was at the police station visiting a new client, I happened to overhear a conversation. It was about a certain someone by the name of Dennis Rudkowsky and his possible involvement in Marco Conti's murder. I also heard other people, not as noble as the police, might be interested in finding Mr. Rudkowsky." He motioned toward the corpse. "I take it that's the man in question and unfortunately, someone found him before the police did."

"What does that have to do with you being here?"

"Before I address your question," he templed his fingers and his voice took on the solicitous tone of a funeral director, "how are you holding up, Claire?"

I just found a dead body. How do you think I'm holding up? I exhaled deeply, controlling my temper. "I'm fine. What do you want, Harold?"

He shook his head and tsk'd. "It's such a shame about Mr. Rudkowsky's demise. Don't you find it interesting, though, that the recently departed also worked for Martin Beckman, the man to whom the late George Dixon owed money?"

Even though I'd put those two pieces together, I wasn't about to let him know. "What's your point, Harold?"

"Merely that Iola Taylor's innocence in Mr. Dixon's murder is becoming clearer. I thought you might consider changing your mind about, shall I say, backing the winning horse." He chuckled softly. "What I mean is, Ms.

Taylor is once again offering you a chance to redeem yourself as well as collect the hefty fee she's willing to pay."

I rubbed my forehead as I pictured that money just beyond my reach. "She's still the prime suspect in Dixon's murder and I'm still the primary witness, so it's still a conflict of interest for me."

He harrumphed. "At this point, that is a mere technicality. Just think about it. I'm sure you'll come to the correct conclusion. Let me know when you do." He turned on his heels to leave, but paused and faced me once more. "You know, given the, um, situation here, you may need an attorney. If so, you have my number." When I didn't respond, he nodded good-bye and made his way out the door.

My legs felt as if they were made of licorice strings, and I collapsed into the client chair across from my desk. Although my body felt limp, my brain spun with Harold's offer and the link between the murders of Dennis, Marco, and George. I was pretty sure Bucanetti arranged Dennis's demise. But how to prove it? I dropped my head into my hands.

Not two minutes later, police sirens assaulted my ears, followed by a throng of uniformed cops and medical personnel invading my office. The crowd split, and in walked Corrigan, like Moses parting the sea.

"God-bless it, Claire. Why are you always the one discovering the body in cases we're both working? If I didn't know better, I'd think you'd be happy to have Rudkowsky's body dumped here just to get ahead on this case."

I was so mad tears sprang to my eyes. "You're right. You should know better, even if that was supposed to be a joke." I crossed my arms over my chest.

I waited for him to say something. Instead, he went toward the body and conferred with the medical examiner.

Corrigan eventually addressed me again in a just-the-facts tone. "I need a statement." He pulled out his notepad.

I whispered, "You're acting like a jerk. How's that for a statement?" I could feel my face heat up.

He glanced around the room, no doubt hoping nobody heard me. Then he scribbled on his pad and read it in a voice only the two of us could hear. "Witness is uncooperative, so maybe I owe her an apology."

I pressed my lips together to stop from smiling. But I wasn't about to cut him any slack, despite him looking as contritely adorable as a puppy caught chewing on a new shoe.

He led me into the hallway and kept his voice low. "I apologize for being a horse's ass. My only excuse is that the Captain is on my back to solve George Dixon's murder and allow Marco's case to cool down for a bit. You know, one less hood on the street, versus a famous critic's grisly murder. Now that someone liquidated Rudkowsky, a person of interest in Marco's murder, the Marco Conti mystery is heating up. Captain could reassign the case to another team. I wouldn't like that. If I start something, I want to finish it."

I felt the urge to give him a hug, but with other cops still mulling around, I restrained myself. I tried to convey my understanding by nodding and making clucking noises.

"Are you going to be sick?" His eyes darted around, probably searching for a trashcan or other container.

"What?" I waved my hands like windshield wipers. "No. I'm fine." I paused. "What if all three victims, Dixon, Marco, and Rudkowsky, were killed by the same person?"

Chapter Twenty-Four

Corrigan took my arm and we moved even further away from the bustle in my office. "Do you have someone in mind?"

I debated spilling everything I knew, or thought I knew. *What the heck.* I'd already stuck my toe in the water. Might as well dive all the way in. I exhaled. "Michael Bucanetti."

Corrigan's shoulders dropped. "Okaay."

Nothing like spilling your guts and then not being believed. "Just hear me out."

"I'm listening." He rubbed his brow.

My words poured out as fast as a medicine commercial guy announcing the drug's side effects. "Bucanetti swore revenge on whoever killed Marco, and Dennis looked good for the crime. As for Dixon's mur—"

"Stop right there." He held up his hand. "If you're planning to give me that routine again, about Iola being innocent, save it. She's guilty. You, yourself saw her coming out of Dixon's house at the time he was killed. So I don't believe your theory that one person fits all these murders. Besides, why would Bucanetti kill Marco and then put out a contract on whoever killed him?"

I straightened my spine and gave him a look I hoped conveyed calm professionalism. "Before you point out any more of my, in your opinion, misjudgments, shouldn't you at least admit I'm probably right about Bucanetti having Dennis killed?"

He broke eye contact and stared down at his notebook. "I'll admit *that's* a good call. Now I'll take your statement on what Bucanetti said to you. We can get a warrant and contact the Newark police to bring Bucanetti in for questioning. At the same time, I'll see if Felicity Dixon is willing to corroborate your story."

While I was relieved Corrigan was going after Newark's version of Al Capone, I was also worried. Could the crime lord put out hits and wipe out my family from the comfort of his jail cell? Sure, the cops would watch Aunt Lena and Dad for a while, maybe even through Bucanetti's trial. Then what? Witness protection? Spots formed in front of my eyes and I heard a buzzing in my ears.

"What about my family's protection?"

Corrigan's gaze shifted past me and toward the stairs. I rotated in that direction.

Ed braked, just short of running over me. Crouched and with his hands on his thighs, he rasped, "Ran all the way from the car." He straightened and swallowed hard. "What's going on? Are you all right?"

"As good as I can be after finding a corpse in my chair."

"Huh? Anyone I know?"

"Sort of. He worked for Beckman."

Ed whistled. "Rudkowsky? Somebody had some serious *cojones* to bump off that one." His eyes flickered to

173

Corrigan, then back to me. "You need help finding who did it?"

Corrigan loudly cleared his throat and put on his official cop expression. "The police are investigating the murder and we already have a person of interest we'll be questioning."

Ed gave a curt nod. "Got it."

Corrigan's brow knit. "Hey, I didn't mean to sound so hard-nosed."

Ed shrugged. "No problemo. Anyway, I didn't come here for a job."

I put up my hand to stop him. "Ed, whatever it is, can it wait a minute? Detective Corrigan hasn't answered my previous question."

Corrigan scowled. "As soon as I get back to the station and the warrant is issued, your father and Lena will have protection, for a time." He paused and his voice turned solemn. "After the conviction, if there is one, the only permanent solution is witness protection."

"Claire," Ed's head jerked and his nostrils flared like a horse encountering a snake. "What the hell have you gotten Lena into?"

I dropped my face into my hands, feeling as if I'd been buried by a rockslide. When I looked up, my eyes were wet. I didn't care who saw it, either. "It started when I was saving her life."

"Valcone? The guy Marco used to work for?" I nodded. He sighed and put his arm loosely around my shoulder. "Sorry I jumped on you, kiddo. So what can we do to fix this situation?" This last question he directed at Corrigan.

Corrigan shrugged. "I'll do everything I can. I promise. But, like I said, depending on how far Bucanetti's tentacles reach, the only way I can absolutely guarantee you and your family's safety is through giving you new identities." He didn't look any happier saying those words than I did hearing them.

I didn't respond. I couldn't. A moment passed, then two. Nobody spoke.

Corrigan enfolded my hands into his. I felt his frustration at being unable to make it right for me. I was thankful for his concern, but it wasn't enough. It couldn't be. I had to do whatever it took to keep Bucanetti's poisonous touch from reaching my father and aunt. I would take whatever Corrigan could offer to safeguard them, but ultimately it was up to me. Realizing I was the main show made me dizzy and I wanted to crumple. People say, 'fake it until you make it', but no amount of acting was going to ever turn me into a courageous person.

Adding to my worry was that I had no workable plan on how to shield Dad and Aunt Lena until the natural end of their days.

Corrigan coughed lightly, interrupting my thoughts. "I've got to get back to the station. You can come with me or by yourself, but I need you there. The sooner I have your official statement, the sooner I can get a warrant for Bucanetti."

Ed piped up. "I'll take you, Claire. You can fill me in on the way." The minute Corrigan left, Ed scowled. "Better start at the beginning."

We were almost at the police station by the time I wrapped up the tale of how my family came to be in danger. "Once Bucanetti finds out I talked, I'll have to have a scheme in place to stop him from carrying out his threats."

Ed kept his eyes on the road. "Way I see it, *we* have

to come up with a strategy. We're talking about the survival of the woman I plan to marry, for God's sake."

Maybe I wasn't as alone in this as I thought. "What do you have in mind?"

Chapter Twenty-Five

Ed parked his car. "We'll talk about it after you finish giving your statement." He pulled out his phone. "While you're doing that, I gotta make some calls."

I wasn't going to ask him who he planned on calling. Ed certainly had a past, and surely had made some connections during that time I didn't know about. I preferred it that way.

I got out of his car and walked into the police station. Before going through the door, I glanced over my shoulder at Ed. I was glad to see he was already talking on the phone.

Corrigan looked up from his computer. "Glad you got here so fast. I just wrote up your statement as you told it to me. Read it over and if it's okay, sign it and I'll get the warrant."

I skimmed the document and, after ascertaining it was accurate, I took the pen Corrigan offered me. My hand faltered at first. If Ed and I didn't devise a foolproof plan, my family's lives could be deleted before the ink was dry.

After I read and signed my statement, Corrigan

walked me back to Ed's car. He must have sensed Ed and I were plotting something of which he'd disapprove. Corrigan opened the car door for me and I climbed inside. Instead of closing it, he stuck his head in. "Ed, I'm counting on you to keep your future niece out of trouble. Her heart's in the right place, but sometimes it overrides her head."

Ed, probably remembering he sometimes worked for me, kept a straight face.

I glared at Corrigan. "I'm right here, you know. Nobody has to keep me out of trouble and I'd put my intelligence against yours any day." I grabbed onto the door and tried to close it on him.

"Hey, I just meant I don't want you to get hurt. Your brain is great. And so are all the other parts of you."

I suppressed a smile at his clumsy backtracking. He was a great detective but not exactly a smooth talker when it came to our relationship. Rather than chiding him about it, I ignored his comeback. I was in too much of a hurry to tease him about it. I needed to cement the plan with Ed. "Okay. I'll let this one slide." Corrigan stepped back, allowing me to close the door. I motioned to Ed to floor it.

Ed threw his car in gear and we inched out of the parking lot. Less than a block away from the station, I could no longer contain myself. "Well? Did you find out anything useful on your phone calls?"

We pulled up to a red light and Ed tapped out a rhythm on the steering wheel. "Talked to a guy who knows a guy, etc. Anyway, word is, Bucanetti's got a favorite niece, his godchild, who's getting hitched this Saturday at Holy Rosary on Murray Hill.

"He'll be on our turf?" I imagined throwing holy water at Bucanetti and hearing him shriek as it seared his flesh.

"Bingo." The light changed and he gave it some gas. "Now you're probably asking yourself what could we do, since his bodyguards will be closer than cheese on a burger."

Feeling low, I sighed, "Yeah. Even if we could get to Bucanetti..." I sat up straight, energized. "If Bucanetti's there, his wife will be too. She knew my dad when he was a paperboy." My voice grew louder as my hope blossomed. "Maybe I can appeal to her. I can ask—"

"Whoa, Nellie. Aren't you assuming a lot?"

My shoulders rose in defense. "Do you have a better idea?"

"Nah. Not yet anyway." He pulled into my office's parking lot, but I didn't have the stomach to return to the scene of the crime just yet. "Hey, you didn't just happen by earlier. Did you need something?"

Ed slung his arm over the back of the driver's seat. "Yeah." He chortled. "Sure don't seem like any big deal now. "Well, yeah, it is. The Las Vegas wedding is off."

My mouth dropped open. Was Ed jilting my aunt?

"Wait. That ain't what I mean. The wedding isn't off, just the Las Vegas part. Chapel of Wedded Bliss is a no-go. Place is closing down. We're still getting hitched. We're just moving up the date and it'll be at the Knights of Columbus hall near *Cannoli's*. Won't be as classy but, it'll still be pretty great. That's not the problem. The problem is my bride-to-be plans on catering her own wedding and I need you to talk to her. Don't get me wrong, she's one helluva cook," he patted his slightly convex belly, "but I don't want her frazzled to the bone making every dish and the wedding cake too. I tried talking to her about it, but she gets all unglued, you know, worried I don't think she's Superwoman." He shook his head. "She's already out of my league. I keep telling her how lucky I am she even gave me the time of day…"

I cocked my head and smiled slightly. Ed didn't realize it, but my aunt was a very fortunate lady.

My phone ringing squelched that mellow feeling. "Hi, Felicity."

"Why did you lie to the police?"

"Huh? About what?"

"Michael Bucanetti never spoke to me about going after Marco's killer. Why would you tell that detective he did?"

I shook my head in disbelief. "You came to me and proclaimed, *repeatedly*, Bucanetti told you he would get whoever killed Marco. We even talked about protecting Charlotte, your friend, from him, remember?"

Her voice was ice. "You're mistaken. We've never discussed anything of the sort."

Panic rose in my throat. "Felicity, I'm coming over. We'll talk—"

She hung up.

I must have looked as pale as the upholstery in Ed's car. "What's wrong, kiddo?"

I stared straight ahead, my fingers digging into the seat. "I have an even bigger problem than I thought."

Chapter Twenty-Six

Ed insisted on driving me to Felicity's house. "You never know when you'll need a men's size eleven shoe to block a door from closing."

There was no time to argue. He sped to her home while I dialed Corrigan's number. The phone beeped instead of ringing and Corrigan was on the line.

He said, "I was trying to call you too. Felicity Dixon's statement doesn't corroborate yours."

"I know. She just called to deny that she ever told me about Bucanetti's threats." My insides quivered. "You can still get a warrant on him, can't you?"

"I'm going to try, but it would've been a stronger case with two witnesses. Right now, it's a 'he-said-she-said,' and that's never a sure thing."

"What about the guy Bucanetti hired to kill Rudkowsky? Have you arrested anyone yet? Maybe you could persuade him to talk."

His voice tightened. "We're still looking into who might have pulled the trigger."

I was desperate. "How long until you know—"

"Look, Claire. I've got my hands full right now. I

wish I could tell you something more, but—"

"No, it's okay, really. I have to go anyway." Before Corrigan could protest, I disconnected the call. Turning to Ed, I said, "Forget about Felicity Dixon for the moment. Care to join me in a visit to Charlotte Pusitano?"

Ed made a quick U-turn. "Thought you'd never ask."

I filled Ed in on Charlotte's likely part in Marco's murder on the way to the hospital. "She hasn't confessed to anything, but I think that's why Felicity shot her. I also believe Charlotte either convinced Rudkowsky to kill Marco or at least knew about Rudkowsky's plan to off Marco."

Ed nodded and didn't challenge my thoughts until we pulled into the hospital parking garage. "What about motive? Why kill Marco? If Charlotte was as devoted to Felicity as she seems, wouldn't she want to protect her friend's happiness?"

"He was cheating on Felicity, and Charlotte caught him." I opened my car door. "Are you coming with me?"

Ed joined me and we descended the cement steps to the hospital.

Charlotte wasn't in the same room as earlier and nobody at the Information Desk lived up to that name.

"Corrigan must have had Charlotte moved."

Ed agreed. "Maybe even to a different hospital."

I sent up a quick prayer that wherever she'd been transferred to, she was well protected. For me, I couldn't take the time right then to search for her. "I can't put off seeing Felicity any longer. She may have answers to questions I haven't even thought to ask.

"One necessary stop first." I ducked into the woman's restroom and caught a glimpse of myself in the mirror. With my makeup long gone and my outfit wrinkled,

I looked like someone's date after a rave. I dug around inside my purse for my lipstick. I was asking a lot of that little tube of color, but it was all I had.

I swung open the ladies' room door. "Okay, Ed. To Felicity's house we go."

***

I politely rang Felicity's bell. No answer. Ed took over, pounding on her door hard enough to rattle it in its frame.

Felicity yelled through the door, "Go away."

I shouted, "Not until you talk to me." When she didn't respond, I added, "Listen, Felicity, you hired me to find Marco's killer. I found Dennis Rudkowsky."

I listened to myself breathe.

Felicity cracked open the door. "What does that scum have to do with anything?"

"Why don't you let me in and I'll tell you."

She sighed heavily. "Okay." She stepped aside. "Come in."

With Ed right behind me, I hurried inside before Felicity could change her mind. She hunched her shoulders and guarded her stomach as if she were a prizefighter.

"I let you in. Now what do you know about Dennis Rud-whatever-his-name is, and what's he got to do with Marco?"

"I think you know more about Dennis Rudkowsky than you're letting on."

"What do you mean?"

Though I knew Dennis and Charlotte were more than acquaintances, my next words had to push Felicity toward the truth, not have her run from it. "Dennis was working with someone else."

"Of course he was. He worked for that lowlife, Martin Beckman. My brother was into Beckman for quite a bit of money. Bookies don't like it when someone interferes with their collections. Marco was definitely getting in the way. So Beckman had his henchman do him in."

"Maybe there was someone else Rudkowsky knew who didn't like what Marco was doing."

She waved her hand as if erasing a whiteboard. "Look, I let you in here so we could discuss Marco's killer and my paying the rest of your fee. Not for you to insinuate God-knows-what."

Okay, so maybe I was being too subtle. "Rudkowsky and Charlotte were friendly." I inched closer to Felicity. "Charlotte knew about Marco's, shall we say, indiscretions and she wanted to protect you. You found out."

Her face betrayed nothing, but she couldn't keep her voice from quivering. *Fear of being found out or anger?* "If you're insinuating that Charlotte had anything to do with Marco's death, or that I shot her because she did, you're wrong. I think you should leave."

I bit my lower lip. My last words had taken this too far and I'd lost her. Trying to salvage what I could, I shifted focus. "Did Bucanetti get to you? Is that why you *forgot* his threats to kill whoever was responsible for Marco's death?"

She took a step back and pushed open the front door. "Get out. Now."

Ed opened his mouth to say something, but I gave him a look I hoped he read as, "Save it."

Ed and I had just backed out of the door when Felicity threw a folded piece of paper at me. "Now you're paid in full." She slammed her door and I heard the lock turn. Ed and I collided grabbing for the paper, which had taken a nosedive into the adjacent rosebush.

Regaining my balance, I crouched down and gingerly pried the check from a thorn. I unfolded it and, except for a tiny hole, it was intact. The check was dated a day earlier. I stashed it in my purse while Ed watched on. I didn't want him to know she'd only paid me half what we'd agreed on. I'd never be out of debt at this rate, never mind buying a business for myself.

"Better not ask her to give you a referral."

He ignored my glare and pulled out his car keys. "That didn't go according to plan. Matter of fact, you sorta blew it. Sorry, kiddo. Maybe it's time you took a break. Ya know, put your mind to something else."

I smoothed my hair. Too bad I couldn't smooth my nerves as easily. "What did you have in mind?" The second I noticed him trying to suppress a guilty grin, I knew what he was thinking. "You mean, go visit my aunt."

"It'll take your mind off this case."

Not that I believed the state of my mind wasn't uppermost in his, but I didn't resist. "Sure, why not? I'm sure I can manage to get her mad at me too."

"That ain't gonna happen. Lena will listen to you."

"Of course, because I'm just full of magical phrases today."

***

I'd insisted Ed drop me off at my car. I didn't want an audience while I attempted to make Aunt Lena see reason about trying to cater her own wedding. Ed didn't argue. He was most likely thankful. After all, an exploding bomb might be meant for one target, but it can still cause collateral damage.

All the way over to *Cannoli's*, I scanned my brain for 'voice of reason' arguments about her enjoying her big day rather than dealing with the hazards of separating sauces and wilting salads. But by the time I arrived, I was still minus any persuasive words.

It was almost closing time when I entered Cannoli's kitchen and heard, "That's it, Lena. I refuse to be harassed by a woman who doesn't know how to accept constructive criticism." It was Angie, Aunt Lena's assistant as well as her best friend.

My aunt's voice was strident. "You call that constructive criticism? Telling me I might be distracted and make my wedding cake too dry? That's not criticism, that's heresy."

Angie threw a damp towel into the sink. "No it isn't. And if you keep this...this touchiness up, I may just quit."

Aunt Lena sniffed. "Sure. Desert me. I'm such a bad cook, maybe you'd be happier working for Volterra's on Lorain Road." Her sniffle increased to a full-on sob. "Oh, you know I don't mean that. I'm just so nervous."

Angie and my aunt, as if on cue, both turned toward me. Angie spoke first. "Claire, tell your aunt I love her to death but she's nuts to try to do more than be the bride. By the time the celebration is over, she'll be too tired to enjoy the wedding night."

At the risk of approaching slapping distance if she didn't like what I said, I drew closer to my aunt. "Angie's right. Even someone as talented in the kitchen as you, can't cater, bake, and be a radiant bride at the same time."

Aunt Lena didn't acknowledge my comment, so I grabbed hold of her pudgy hands. "You should enjoy your wedding, not be worrying if the cake is moist enough."

She withdrew her hands from mine and wiped her eyes with the edge of her apron. "So nobody thinks I can do it."

Angie piped in. "It's not that, Lena. It's just better for you and Ed if you let somebody else do the catering and worrying."

Aunt Lena threw up her hands. "Okay, okay. I give in. But it's such short notice, nobody who's any good will be available to do the job." Her eyes bored into me. "Or is some big idea already bouncing around in your head?"

I did have a tiny sprout of an idea. I decided to spread some fertilizer and hope it'd blossom. I grinned and laid out my plan as if I'd been the star pupil at the PT Barnum School of Sales. "I have the very person. You'll love what she can do."

I went on to describe irresistible chicken, beef, and pasta dishes and then napoleons, éclairs, creampuffs, and petit fours so delicate one would suspect fairies made them. Spinning this sugar tale with my hands and words, I watched Aunt Lena. I hoped she was envisioning a wedding cake that, layer by layer, could compete with any she'd ever tasted.

She laid her arms across her belly. "So who is this *sorceress,* and how come I've never heard of her?"

I took a tiny step back. "But you have—heard of her."

Her face scrunched in thought. "Then who is it?"

I swung my hands out in a half-circle. "It's a surprise!" My insides cinched. That response was so lame it should have been shot.

My aunt tsk'd. "Are you making this person up, Claire? Angie, she's making this up so I don't work too hard."

For a wild second, I was afraid my aunt would wallop me on my bottom like she'd done when as a child I'd scooped out a hunk of the chocolate cake she'd baked for my uncle's family. Instead, she grabbed my chin and kissed me hard on both checks. "You're a great kid but a rotten liar."

"I'm not lying. Really. There is someone. I have to talk to her first. Set it all up." I shifted gears before my flimsy plan collapsed like the chocolate soufflé I'd once attempted. "So do you want a white wedding cake?"

As soon as I elicited my aunt's wedding cake idea, her catering plan and budget, interspersed with multiple reassurances, I took my leave.

Outside *Cannoli's* and out of my aunt's radar earshot, I withdrew my phone. Before I could make that call, I spotted Angie speed-walking toward me.

"Listen, Claire, I'm not sure who you're thinking of using for your aunt's wedding, but forget about them making the cake."

I groaned. "Did she change her mind?"

"No, no. She's a little shaky but still on board. I wanna make the cake."

"You're a good friend to her, Angie. Are you sure?"

Her face softened with affection. "Lena and me have been friends for so long. I love her like a sister. This is the least I can do." She dabbed at her eyes with her apron. "I gotta get back before she figures something's up."

Before she turned to go, I reached out for her and gave her a big squeeze. "She's lucky to have you, Angie."

Alone once more, I punched in the number of the

person I hoped could save my aunt from a nervous breakdown and me from disappointing the woman I loved like a second mother.

Chapter Twenty-Seven

"**H**i, Claire. Your father and I were just talking about the party I'm giving for Lena and Ed." Suzy's voice rang with excitement.

I saw my opening and dove in. "Then my timing is great because that's exactly why I called." I sunk my top teeth into my lower lip, then forged ahead. "It's wonderful what you're doing and I'm sure they'd love it. It'd be a nice interruption from all their planning and stressing out. I mean, my aunt plans to cater her whole wedding. On top of getting ready to become Mrs. Ed Horwath. Do you believe that?"

"Yeah, Frankie told me about it. Between you and me, that's crazy."

"I agree." I pressed my lips together for a moment. Then delivered what I hoped was an irresistible idea. "Suzy, how would you feel about helping Aunt Lena and Ed in a big way?"

"Sure, I guess."

She didn't sound as positive about it as I'd hoped. Nonetheless, I continued on, sliding into my idea of Suzy catering the wedding instead of throwing them a party. "I know you could do it. You're a great cook, plus you can bake up a storm."

When Suzy began to moan a negative response, I gave her my best salesperson-of-the-year pitch. "Just think how much my aunt and Ed would appreciate your making the food for their wedding. You'd really be contributing so much to making it special." I grimaced, hoping I hadn't laid it on too thickly. "I'll help you do it. I'm positive my dad will too." Of course, I knew no such thing. But I'd said the magic words. The rush of air I heard in my ear was her resistance dissolving.

"Okay, but I'm definitely gonna need both of you to help. Now, how many mouths am I feeding?"

"About fifty, give or take a few." I held my breath, hoping Suzy wouldn't freak out.

"Okaaay. I guess the three of us can manage that."

My shoulders dropped in relief. "Thank you!"

"Wait until the wedding's over before you thank me." She sounded as if her mind was already focused on grocery lists and recipes. "I better get going."

No sooner had that call ended than another came in. When I saw who it was, my mouth went dry.

"Hello, Claire." It was Bucanetti.

Words rushed from my mouth. "I found the man who killed Marco. He was sitting at my desk, dead." I clutched the phone with both hands to stop it from trembling. "I'm sure you already knew that. Just like I'm sure you ordered his death."

"I don't know what you're talking about. I worry, though, you've been blabbing to the cops about what you think. And I hate to worry."

"What? No, no, of course not."

Bucanetti tsk'd several times. It sounded like the tick-

191

ing of a time bomb. "You never know what can happen when the police get involved."

The bones in my legs seemed to liquefy and I grabbed onto the hood of my car to steady myself. He went on. "I hear your aunt's getting married. Whole family oughta be there."

I squeezed my eyes shut to block out the vision of my family's potential massacre. I shuddered to envision the hot pink rose on my aunt's wedding dress turning red from her blood. Anger tangled with worry in my chest. "Is that why you called? To threaten my family and me? It won't work."

He released his breath, reminding me of the hiss of a snake. "Who's threatening? Listen. I still want Charlotte. Me and her need to...talk. That's where you come in. You find her, I forget about you blabbing to the cops. Provided you don't keep shooting your mouth off. Hey, I'm giving you a second chance." His voice grew harsher. "But don't take too long. I'm not a patient man."

"I don't know if I can find..." I stopped, realizing he'd hung up.

I just stood in place for a moment, numb. I don't know how I managed to get into my car, but there I was, staring straight ahead, seeing nothing. My thoughts spun around like a spool but I couldn't find the thread's beginning. I rested my forehead against my steering wheel, telling myself there was a solution to all this. I just had to think it through. A tiny voice inside tried to warn me there wasn't, but I muzzled it.

I mentally reviewed my choices, poor though they were. Giving Charlotte to Bucanetti, assuming I found her, would mean her death. I couldn't do that, even if she did have a part in Marco's murder. Nor could I sentence my family to abandoning their lives to go into protective custody, or worse, getting them killed. Instead of feeling the righteousness of Joan of Arc going into battle, the heaviness in my body felt as if her horse had fallen on me.

It began to drizzle and I watched the raindrops cover my windshield, blurring the outlines of the buildings and other cars, softening borders. Right and wrong, smart and stupid intertwined. I turned on the ignition and hit the windshield wipers. My eyes followed the back-and-forth of the blades. What do I do? Hope there's a warrant out for Bucanetti? Hold a gun on the gangster until he agrees to leave my family alone? Almost in sync with them, I realized what I had to do first.

I called Corrigan to find out the status of Bucanetti's arrest. When he picked up, my question came out so thick it was as if I'd just eaten a peanut butter brownie and had no milk to wash it down.

"Were you able to get a warrant on Bucanetti?"

His heavy sigh blew away any hope I had of a reprieve. "I tried like hell, but the judge wouldn't go for it. He told me he wanted more evidence. I'm sorry, Claire. "

I slumped in my seat. "I understand."

"That doesn't mean it won't happen. Believe me, I'm working on it."

"I'm sure you are. Look, I have to go."

"Don't go crazy and—"

I cut the conversation off before he could warn me not to do what I now fully intended to do.

Chapter Twenty-Eight

Although it was a chilly, late September evening, my car's interior felt like 90 degrees, and I could feel perspiration seeping through my blouse. I could have made my next call from my apartment, but it was already close to 6, and if I waited much longer, I'd never get the information I needed. So before either my resolve or my opportunity disappeared, I made my next call.

"Come on, Ed. Pick up." I bounced up and down as if I was riding a bronco instead of sitting in my car.

At last he answered. "Whatcha need, Claire?" His voice was low. He was probably at his part-time security job.

"I'll make it quick. Where is Bucanetti's niece having her wedding reception?"

"Why? You planning on sending a gift?"

I gritted my teeth, hoping to sound tough and determined. "Yeah, Bucanetti's head on a platter."

"Whoa! Talk to me, Claire. You can't just walk into the wedding and go Samurai on the guy."

My false bravado fell flat as an under-whipped meringue. "I don't have a plan exactly, but I will be at the wedding. Now, do you know where the reception is going to be?"

I could hear him sucking his breath in through his teeth. "I'll tell you, but you gotta promise you won't go half-cocked after Bucanetti. He'll have more protection than that short guy in North Korea."

"I know." That was my problem.

"Okay. My source told me it's a fancy-shmancy place in Chagrin Falls called Belle Fontaine. Niece's last name is LoRusso."

"Thanks, Ed."

"Promise me whatever you decide to do with that info, you let me know. I'll make myself available."

"I promise." I crossed my fingers. I just couldn't involve Ed in what might be a suicide mission.

I wiped my moist palms on my pants, looked up Belle Fontaine's phone number and called. The phone rang five times before going into voicemail. I inhaled to leave a message but miraculously, a woman's voice interrupted the machine's message. "Belle Fontaine, where your vision can become a reality. How may I help you?"

I cleared my throat. "Hello, I'm Claire, with the *Plain Dealer*, and I'm putting together the announcement for the LoRusso wedding this Saturday and need to know who's doing the catering."

"Hmmm. You should probably get that information from the bride, but I suppose it wouldn't hurt..."

I could hear her pressing computer keys.

"It's Valducci's."

A grin spread across my face. Aunt Lena knew the owner. "Thank you so much. Goodbye."

"But don't you want to know—"

"No, that's it. Thanks again." I cut off the call, put on

my most innocent expression, and marched back into *Cannoli's*.

Angie, her car keys in her hand, spotted me first. "Claire?"

My aunt came back into the kitchen carrying an empty pastry tray. She dropped the aluminum pan. "What's wrong? Whoever-you-had-in mind for catering my wedding can't do it?"

I couldn't tell if she was hoping for or against that being the case. "No, nothing like that." I glanced down at my feet. "You know Gloria Valducci pretty well, don't you?"

One of Aunt Lena's eyebrows rose. "Sure. Why?"

Using my fingertip, I made a squiggling design in the tray's crumbs. "They cater weddings and stuff don't they?"

My aunt's eyes bored down on me. "Tell me that's not who you asked to cater my wedding? I love Gloria, but she can't make a good crème cake to save her life!"

"No. That's not why. I could use some extra money and since I already have some waitressing experience, I thought maybe you could put in a word for me at Valducci's. I can get some work helping them cater at weddings and other events."

She set her hands on her hips. "If you want, I can use the help. Work here sometimes. I'll pay you."

I should have seen that coming. With a smoothness that surprised me, I said, "But how could I take money from you to buy you a wedding gift?"

She clucked. "You don't need to get Ed and me a present. Your being there is enough of a gift."

I threw my arms around her. "How could I not give my most favorite aunt a present on one of the happiest days of her life?" I smiled, banishing any thought of her in danger because of me.

She pushed me away and stared into my eyes. She pinched both my cheeks. "Ooh, you! Okay, I'll call Gloria tomorrow morning. Angie, remind me."

I hugged her again, but all the while my heart felt as if it'd been wrapped in cement and was sinking.

Chapter Twenty-Nine

That night I tossed and turned in bed, finally trudging to the kitchen to defrost a chocolate, chocolate chip muffin. I placed it on a plate, and opened the door to the microwave, but slammed it shut without placing the goodie inside.

I drooped into a kitchen chair. This was one time chocolate couldn't make things better. It couldn't keep my family safe. It couldn't tell me if what I was planning was the right thing to do. Or if it was even sane. I pushed the plate away, wrapped my arms around myself and rocked back and forth.

***

My head snapped forward and I woke up, still in the kitchen chair. I checked the time. I'd been asleep for a whole ninety minutes. I shuffled off to bed, but again was unable to sleep. After forty frustrating minutes, I rose and prepared to shower.

I was massaging shampoo into my hair when it hit me that it was now Thursday. I had a bit more than 48 hours before I'd be facing off with Bucanetti at his niece's wedding. My elbows caved in toward each other and my chin dipped down onto my chest. A groan rose from deep inside my belly and I let it out, knowing nobody else was there to hear it.

I allowed myself just a minute to wallow and then forced myself to straighten up and finish showering. I dried off and dressed, squelching any worries or fears about my plan with Bucanetti. I focused on the muffin I'd left on the counter. Maybe now the chocolate would soothe my burning stomach.

The sun was just coming up when my tea was ready. I heated up the muffin and took a bite. It never got as far as my tummy. It hardened in the back of my throat as if it was made of plaster of paris. Apparently, eating wasn't on today's agenda.

I threw it in the trash, grabbed my keys and purse and headed to my office. Thankfully, the police had removed the crime barrier tape. Maybe I could make some headway on the George Dixon murder. Since the whole matter with Bucanetti and Marco's death, I'd let my investigation into the literary critic's murder case slide. I harrumphed when I recalled how concerned I'd been on that investigation about playing by the rules. Now, in dealing with Bucanetti, I was preparing to break some of the biggest precepts around.

I hit rush hour traffic, so it took me longer to get to my office than I'd expected. I confess, I used my horn a few times. Ordinarily, the performance of other drivers doesn't affect me. This morning, though, I felt like Atlas, holding the weight of the world on my shoulders. An incident with one careless driver could tip me over and my world would crash down around me. Not only hurting me, but destroying those close to me.

I somehow reached my office without any trouble,

and had just flicked on my computer when my phone rang. It was Gloria Valducci. My aunt had worked fast.

I explained that I was looking for a job and expressed my desire to start right away.

"Well, we could use an additional server. Lena told me you're a good worker—on time and polite." Her words were crisp and commanding. A woman used to giving orders. "Okay, you need a black skirt, at or below the knee and a white shirt. Nothing tight or revealing. We're a classy business. Come by later today, around 10, so I can have a look at you, and you can see our setup. If we both like what we see, you're hired."

She gave me her address and we ended the call with the usual pleasantries. I put my phone down and pressed my lips together.

Before I could sit down and try to process my jumbled-up thoughts, my aunt called. When I told her I appreciated her contacting Gloria Valducci for me, she interrupted.

"Don't thank me until you get the job. Just make sure you dress tasteful when you go see her."

I shook my head. "So I shouldn't wear a bikini?"

She clucked. "Such a funny girl. You know what I mean. And put some makeup on."

"I will." I didn't add that as part of my uniform, I'd also be wearing a gun.

I spent the next few hours in a haze, accomplishing little. My mind returning repeatedly to what lay ahead if Gloria Valducci hired me. I retrieved my gun and felt the weight of it in my hand.

***

I arrived at Valducci's ten minutes early. I had to

make a good impression. A guy, late thirties, apron tied around his waist opened the door. "You must be Claire. I'm Leo, Gloria's second-in-command. Come on in. Gloria's waiting for you."

I followed him to a small empty office. Within seconds, a tiny-waisted, buxom woman with a straight Roman nose and black but graying hair worn in a French twist appeared. Gloria Valducci looked like she stepped out of a mid-twentieth century Federico Fellini movie.

"You're Claire?" She looked me up and down. "Lena told me you're trying to get enough money for her wedding present. That's sweet." Her lips pursed and she got back to business. "Well, you look clean enough."

She grabbed my arms and pulled them out straight toward her, turning them elbow-side down. "No needle marks. Good." She released them with just as little fanfare. "Not that I thought you, being Lena's niece, would have that problem, but you never know."

I nodded, rather taken aback by the abruptness of the woman.

She thrust a hairnet at me. "Here. Put this on and I'll show you around."

After walking past racks filled with cookies and cakes, she described the workings of Valducci's. Twenty minutes later, we were back in her office and she offered me a job.

"You can start right away. We've got a wedding this Saturday at Belle Fontaine over in Chagrin Falls. You know it?" I assured her I did and she continued. "Be here, in uniform, black skirt, white blouse, at 3. Leo will show you the ropes and you'll be good to go."

I felt a tinge of victory, knowing that now I was one step closer to stopping Bucanetti. Plus, I would actually have money for my aunt's wedding gift.

We discussed the pittance that would be my salary and the interview was over. All the way back to my office, I ruminated on the idea of confronting Bucanetti at his niece's wedding before he could ruin my aunt's. I caught myself in my rearview mirror wearing a grim smile.

Chapter Thirty

By late afternoon, I'd exhausted my brain with all the 'what-ifs' in taking care of the Bucanetti problem and decided to call it a day. I didn't want to go back to my apartment, though. I wondered if my father was home. I could have used one of his comforting daddy-hugs. Then I recalled that I'd forgotten to talk to him about helping Suzy cater my aunt's wedding. I slapped my palm against my forehead and quickly tried to reach him on the phone.

"Hey, Dad."

"Ah, ha. Is this my daughter who volunteers my help without asking me?" He didn't sound angry but I still winced at being caught.

"You know about that, huh? I'm sorry, Dad, but it's for a worthy cause."

"Yeah, yeah. Ya did good, kid. Your aunt shouldn't have even been thinking about catering her own wedding. Even though Lena's a great cook, I bet Suzy'll show her a thing or two." I could hear the pride in his voice when he mentioned Suzy. "Maybe after the wedding, Lena will see what a hell of a woman Suzy is."

"You're right. She is—" I was getting a call from Corrigan. "Dad, another call's coming in. We'll talk later, okay?"

Believing he was only calling with more bad news, I greeted Corrigan with all the enthusiasm of an IRS agent.

"Is that any way to talk to the man who's going to take you to dinner tonight?" His voice was light and so full of affection, it tickled my heart.

I lightened my tone. "I'm sorry. I didn't realize this was a social call."

"I know. Lately our conversations have been less than fun. That's why I thought dinner out would cheer both of us up. But if you don't want to..."

My stomach felt so empty by now it could pass for an echo chamber. Still, I didn't want to even think about making a decision about what to eat. "I'd love to see you and I should eat, but could we just do a pizza?"

"Yeah. Sure. I'll pick one up and bring over some wine. If you play your cards right, I might even give you a neck rub."

"Mmmm." My hormones hoped he wouldn't stop at my neck.

***

By the time I heard Corrigan's knock at my apartment door, I was ready for some relaxation. A spark of optimism hit me. Maybe, if I was extra adorable, Corrigan would give me a hint as to Charlotte's whereabouts.

He stepped into my apartment dressed in a casual shirt and jeans that fit him well enough to draw my attention away from the grease-stained pizza box and bottle of wine he carried. The combination of his clothing and the food set my stomach growling and my lower regions purring. Thoughts of Bucanetti, at least for a time, vanished.

We ate at my miniscule kitchen table, making small talk and flirting with each other. After he devoured the last piece of crust, we sat across from each other in companionable silence. He reached over and took my hand bringing it to his lips. I melted like the mozzarella on my pizza.

We both stood and embraced, mouths searching each other's. He pressed his body into mine and my heart thumped in double-time. I broke away for a minute to catch my breath, but as soon as he looked at me with his half-closed blue eyes, I zoomed in for more. My nether-regions were screaming for a horizontal position and by the swelling I felt against me, he was wanting the same thing. We'd just started doing the entangled tango toward my bedroom when his phone rang.

He cursed under his breath and his hands dropped to his pocket. He checked his phone and answered. "Corrigan." He turned to me and mouthed, "Sorry." When he returned his attention to his caller, his eyes went from soft and loving to hard and cold. "When? How the hell did that happen?" After a few more heated exchanges, he ended the call.

"I've gotta go. Charlotte Pusitano's disappeared from custody."

His words threw ice water on the fire we'd had a moment ago. My detective persona quickly roared back. "Any idea where she went?"

He tucked his half-out shirt back into his pants. "No. They've already put out an APB on her. She was still pretty weak. She couldn't have gotten far." His hand on the apartment door, he kissed me hard on the lips. "Don't want you to forget where we left off."

As if I could.

Chapter Thirty-One

I didn't have time to dwell on Corrigan or anything else before my phone rang. It was Bucanetti. Was it to tell me he didn't need me to find Charlotte? Had somebody tipped him off as to where Corrigan had hidden Charlotte? Would she soon be joining her old boyfriend, Dennis, in the morgue?

He didn't even wait for me to greet him.

"What the hell's happening, Claire?"

"What do you mean?" The pizza I'd eaten threatened to reappear.

"I hear things. Ya know, like Charlotte's disappeared right from under the cops' noses."

It felt as if barbed wire was squeezing my throat closed. I croaked, "You don't have her?"

The ogre raged. "What are you, stupid?" He took in a deep breath, pulling in oxygen to burn me with his next words, "I want her. This time, no excuses. You got until midnight this Saturday." His words were like the sizzling sound of a bomb. "Clock is ticking."

Protesting would've been as helpful as wearing a

leaky lifejacket. Besides, he'd hung up. I shuddered, thinking how he'd merrily dance with his niece at her wedding all the while knowing what he'd do to Charlotte the next day.

I made up my mind to find Charlotte and turn her back over to the police. Not that I owed her anything, but nobody deserved to be executed without a trial.

***

I pounded on Felicity Dixon's door, with the improbable hope Charlotte was there.

Felicity appeared and just about snarled at me. "You and the cops should coordinate better. They've already been here and I told them the same thing I'm telling you. I don't know where Charlotte is, but she's not here. Now leave me alone." Before I could say a word, she slammed her door so hard the knob rattled. I stood there wondering what to do next.

My phone buzzed with a text message. I glanced at it, hoping it was Corrigan, announcing Charlotte had been located. I groaned and cast my eyes to the sky. It was Gino, wondering if I'd finished writing the announcement of his return.

A second text followed. The list of recipients for that announcement.

I stomped off Felicity's porch, cursing under my breath.

***

By 11, I'd talked to everyone I could think of who might have some clue as to where Charlotte might be. All I came up with was a big, fat headache. I rubbed my eyes and told myself Charlotte's disappearance was a police matter and, as long as I wasn't responsible for Bucanetti laying his paws on her, my conscience was clear.

Besides, I had just 48 hours to perfect my plan to defuse Bucanetti and his threat to my family. Tomorrow I'd spend some time at the shooting range.

Chapter Thirty-Two

Friday disappeared in a haze of gun practice, worry, and shopping for a black skirt for my new job as a server for Valducci's.

I laid awake most of Friday night, curled up under the covers in one position until my limbs stiffened. Finally sleep had come in the early morning, but was filled with a nightmare in which I was hunting a T-Rex with a bee-bee gun.

Saturday morning appeared as a bleak, cloud-covered day. The gray of the sky mirrored my mood and I had to force myself out of bed. After dressing, I sat in my kitchen with a cup of tea I'd barely touched. Eating was out of the question. My stomach was jumping around so much, food wouldn't have a chance of landing in it.

My tea had long since grown cold when I checked the time. Noon. I interlaced my fingers and squeezed my palms together as hard as I could, hoping to relieve some of my tension. Before I could even tell if that move was successful, my phone rang. I jumped as if I'd been sitting on Mount Vesuvius and it had just erupted.

I glanced at the caller ID and murmured a prayer of

thanks that it was Corrigan and not Bucanetti. I steadied my voice and greeted him.

"Hey Claire. Sorry I had to disappear on you Thursday night."

"It's okay. A policeman's duty and all that. Did you find Charlotte?" I sat still, as if my not moving would produce the answer I wanted.

"No. You haven't heard anything either, have you?" When I told him no, he continued. "Didn't think so. We checked all the places she could be, but haven't turned up anything. We will, though. I just hope we do before anybody else gets their hands on her."

I grimaced. He didn't say Bucanetti's name, but I knew who he meant.

His voice went from determined detective to playful boyfriend. "Anyway, I called to see if you'd like to, um, continue where we left off Thursday night." He backtracked. "I mean, we can do dinner and then, you know…"

I smiled at his sudden and unexpected awkwardness, but shook my head. I had a different sort of arrangement for the evening. "I'd love to, but I have…other plans." I wrinkled my nose. "I mean, I'm working tonight?"

"You mean, like a stakeout?"

"Not exactly." I blew out a breath. "I'm helping to cater a wedding."

"For Lena?"

Did he sound suspicious, or was that my paranoia kicking in? "Not exactly."

"Well, what, exactly?"

I felt trapped and, unjustly angry with Corrigan. I wanted to sass back, "None of your business." I took the adult way instead and said, "A friend of my aunt's. Gloria Valducci. I'm helping her out." I quickly added, "What about Sunday?" *If I wasn't dead or in jail.*

"Okay. How about I pick you up at 7. Casual dinner?"

"Yeah, great."

I succeeded in getting off the call as fast as I could before he could catch on to my real plan. Corrigan hadn't made detective by being guileless.

I pushed myself back from the kitchen table to get ready for my appearance at Valducci's. I completed my morning rituals on automatic. It felt as if all my thoughts and emotions had been vacuumed from my body and I wondered if that emptiness was how assassins dealt with knowing they were about to kill somebody. I checked to make sure my gun was loaded and stuck it, for the time being, back in my purse.

As I was about to leave my apartment, I took a quick look around as if for the last time.

It took me just thirty minutes to reach Valducci's and in that time, to my great relief, my phone remained silent.

Leo greeted me with a wave of his hand as soon as I walked through the caterer's entrance. "Hiya, Claire. Sure am glad you're here. You wouldn't believe the number of people who hire on and then never show."

I half-smiled. "I make it a point to do what I say I'll do." *Like stopping Bucanetti from destroying my family.*

He gave me a quick rundown of what I was supposed to do and then grabbed his jacket and keys. "Come on. Time to get over to Belle Fontaine. Gloria and the other servers are already there setting up."

The comforting scents of vanilla and chocolate filled the Valducci's van as we drove to the ballroom. Leo told me about his history with the catering company while I surreptitiously checked my phone, relieved Bucanetti hadn't called, yet worried that he hadn't.

A few minutes later, we pulled into Belle Fontaine's back entrance. Leo nodded toward my phone. "Word to the wise. I know you young people can't do without them, but turn your phone off when we get into Belle Fontaine. Cell phones on a job are a big no-no if you're working for Gloria."

I took a last look at my phone and turned it off. I inhaled and exhaled, hoping to stretch out the girdle I felt around my lungs. No telling what Bucanetti might do if he couldn't reach me.

Leo handed me a large metal tray of petit fours, each covered in a chocolate ganache and topped with delicate fondant hearts. "Here. Take these inside."

Carrying the sweets into Belle Fontaine, I had the definite feeling I was plunging into an unfathomable tunnel. I wasn't sure what lay on the other side.

I deposited the tray and Gloria looked me over. She must have decided I passed muster because she instructed me to follow Leo into the ballroom. He demonstrated how I was to position the wedding favors, lavender Jordan almonds wrapped in netting, at each place setting. After I did so, I scanned the ballroom wondering where my encounter with Bucanetti might occur.

There was one entrance at the front of the room through which guests would enter. They'd go through a grand-looking arched foyer to then come into the ballroom. An alcove leading to the coat checkroom stood on the left of the entrance, and behind the dance floor were two glass doors leading to the outside garden.

I decided the alcove would be the best place for a showdown with Bucanetti. It was still fairly warm today, so with luck not many guests would be using the coatroom. Of course, getting the mobster alone there would be only the start of my challenges.

My hands were as cold as the bottle of champagne with which the bride and groom would be toasted. I rubbed my palms together to warm them and slunk back into the kitchen to see what my next task would be. Maybe whatever it was, my mind would allow me to lose myself in it for a time.

No matter the task, time inched by but at long last it was 4:30. The wedding party was due at 5. They would be fed first, then the guests would begin to arrive at 5:30 and be served hors d'oeuvres followed by a buffet dinner. My assignment was to keep the guests' appetites at bay while they mingled. I could only hope my arms wouldn't tremble so much that the tray would slip and somebody would be wearing the canapés.

***

Wedding guests began to filter in. So far, though, no Bucanetti. At least nobody that looked like the fuzzy picture I found of him. Nonetheless, I circulated with my tray of shrimp puffs, straining my neck to view those around me.

Passing around my second tray of those puffs, I heard a familiar voice call my name. I spun around so quickly some unfortunate woman in a black sequined dress was almost wearing the pastries as a necklace.

"Claire!" It was Alex Carpenter. "I didn't know you'd be working here."

I hesitated. Then plastered a smile on my face. "Hello, Alex. It's nice to see you again. They were short a server so I'm just helping out. So…are you here alone?

Or did you come with someone?"

He gave me a crooked smile. "If I thought you might actually be interested, I'd make sure I was alone. But that's not the case, so I'm here with a friend of the bride, Rebecca Castellano." He twisted around, searching. "She's over there, talking to my Aunt Carmella." He frowned. "And of course, the flashy-looking guy surrounded by his goons is my Uncle Michael." His face screwed up as if he smelled sewage. There was no love lost between Alex and Bucanetti.

"You know, my aunt's the reason I'm not like my uncle. The sweetest woman who ever walked the earth. She knew your father, too. Remember? She claimed he was her paperboy before she moved to Jersey." His hand skimmed my elbow. "Come on. I'll get her away from Uncle Michael, whom I know you don't want to have any dealings with. I bet she'd love to meet you in person."

My heart skidded to a stop. "I...I don't think I can. Uh, I'm not supposed to mingle with the guests. It's against the caterer's rules." My voice trailed off at the end of my lame excuse. I wasn't ready to face Bucanetti yet. If he laid eyes on me now, I'd lose the element of surprise. I had to be in control with this plan or I might as well kiss Aunt Lena and my dad goodbye as they became Jane Doe and John Smith and relocated to Wisconsin or Idaho.

Before he could respond, I shoved the tray under the nose of some older gentleman who was passing by. "Have a canapé, sir."

After unloading three shrimp puffs on the unsuspecting guest, I dashed back into the kitchen leaving Alex in my wake.

I dropped my tray onto the counter and took hold of the back of a nearby chair to steady myself. My breaths came out ragged and I felt as if I'd just avoided a car crash with an eighteen-wheeler.

"Claire? Shouldn't you be offering the hors d'oeuvres?" Gloria peered at my face. "Good Lord, you're not sick, are you?"

"No, just a bit dizzy. I haven't eaten much today."

"Not smart. You knew you'd be on your feet. Go grab a couple of the leftover hors d'oeuvres." She fumed. "Then get back to work. Dinner is about ready to be served and I need you functional!"

"Yes, ma'am."

I slunk over to the back counter where there were some smoked salmon and cream cheese toasts and some bruschetta with green olive tapenade that had been abandoned. Since Gloria was watching me, I shoveled one of each without tasting either. To wash them past my constricted throat, I drank almost a full glass of water.

"Feel better?" Gloria asked as if she knew what the answer had better be. When I nodded, she motioned toward a stack of small plates. "Set those out by the salads. Dinner's about ready. Don't forget, your job once the buffet opens is to make sure all the chafing dishes stay full."

As soon as I laid the heavy dishes down on the table in the ballroom, Alex approached me. "Claire, are you okay? You ran off as if my uncle was chasing you."

I wished people would stop asking me if I was okay. Of course I wasn't. My skin felt clammy and my stomach had turned to stone. Now that the time to confront Bucanetti was so near, I started second-guessing the wisdom of my plan. *Maybe witness protection wouldn't be so bad.* I mentally slapped myself. I had a job to do.

I smiled, knowing it wouldn't reach my eyes. "Sorry, Alex. I just, you know, my previous experiences with your uncle have been pretty unpleasant. But I would like to meet Carmella." I saw the opportunity to push my plan through and I took it.

My words dripped pure innocence. "What about your getting your uncle to go outside into the garden? Then I could approach your aunt and introduce myself. But please make sure your uncle doesn't know I'm here."

He gave me the sweetest smile and the guilt I felt for involving him in my scheme brought heat to my face.

"I know she'd love that. Not a word to him. Thanks, Claire."

Gloria appeared and announced that dinner was being served, and with a squeeze of my hand, Alex returned to his family.

The guests filed up to the serving table, while I stayed safely in the kitchen, quickly filling and refilling pans with more potatoes, pasta, veal, chicken, and vegetables. All the while, my thoughts were on a permanent loop. Would my counter threats to Bucanetti work? Would it come down to his life or mine? *Slowly, breathe in, breathe out. Repeat.*

As the return of empty pans to be refilled slowed, I wiped my damp forehead with the back on my hand and leaned over the counter.

Leo ducked out of the kitchen and quickly returned. "Looks like we're done except for the cleanup. Good job, Claire."

"Thanks, Leo. Do we start that now?"

"Nah. They eat. Some come back for seconds or thirds. When they stop coming up to the table, that's when we clean. For now, relax and take ten."

Ten minutes. Would that be enough time to settle things with Bucanetti? And, would I be able to come back to the kitchen? Or would I be carried out of the building on a stretcher, sheet over my face?

I grabbed my purse, which still held my gun, and made my way out of the kitchen into the ballroom. My feet moved as if they were walking through molasses.

Alex spotted me almost instantly and gave me a quick nod. In the next moment, he and his uncle headed out through the glass doors into the garden. My stomach dropped when Bucanetti's bodyguards followed.

An abandoned metal tray displaying four éclairs sat on the table next to me. I picked the platter up with the intention of pretending I was offering Bucanetti and Alex the pastries. That would get me close enough to the mobster without his bodyguards suspecting anything.

A nervous snicker escaped from my mouth. The idea that maybe I might have to use the serving piece as a shield blackened my already dark thoughts.

I drew my gun from my purse, stashed the purse under the table, and hid the weapon under the tray. Fighting the desire to throw up, I started toward the garden doors.

The band's tempo picked up and I wound my way through the dancing couples. I might have heard my name called from behind. I couldn't stop, knowing if I did, I'd lose the will to finish. I used my shoulder to push the glass door open and forced my feet to step into the garden.

Bucanetti and Alex were sitting on a bench behind the lit fountain, their backs to the two muscular guards and to the glass door. Making a big show of offering the éclairs to the guards, I stood between them, directing the tray toward one, then the other. The second man took a pastry and murmured his thanks loud enough for Alex and Bucanetti to look over their shoulders.

"Claire? Why are you here?" Alex half-rose.

I dropped the tray and swung my gun around so it pressed against Bucanetti's back. My revolver was wobbling so much I had to grab it with both hands. Time seemed to stop until I found my voice. "Don't move."

Bucanetti didn't even twitch. To his henchmen he said, "Relax, boys. It's all right. Lemme guess." He gnashed his teeth as if he wished I were a piece of meat. "It's little Claire DeNardo, PI extraordinaire, hoping to scare me."

My lips felt so dry I had to lick them to stop them from cracking. "You're right. It's Claire and there's more to this than just scaring you. I want to discuss my family and—"

"Police! Everyone, hands in the air. Now!" Corrigan jumped from the bushes surrounding the garden, gun drawn. He frisked the bodyguards, Bucanetti, and even Alex and laid the weapons by his feet. Without looking at me, he said, "Claire, put your gun away." He scowled, watching me fumble and finally manage to stick my weapon into the waistband of my skirt.

I moaned, "It's not what it looks like." To hide my quivering chin, I leaned over and picked up the tray, pressing it against my chest. *Could this have gone more wrong?* Any hope of protecting my family was as smashed as the éclairs that had been on my tray.

Bucanetti chuckled, but there wasn't any humor in it. "It appears my niece has a few uninvited wedding guests. First Claire, now the cop."

The words were no sooner out of his mouth when,

darting over from the far side of the fountain was Carmella Bucanetti. "Alex, look! I met another friend of yours." Turning toward the accompanying woman, Carmella added, "Her name is—" She finished with a guttural sound as the woman stepped from the shadows and locked her arm around Carmella's neck. Her other hand held a gun against Carmella's temple.

It was Charlotte, wearing a black wig and heavy makeup. The edge of her bandage from the chest wound peeked out from her dress.

She commanded everyone who hadn't yet surrendered their guns to do so. "Detective, that means you and Claire, too." After we did as she ordered, Charlotte tightened her grip around Carmella's neck and taunted Bucanetti. "You know, I could just squeeze the trigger and 'boom' this nice lady would be gone. So, *Mister* Bucanetti, how does it feel knowing you might lose someone *you* love?"

Bucanetti's hands became fists and this king of the jungle growled, but it was Corrigan who spoke up. "Charlotte, let the lady go. This isn't going to solve anything. Let's talk about this."

"No! This scumbag had Dennis killed in revenge for Marco's death." Her upper lip curled. "Dennis was worth ten Marcos."

Carmella whimpered and Alex pleaded, "My aunt never hurt anybody. Take me instead."

He reached out for her only to have Charlotte yank Carmella backwards, almost bumping into me. With that last effort, Charlotte breathed harder and she tottered a bit.

I tilted toward her. "Charlotte, I can tell you're still weak. Why don't you—"

"Shut up!" She shook her head slightly, as if to clear her thoughts. Then cocked her gun, ready to shoot. "All right, Bucanetti, confess what you did to Dennis, or I'll blow your wife's head off."

Carmella's helplessness triggered my memory of the time thugs kidnapped Aunt Lena. My mind blanked and sheer instinct took over. I slammed Charlotte's head and right shoulder with the metal tray I'd been holding.

She stumbled and fell to her knees, pulling Carmella down with her. Her gun went off and the bullet went wild, grazing the arm of one of the bodyguards. I tore Carmella from Charlotte's grasp and knocked the woman out of the way. Corrigan went for his gun and shouted at Charlotte to drop hers.

Ignoring his command, Charlotte aimed her weapon at Bucanetti. The shot from Corrigan's gun found its target. Charlotte dropped her weapon as her body slumped against the fountain.

Carmella, weeping and screaming, dove into Alex's arms while his uncle watched, hands folded in front.

In a heartbeat, Corrigan was on his phone calling for an ambulance, telling them to rush it. Charlotte was losing so much blood it didn't look like she'd make it. Barely conscious, she signaled to me. I knelt and lowered my ear to her lips.

A bubble of blood-tinged mucous appeared in the corner of her mouth. "I'm not gonna make it."

I took her hand. "Hang on. The ambulance will be here any minute."

She squeezed my fingers. "Need to tell you." Her breath rattled. "Dixon-hurt-both-of-us." She dropped my hand and with a shudder, she was gone. I said a prayer for her and blinked back guilty tears. It wasn't my bullet that killed her and I wasn't the one who held Carmella hostage, but I was responsible. I was the one who set this all in motion by tricking Alex into bringing Bucanetti outside, thereby leaving Carmella alone. In all likelihood, Corrigan showed up here because of me. I dropped my head into my hands and wished I could rewind time.

Bucanetti slid next to me and stuck out his hand to help me up. His grip was strong yet his hand was soft, with manicured nails. His lip curled in a snarl. "Looks like both of Marco's killers are dead. The one who planned it and the one who did it." He expectorated beside Charlotte's fresh corpse. "Now you and me gotta settle up."

Blood coagulated in my head and I couldn't think, sure he was ready to pop me and create an additional corpse.

He must have read my mind. "Nah, nothing like that. You saved my Carmella and probably me, even if this all started because of your half-assed plan."

"So that makes us even?" My voice went up so high it almost got caught in the trees.

He rubbed his chin. "Yeah, we're even. You and your family are safe. And I ain't even gonna press charges against you."

It was as if he were a genie granting me three wishes. I felt the weight of my family's fate lifting off my shoulders. All I could do was nod. With a return nod, he turned back to Alex and Carmella, his arms sloped around each of them while his guards watched.

Avoiding Corrigan's gaze was my next objective. I failed miserably and when he caught my eye, all that recently found lightness disappeared.

He shouted over the scream of the oncoming ambulance. "What the hell did you think you were doing?" He rubbed his temples. "It's a good thing I talked to your aunt. Otherwise, I would have thought you were staying out of trouble. When am I going to learn? You and trouble are like twins."

Lucky for me, the ambulance had arrived, along with more police, who cordoned off the garden. Corrigan's tirade against me would have to wait, especially since curious guests had started pouring out from the ballroom. He was herding them and shouting for them to go back inside. Everyone, except the bride and her mother complied. I didn't catch all of it, but the mother had some choice words for all concerned regarding the spoiling of her daughter's wedding.

***

It seemed to take forever, but Charlotte's body was removed. Everyone gave a statement. Bucanetti and Alex insisted I was only demonstrating how to hold a revolver, not threatening anyone. One glance at Bucanetti's face and his guards backed up his story.

Corrigan made a last ditch effort to detain Bucanetti, but, still unable to obtain a warrant, he had nothing with which to hold the man.

Assuming he'd let me go too, I cleaned up the tossed éclairs from the garden path. I was wrong. "What did Charlotte say to you before she died?"

I repeated what she had whispered and his eyes crinkled.

"What does that mean?" He eyed me suspiciously. "What else did she say?"

"That was it." I shrugged. "Maybe she just wanted me to know George Dixon, Felicity's brother, hurt both

222

of them." I crinkled my nose. "Or maybe she killed Dixon because of Felicity?"

He rubbed his chin. "There's no way we could get a confession from her now. But it's an angle I should look into."

I had nothing else to offer and Corrigan had run out of questions for me, so he let me go.

Once freed, I searched for my purse where I'd left it, but it was gone. Before anger or upset registered, Gloria Valducci tapped me on the shoulder. My bag dangled from her fingers.

"This yours?"

I gave her a guarded grin. "You found it! Thanks." I reached for my purse, but she pulled it away.

Her face impassive. "Kitchen. Now."

We had no problem getting to the kitchen, as the guests, without a word, cleared a path for us. I didn't know where to look, knowing they were staring. I felt like I had a big 'S' on my chest, for 'Screw-up.'

We almost reached our destination when one of the groomsmen quipped loudly, "And she can cook too."

An uneasy twitter arose, quickly followed by the band striking up a well-worn but lively tune.

As soon as the kitchen door closed behind us, Gloria thrust my purse at me. The cords in her neck stood out like the thin straps on my bag.

"I understand you're a bit of a hero." I started to respond and she snapped her fingers to silence me. Gritting her teeth she continued, "Why the hallelujah did you really come to work for me? Do you have any idea what your little adventure could cost me? One of my servers involved in a shooting while she's on the job?"

Knowing I had no real defense or answers that would

placate her, I responded with, "I was just passing out éclairs." I clasped my hands around my handbag to stop from fidgeting.

She scowled. "Thank God you weren't hurt or I don't know what I'd tell Lena."

"I'm so sorry. I'll never do it again."

The bride's mother stuck her head into the kitchen. "Excuse me, if you're done shooting people, my daughter wants to cut the cake."

Gloria's face transformed into that of a gracious businesswoman. "Of course. We'll be right out to serve it."

The door closed and Gloria addressed me, "I'd planned to have you pass out the cake. That's not possible now. Stay back here and help Leo clean up."

She marched out the door into the ballroom without another word. I let out a big breath, glad she hadn't fired me. Let's face it. I still needed that paycheck.

Leo tapped me on the shoulder. "Heard you saved the day. What was that all about, anyway? Come on, you can tell me."

I recapped what I deemed shareable. Afterwards, we cleaned in mutual silence. While I washed and wiped off trays and pans, I thought about what Charlotte had said to me. *Dixon-hurt-both-of-us*. The explanation I'd given Corrigan still seemed the most likely to me.

Chapter Thirty-Three

It was past midnight by the time the cleanup was done and almost 1 in the morning when Leo dropped me off at Valducci's. Too tired to do any work, I drove home and made myself some tea, wishing I had one of those éclairs that had been on the tray. Digging around in my cupboard, I found a bag of chocolate bridge mix left over from the last get-together Aunt Lena had. I made a face. The chocolate had partially melted, but it was better than nothing.

As I picked out the chocolate-covered almonds and popped them into my mouth, I grabbed a scrap of paper and wrote down Charlotte's final statement. I put the emphasis on various words and changed where I imagined the punctuation belonged.

The conclusion came to me and I almost choked on a raisin. What if Dixon hurt Felicity and Charlotte, and so Charlotte hurt him. In fact, killed him? Could Charlotte have been confessing to the murder of Felicity's brother?

My exhaustion disappeared and I felt ready to return to the wedding to dance the tarantella. In this wave of optimism, my mind turned to Iola. If she wasn't Dixon's

killer, she could hire me again. I let out a whoop, thinking of that big, fat fee she had offered me. Gino could
have his business back and I'd have the money to start
my own.

Forgetting about the lateness of the hour and barely
able to contain my enthusiasm, I called Corrigan. He answered on the first ring.

"What is it, Claire?" If his voice was any indication,
the man was worn out. Regardless, I pressed on.

"What if Charlotte's last words were a confession?
What if *she* killed George Dixon to protect Felicity?"

The silence on Corrigan's end of the phone had me
fidgeting. Finally, "Could be. But again, how to prove it?
There's still you witnessing Iola Taylor running out of
Dixon's home. Yeah, Charlotte may have confessed, but
her confession wasn't exactly clear."

I ran my fingers through my hair. "Iola could be telling the truth. Maybe Charlotte got to Dixon before Iola
arrived at his house. Iola finds him already dead. Panics
and makes a run for it, only to be observed by me."

"Claire." He paused and blew out a deep breath. "I'll
think about it. Tomorrow. Probably won't finish my paperwork until 3 if I'm lucky."

"Okay. You do sound beat. Is the paperwork about
tonight?"

"Yeah. Hey look, I'm sorry if I came down on you
too hard."

"I know. It's your job." Adult speech, childish pout.

"It's more than that. You mean a lot to me. If anything ever happened to you…"

A smile sneaked across my face. Before my brain
could stifle my mouth, I whispered, "I love you." As
soon as the words were out, I hoped the line had discon-

nected before he heard them. My face felt hot enough to melt the phone. Foolish to be the first to say it. Even worse over the phone.

It seemed forever before he responded. Clearing his throat, he said, "Uh, yeah? Me too. "Hey! You know I'd come over right after I was done here if I didn't have to meet with Internal Affairs in about seven hours."

"Okaay, well I better sign off now." I sounded as chipper as the activities director on a cruise ship. I ended the call before he could say another word.

I left everything on the table and made it to my bedroom, flopping onto the bed. Did he say what he did just to help me save face? Did he feel trapped now? Did I? Would things be awkward now? I popped back up. If he did mean it, what did it mean for us? I laid my hand on my belly and took a few slow, deep breaths. It was going to be all right.

The playful tune on my phone woke me. I had fallen asleep fully clothed and it was now early morning. "Hello?"

"How could you? I recommend you to Gloria and you go playing cops and robbers."

It was my aunt. "It wasn't cops and robbers. I was just passing out éclairs. It wasn't my fault somebody got held hostage. Anyway, everything's okay. I'm good, in case you wondered."

"You know I care how you are. It's a lucky thing I told Brian where you'd be so he could save you."

"He didn't *save* me. I was doing perfectly fine before he came along."

"Well, you still almost spoiled that poor girl's wedding. I hope you're not planning on doing something similar at mine?"

I threw up my hands. "Not unless you've hired some 'rent-a-mobster' to perform the ceremony." I bit my lower lip. It wasn't right to argue. She was getting married in two weeks, and I'm sure her nerves were nearly as frayed as mine. "I'm sorry. No, nothing like that will happen at your wedding. The food and the whole event will be as lovely as the bride."

She chuckled. "Oh, is someone standing in for me?"

Good humor was re-established. I was relieved. And I knew she was no longer in danger.

***

By early afternoon, I was on my way to Felicity's home. I wondered if she had been informed of Charlotte's death. Being the one to break the news to her wouldn't be my first choice. Though if I were, it could be my best chance to get some information out of her. She wouldn't have had a chance to come up with a story to explain Charlotte's last words.

No police cars were around when I arrived. Maybe I beat them to it. I walked up to Felicity's door and knocked, fully expecting her to scream at me to leave.

To my amazement, as soon as I identified myself, she opened the door and let me in.

Unsure what to expect, I slinked into her house. She trudged to her sofa and plopped down.

"Hello, Felicity." My voice was hesitant.

She didn't even acknowledge me. Her face was splotched, her nose red, as if she'd been crying.

"Have the police been here?"

She shook her head. "No, but Mr. Bucanetti called to tell me."

While I was disappointed not to catch her with her

guard down, I was also relieved at not being the one to break the bad news.

Staring down at a used tissue, she nodded. "Marco and now Charlotte." Her voice broke.

I kept it low key. "I'm sorry."

"Now they'll come asking me if I think Charlotte could have killed my brother." She sniffed. "It's all his fault, you know."

I drew closer to her until I was right beside the sofa. "Who's fault, Felicity?"

"George's."

I swallowed my excitement and forced my voice to remain soft. "Really? How?"

"His gambling. His cruelty." She spoke into her chest.

To better hear her, I lowered myself onto the sofa beside her. "I don't understand."

She sighed. "Marco died because he tried to help my brother. If Charlotte hadn't had to protect me from George, she'd still be alive."

"Wait. Charlotte died because she held Bucanetti's wife at gunpoint." The answer to my next question could mean the difference between knowing Charlotte killed Dixon or just guessing at it. "Or did you know Charlotte was George's killer?"

"Charlotte protected me from my brother. She loved me!" She looked straight at me. "You saw that. She loved me!"

I went for it. "You're saying Charlotte killed George?"

"I don't know." She dabbed her eyes.

"Charlotte was your alibi for the time of his death. Was she lying?" She hesitated and I didn't move a muscle.

At last, "I was alone at home when George died. Charlotte offered to be my alibi and made me promise not to disagree. For my own good."

My gaze narrowed. "So you don't know where Charlotte was at the time of his death?"

"No. I assumed she was home alone, too." Her eyes pleaded with me. "Please don't tell the police!"

I couldn't agree to that. She'd lied to the cops. Never a good thing. I didn't want to dwell on that, though. A lot more needed to be uncovered.

"Did Charlotte know your brother well?"

She sighed. "Well enough, I suppose. George was so awful to me. And to everyone else too. The last time the three of us were together, he and Charlotte got into an awful row. He called her a leech, right to her face. He was such a bastard!"

Touching her lightly on the shoulder I said, "Felicity, you have to tell the police about this. They have reason to believe Charlotte killed your brother."

"How could you say that?" She was nearly shrieking. "She was a good person and she cared about me." She pounded her fist into her other hand. "I can't do that to her memory."

Keeping my voice balanced between gentle and strong, I kept on. "When you shot Charlotte... wasn't that because you believed she'd murdered Marco?" Felicity's tears flowed freely now.

I coaxed her, "Charlotte may not have meant to kill him."

The doorbell rang. "Police."

Felicity gave a slight shake to her head, as if giving up. "It's open."

My opportunity to get to the bottom of this mystery ended with that bell.

Two detectives entered. The first, Mike Something-or-Other, was Corrigan's partner. My heart lurched when I saw Corrigan behind him. I couldn't look him in the eye. Yet I sure didn't want to leave at this critical point. I scooted as far back into the sofa as I could, hoping it would enfold me enough so I disappeared. Making matters worse for me was my hasty proclamation of love. The memory of it was like splashing hot water on my face. It felt like it was burning up and was no doubt as red as a pomegranate.

For his part, Corrigan acted every inch a policeman. Mike glanced at Corrigan, apparently waiting for him to start talking.

Felicity spoke first. "I already know. Charlotte's dead. I also know you think she killed my brother."

Corrigan found his voice. "You and Ms. Positano stated you were together at the time of Mr. Dixon's murder. Care to revise your alibi?"

Felicity took in a breath and demanded her lawyer be present, shutting down the conversation.

Even after the police left and it was just the two of us again, she stayed quiet. Frustrated, I took my leave.

Mike and his car were gone. Corrigan was waiting for me. My first instinct was to flee. Unfortunately, he was leaning against my car. I plastered a smile on and ignored my churning stomach.

Too bad I couldn't stop my mouth from babbling like the proverbial brook. "Sooo, why are you still here? Did you get the information you wanted? I just got here a little bit before you. You know, Felicity doesn't want to admit it, but I think she thinks Charlotte may have killed her brother. Maybe check into Charlotte's alibi. In fact, it could be that Charlotte killed George Dixon and had Dennis murder Marco. What do you think? Of course, you may not see it that way. We don't always agree on things, do we?"

Corrigan didn't say a word until I stopped for a breath. "I agree. I think she either suspects or knows Charlotte did it. Which would thrill my captain. He's been getting pressure to close this case." He curled his lip. "What better way than with a deathbed confession, albeit an unclear one."

"Yeah, yeah. That's right. That's right." *Somebody, slap me so I stop talking.* "Well, I guess I better go."

"Claire, wait." He put his hand on my arm. "Why are you acting so, so weird? Is it because you said it first?"

I played innocent, but my stomach was rising so fast it would soon meet my brain. "What do you mean?"

"There's nothing for you to feel strange about. I thought it was pretty clear how I feel about you."

"You mean..."

"Yeah, I do and I have for a while. Okay?"

I'm sure I glowed bright enough to light up all of Cleveland. I leaned toward him, hoping for a big embrace and kiss. Instead, I got, "Can you give me a ride back?" So much for romance.

On the way there, I broached the subject of Felicity's alibi.

"We could probably charge her with *obstruction of official business*," he shrugged. "But she's been through a lot. Most she'd get would be 90 days."

We'd gotten a block from the police station when he told me to pull into a lot behind an office building. Puzzled, I did so and turned the car off. "Now what?"

He unbuckled his seatbelt and planted the most passionate kiss on me a guy could achieve with a console between us.

I dropped him off, my lips still tingling.

By the time I reached my office, the magic of his kiss had worn off a bit and I began contemplating my next move.

I didn't have to think for too long. Within fifteen minutes, Iola Taylor was tapping on my door. Her face was as pale as computer paper and her ample figure was less ample than the last time I had seen her. She pressed her hand to her heart. "Thank goodness you're here."

Afraid she'd collapse, I offered her a seat across from my desk. She dropped her still-considerable heft hard into the chair and removed her signature-oversized sunglasses and floppy hat, revealing thin, oily hair plastered to her head.

I sat behind my desk and my fingers tapped out a nervous beat. When she didn't start, I asked, "Why are you here, Iola?"

She intertwined her fingers. "Do you handle blackmail cases?"

I slumped in my chair and folded my arms across my chest. "You better start from the beginning."

She cleared her throat. "First, let me say I've learned Charlotte Pusitano, even though she's dead, is considered the prime suspect in George Dixon's murder."

"Okay." With a tilt of my head I asked, "What's that got to do with blackmail?" My imagination spun. Anything was possible.

"Now you know I am not a murderer. George was dead when I got to his house."

I closed my eyes for a moment. "Let's say for a minute you're telling the truth and you didn't kill Dixon. Again, what's that got to do with blackmail?" My eyes popped open. "Did somebody beside me see you running away from the scene? Are they putting the squeeze on you?"

She shook her head, no. "But, this is just as devastating." She scooted forward on her chair. "When I first hired you, it was to find out if that weasel, Dixon, had any dirt on me. Well, he did. I saw his research page before he snapped the folder shut." Her voice broke and she whipped out a wrinkled handkerchief.

I took a deep breath. "Do you know who the blackmailer is?"

"I have no idea who might be doing this to me."

"How do you know if he or she even has George's information?"

Her expression was grim. "I'm sure of it. What I'm not sure of is, what the vile creature wants. I'm also sure that if you don't agree to help me, I'll have no choice but to do as they demand."

"If you're willing to give this blackmailer whatever he or she wants, the information must be pretty horrendous."

She dabbed her eyes and remained silent.

"Iola, if you want my help, you'll have to tell me what the dirt is the blackmailer has on you. I assume what they've learned is true."

"This must go no further than this room. You have to promise me!"

"In all good conscience, I can't promise that. If you're honest with me, I'll try to do what I can so your name isn't smeared everywhere."

"Very well. Years ago, I was a private duty nurse taking care of a fine man afflicted with a terrible degenerative disease." She paused, as if summoning her courage. "After he passed away, I discovered manuscripts he'd written but never had published." She stared down at her lap.

I tried to keep the shock from my face. "You stole those manuscripts and put your name to them?"

She nodded, avoiding any eye contact. "He had no family. At the time, I didn't think what I was doing was so wrong." Her tone was somewhat petulant.

Struggling to keep my voice even, I asked, "When did you receive the first blackmail note?"

"Friday evening. I shredded it. It was the type that had letters pasted on it from a newspaper or magazine." She pulled a sheet of paper from her bag. "I received this one late Saturday afternoon."

She read it aloud. "Meet me Monday at 3. Outside West Side Market Café on Lorain."

A busy public place. It didn't seem like the blackmailer was planning to kill or hurt Iola. *Then why meet?*

Concerned that more handling of the note would further destroy any fingerprints, I picked it up with a tissue and slipped it into an envelope. "You shouldn't meet with this person." Whoever the blackmailer was, they didn't ask for money. They wanted something and it was most likely a thing Iola wouldn't freely give. "I understand why you don't want the police involved, but this is a matter for them to handle."

"No!" Iola leaned forward and tried to grab the envelope. "Nobody else must know about this. That's why I want to hire you to find out who's doing this to me and retrieve the information. Believe me, it will be very worth your while. $15,000 advance and $15,000 when you complete the job. Plus expenses, of course."

I templed my fingers and rested my chin atop them, picturing how that money could help me establish my own PI business. Tempted as I was to accept the advance, something told me there was more to her story.

I needed time to think. "I'm going into the kitchen to make some tea. Want some?"

When she declined, I disappeared into the office kitchen. Waiting by the cupboard until the water in my cup darkened, I thought through what theories I had.

First, Iola visited George regarding his dirt on her. They argued and she left. Charlotte entered, hit George in the head and killed him. Afterwards, Iola showed up again to get her scarf and found Dixon dead.

I zoomed back in on Charlotte's involvement in Dixon's death. She was the last one to see him alive. Did Charlotte swipe the information after she killed him? She couldn't have started sending the anonymous letters until she left the hospital and got away from the police. Would she have had the time to send them before she came to the wedding and nabbed Carmella Bucanetti?

This case had more questions than answers. Dixon had a knot on his forehead at the time of his death. Why would Charlotte smack him in the face with something, then cut him and leave him for dead? If she had wanted to kill him, she had a gun. I understood why the police would be happy to close this murder case without further investigation.

My thoughts returned to Iola and Dixon's argument. Under what circumstances did she leave? Was she in a hurry? If so, why?

My phone vibrated and I grinned seeing Corrigan's text reminding me of our Sunday night dinner plans. At least some of the questions about our relationship were clearing up.

Cup in hand, I sat at my desk. Iola was coiled and ready to spring. "Well? What have you decided?"

I opened a notebook and picked up a pen. "Iola, I want you to tell me everything that transpired between you and Dixon the night he died."

She moaned, "I already told the police. We just had a small disagreement. Then I left."

I put down the pen. "How can I help you if you're not going to be completely honest with me?" This was a huge gamble on my part.

She started with, "I don't see how what happened that night would have any bearing on—"

"Was someone else at Dixon's house that night?"

Iola rocked back and forth slightly. "I don't think so."

I leaned across my desk. "You don't know for sure? Think."

She patted her cheek lightly with her palm. "There was another car parked in front of his house the first time I was there. A red one. I didn't see anyone else, though."

I tried to catch Iola's eye but she was looking past me. "Iola," I took a breath, wondering how to phrase my statement. "You and George argued when you realized he actually had the information you didn't want released."

"Yes. I told you that before." Her expression as cautious as a deer's spotting a hunter in camouflage.

"Did the argument get physical at any time?"

"Of course not. I'm no animal."

No way was I buying what she was selling. "I didn't say you were. It's just, sometimes, emotions run high...You know, there are times when arguments don't stay in the talking phase. In fact, Dixon had an altercation just a short time before you met up with him. He wound up with a bloody nose. Can't say he didn't deserve it, either. From what I've heard, lots of people detested the man. Even his own sister. I could see why somebody would take a swing at him, especially if he was trying to hurt her."

Iola bit her lower lip and closed her eyes. "All right. I was in total control of myself until he called me a thieving hack and threatened to tell everyone the truth about my books." She pulled out the handkerchief she had previously used. "I couldn't abide that."

Trying to lead her, I asked, "So you slapped him?"

"Worse." Her voice broke. "I struck him in the face with my latest book. He collapsed and there was some blood." She half-rose from her chair. "He was alive when I left. I swear it!"

"You left in such a hurry. Why didn't you take the information?"

She lowered herself back down and released a deep breath. "I thought I heard somebody. I ran out. Didn't even notice my scarf was gone until later and went back to get it. That's when I saw him in the chair, dead." She clenched her fists. "The police already have the killer. I just lost my temper. No real harm done."

"You're kidding, right?"

"Nobody else has to know about that little quarrel. Do they?" Her eyes pleaded with me.

I tucked my hair behind my ears. "Under the circumstances, I cannot take your case, Iola. On top of stealing a deceased man's work, you assaulted another man and left him unconscious."

My dream of starting my business vanished like a

pizza in a room full of teenagers. "That doesn't mean I changed my mind about your meeting with your black-mailer, though."

Iola cried, "What am I supposed to do? You just told me not to meet with that...that piece of garbage. Please! I need your help."

I rubbed my stiff neck. I didn't want hers to be the next corpse found in relation to Dixon's murder. "Okay. I'll do some investigating and get back to you tonight. Tomorrow morning at the latest." Would I get my reward in heaven, because I certainly was not going to get it here on earth.

Her head bobbed up and down and she grabbed my hand, holding it to her cheek. "Thank you! I'll write you a check right now." She ignored my protests and slid her check toward me saying, "For your trouble. In case you change your mind."

Leaving the advance on my desk, I escorted her out. For a moment after she left, I stared at the check, realiz-ing I couldn't cash it. I have a conscience and it wouldn't let me. Iola had crossed the line and chosen expediency over decency too many times. I should have turned her in. Questioning my judgment, I placed the check in my desk drawer and locked it. I would decide what to do with it later.

It was already 4 when I left my office. I had to find a blackmailer before having dinner with Corrigan. Talk about trying to multi-task.

My first stop was Charlotte's apartment. I didn't know if I'd be able to get inside, but I knew someone who could, Ed. On numerous occasions, he had demon-strated his ability to get past doors and locks. I hated ask-ing him. I didn't want a reputation as a B&E kind of gal.

I held my breath while his phone rang and blew it out when he answered.

"Ed? It's Claire. Are you busy right now?"

"Matter of fact, I am. I'm in the middle of a meeting with the florist."

"Is my aunt with you?"

"No. She's busy with *Cannoli's* so, I told her I'd take care of this."

I couldn't help but ask, "She trusted you with the flower arrangements and the bouquets? That doesn't sound like her."

"Well, see, I told her I used to work for a florist and she figured I'd pick the right flowers for our wedding."

"You worked for a florist? What did you do there?"

"After high school. I drove the delivery truck."

I chuckled. "Does Aunt Lena know that?"

"No. And don't you tell her. I wanted to make it easier for her. It'll be all right. This flower lady knows her stuff."

"Okay. I won't breathe a word. How long will you be there?" Maybe I could wait another twenty minutes to visit Charlotte's place.

"Fifteen minutes maybe. Then I have to get fitted for my suit. Haven't worn one of those since my uncle died. Whatever you need, can it wait another hour or so?"

I looked at the time. "No, it's okay. I'll figure out something else." Any idea what that something might be hadn't come to me yet.

Nor did it arrive once I reached Charlotte's apartment building. At least there were no police cars around. Maybe I could sweet talk a maintenance man into letting me into the dead woman's place.

As my luck would have it, nobody who worked there

was on the premises. Just as I believed bad luck would continue following me on this case, I spotted a young woman with two heavy-looking bags of groceries and a small child in tow entering the elevator. I crossed my fingers and dashed in just as the doors were closing.

I offered her a hand, "Here, let me carry one of those for you."

She eyed me cautiously until I said, "I'm Claire. A friend of Charlotte Pusitano, Apartment 302. We worked at Cicarelli's together."

She smiled and handed me one of the sacks. "Nice to meet you."

As we made it to her place, the child began to whine. She shouted over him, "Appreciate it. Tell Charlotte hello for me."

I set her bag down inside her door. "I would, but she's not home."

She opened a juice box for her son. "She must have had a great time last night. I didn't even hear her come home. I'm a night owl, even though nowadays I'm up and out really early. Like today." She tilted her chin toward the child. "I was going to ask Charlotte to watch Jonathan tonight. Do you know if she'll be home?"

"Highly unlikely. In fact, she needs a fresh set of clothes."

The woman looked disappointed. "I suppose I'll have to ask Jonathan's father." She made a face. "Well, I guess I'll put this ice cream in her freezer so she can have some tomorrow."

She had a key! I was almost giddy with possibilities. "I can do that when I pick up some clothes for her. It'll only take a minute extra." I gambled with my next question. "I forgot to get Charlotte's key. Can I use yours?

I'll bring it back in a second." I paused, trying to look sincere. She looked unsure, so I offered, "Or you can come with me."

The neighbor bit her lower lip. "No, that's okay. You have an honest face."

The trouble came when I opened Charlotte's door. Somebody had tossed the place. My breath caught in my throat. Had the police done it, or an accomplice? Who else had a key? The one person I could think of was Felicity. It seemed all roads led back to her.

After placing the ice cream in Charlotte's freezer, I hunted for anything that could indicate Charlotte was involved in the blackmail scheme. Nothing.

Since my supposed purpose here was to find clothes for Charlotte, I grabbed an old pair of jeans and a sweatshirt and returned the key to the neighbor. In doing so, I asked, "Do you know if anybody else came by here last night or early this morning?"

"I've been out since late morning, so maybe. Why?"

The last thing I needed was a suspicious neighbor. "No reason." I had to make a quick getaway. "Thanks for the key. Ice cream is in her freezer so it won't melt."

I was out of the apartment building in a flash. Next on my agenda was dinner with Corrigan.

I made it home in time to apply some makeup and brush my teeth. So much for primping for my date.

Corrigan, on the other hand, looked good enough to have just stepped off the fashion runway. He'd replaced his tired dark blue suit for jeans and a shirt that emphasized his muscles as well as concave and convex areas.

I mused how long it would take him to react if I wrenched off his jacket, tore off his shirt, then ran my hands over his tantalizing contours and warm skin. *Who said dessert couldn't come before dinner?* I needed to fan myself just thinking about it.

He kissed me briefly. "Do you need time to get ready?" His expression betrayed no sarcasm.

I looked down at my outfit, noticing for the first time, I'd spilled tea on it. Head high, I pronounced, "I *am* ready. You said 'casual' remember?"

"Yeah, I did." He nuzzled my neck and my body shifted into ready-for-anything mode. Too bad my mind didn't shift with it. "What did you mean about me needing to get ready?"

"Nothing." His embrace tightened and all systems were a go, until my stomach growled loud enough to drown out any passionate breathing.

Wondering why abdominal noises never happen in movies, I pulled away and let out a deep breath. "I think we better go eat or my stomach will be serenading us all night."

He pulled me back into his arms. Unfortunately, my belly's protest of the meal delay was so thunderous he finally gave up. "Sure. Might as well satisfy something."

Once we placed our orders at Rocky River Brews and Burgers, he sipped his beer and I practically downed my chocolate martini. I just sampled my second one when our dinners arrived. One glass of wine is usually enough alcohol for me, but chocolate martinis are, in my opinion, one of life's treasures. So when the second liquid gem appeared before me, I couldn't resist. I should have because that much alcohol was sure to separate my tongue from my brain.

Between bites of my salad and with no prelude, I asked, "Brian, do you happen to know if anybody, I mean to say, the police, searched Charlotte Pusitano's place?"

He put his burger down. "Why?"

"Can't I ask a simple question?"

I could see that tiny vein in his temple boogying. "You never ask a question unless something's behind it. Have you been to Charlotte's apartment?"

He'd find out soon enough. "I was in her neighborhood." *Lame.*

"Sure, you looked up her address then just happened to find yourself there." Sarcasm dripped from his words. "Or, let me guess, you were in the market for an apartment in her building and knew there'd be a vacancy."

I used the tone of voice I often heard parents use with errant teens. "Will you answer my question or not?"

Silence for a moment. Then, "Yes. This morning. Now will you tell me why?"

Worried he might explode if he knew I was associating with a story thief, I chose my words as a soldier in a minefield chooses his steps. After all, I still didn't know whether I would take her case or not. That fee could provide the solution to my Gino problem. "Before I answer, did you find anything...interesting?"

"Do you mean like, anything about Iola Taylor?"

Praying he couldn't have heard me gulp, I said, "Yeah, like that."

"Funny you should mention it." That double-edged tone of his again. "There was nothing."

I lowered my head and scooped a loaded forkful of salad into my mouth. "Mmm hum." I knew to avoid eye contact at all costs.

"Claire, I thought you were staying out of the Dixon murder case after what happened with Charlotte." His eyes narrowed. "Why are you still involved with Iola

Taylor?"

I chewed my salad for a long time, trying to formulate a response that wouldn't get my head bitten off. "She came back to my office and told me what I believe is the truth. I think Charlotte killed Dixon and while she was there, made off with some information that could destroy Iola's writing career." If a lucky star were shining upon me, Corrigan wouldn't ask what that information was.

Too bad that star didn't exist.

"What information?"

I spoke slowly and softly. "That maybe Iola isn't the great writer people think she is."

"Iola's claiming Charlotte was blackmailing her?"

"She doesn't know who it is."

"And what were you going to do with that information? Is Iola you're client now?"

"I don't know. Maybe." I lowered my voice. "I don't see why you're getting so upset. We know Iola didn't kill Dixon. Charlotte did."

"Something's not right here. Iola's dirty and you shouldn't be involved with her." He threw his napkin on the table. "My God, you never listen. How often do I have to warn you to stay away from her?"

I followed suit with my napkin. "Well, it won't be any more tonight. I'm going home. Alone." I stood up.

So did he. "Wait. I'll take you."

On the way home, the atmosphere in the car was chilly enough for cardiac frostbite.

Even angry, Corrigan was polite enough to walk me to my door. Then he left without so much as lips brushed against my cheek. Childishly, I was glad I hadn't shaved my legs for tonight's date.

I plopped down on the couch, rose and dug through

my freezer for something chocolate. There in the back was a slightly freezer-burned brownie. It'd do.

I gnawed on the still-frozen goodie thinking of snappy retorts to Corrigan. Then switched to theories of what happened to the blackmailer's information.

The brownie gone, I licked the chocolate from my fingers and decided to make one final visit to Felicity. The woman was like Rome. All roads led to her.

Chapter Thirty-Four

I drove around Felicity's neighborhood for twenty minutes, trying to come up with a plan to get her talking and telling the truth.

My opportunity materialized when I spotted her in her driveway, getting into her car. I spun my vehicle around and pulled in behind her, thereby blocking her chance to leave.

She blew her horn, but I didn't budge. After motioning impolitely, she got out of her car.

"What do you want now, Claire? You've got one minute. If you don't move your car by then, I'm calling the police."

Courtesy before questioning. "First, I'm really sorry to keep dropping in on you, but I've got some new information and wanted your take on it. Did you know Charlotte was blackmailing someone?"

For a second, I thought I saw a flicker of knowledge pass over her face. It was so quick and the light so poor, I couldn't be completely sure.

"That's ridiculous. Even if it were true, what does that have to do with me?"

"I thought maybe you knew where Charlotte got the information. Or what happened to it?"

She waved her hand. "Your minute is up." She stomped back to her car and over her shoulder yelled, "Now get your car out of my driveway."

So much for being courteous. Having no other choice, I complied with her wish. As she sped away, I even considered giving up the whole messy case. But if I could find who was blackmailing Iola and exonerate her in Dixon's murder, I could accept Iola's fee and have it in the bank before Gino came home. Sure, she was a plagiarist, but she didn't murder anyone. The plain truth was, I needed that money to have a business and a livelihood.

I shoved any murmurs of misgivings from my conscience about the evils of plagiarism and drove my car to the end of the block, returning to the house on foot. In a flash, I saw my next step. Felicity's trash. PI's know you can tell a lot by a person's trash. Maybe hers would hold the proof of what happened to the information Charlotte stole.

The cans were on the side of her home. One look and I chose the recyclables first. They were the cleaner of the two bins. I quickly scanned the neighborhood. Nobody was about. Still I hesitated. Who knew what kind of germs could be breeding and flourishing on the cans, bottles, and who-knew-what in that bin. I grimaced and rooted around in my purse until I located the two thin rubber gloves I kept stashed there. My job is dangerous enough without opening myself up to attack by bacteria and viruses. I pulled the gloves on and stuck my arm in the bin. I held my breath lest some aggressive germ bypassed the rubber barriers I wore and became airborne.

Blessedly, since I needed to breathe, I latched onto a manila folder. Or one-half of it. My hand began to tremble and I was ready to whoop. Someone had printed the letters 'I.T.' on the tab.

I dug through the rest of the receptacle like a dog looking for scraps. At the bottom, I found the other half of the folder. Any documents that might have been inside were nowhere to be seen. Putting aside my pride, I called Corrigan to tell him of my find. After all, this was business.

I tapped my foot, waiting for him to pick up. "I found the folder. It's got Iola's initials, I.T., on it."

"Where are you?"

My words tumbled over each other. "Felicity Dixon's house. The folder was in her trash. She must have removed whatever her brother wrote about Iola. You'll have to come here with a search warrant."

"Wait. You went through her trash?" He sounded almost indignant. "And just because you found a folder with 'I.T.' written on it, you think it's about Iola Taylor? Do you think maybe it's Internet Technology, or something like that?" He didn't even wait for me to respond. "Now get out of there before you get into trouble."

"You aren't even going to consider—"

"Claire." His tone was similar to a dog owner warning Fido to drop the shoe he was chewing on.

"Fine. Goodbye." It was clear I needed more proof and I was sure the blackmail information was inside Felicity's house. I'm no break-in expert and there was no time to call Ed. I was on my own.

Felicity's home was like the others in the area, built sometime between the 1930's and 1940's. I studied the milk chute and sighed. Even if I could get the small door open, my hips would never make it through.

I walked around the house and spotted the opening to

the coal chute. In years past, homeowners had coal dumped into their basements for heating. Someone in the house would pull a lever, which would cause springs to open the door.

It was closed, but slightly askew. If I could get through, how far was the drop to the basement floor? Only one way to find out. I tried to push it open, but nothing happened. Desperate, I turned around and butted it with my rear end. The springs on the inside squeaked. I stopped cold. If I actually succeeded in opening the chute and crawling in, I'd be trespassing. I got dizzy just thinking about the consequences of being caught, like Felicity shooting me.

I blinked hard a couple of times and the spinning disappeared. I took a deep breath to steady myself and tried the chute. It opened and I stared into blackness. I wondered if this wasn't my own personal gate to Hell. For a moment, my panic took complete hold and my mind screamed that this wasn't worth it. Nothing was if I died. I stepped back ready to bolt.

Only the possibility of continuing as a PI in my own business stopped me from running. If I didn't go down the chute, I would have to give up any dream of having a PI business. I closed my eyes and visualized Iola's check.

I rammed the chute again with my behind and shimmied through. If something happened, like a fracture from the fall, I prayed my cell phone would work.

Thankfully, it wasn't too bad of a fall. I dusted myself off as well as possible and hurried up the stairs to the house's main floor. My breathing was so shallow, I feared passing out. Felicity might come home any minute, so I couldn't slow down.

I began my search in the study. Rummaging through

the desk drawers and bookcase yielded nothing. Moving on to her bedroom, I could feel my armpits getting damp. I pawed through the closet and drawers, even peered under the bed. The kitchen, with all its cupboards and nooks took me more time. My nerves jangled with each loud tick of the wall clock.

I was out of rooms and I feared, close to being out of time. I barreled back downstairs to the basement, hoping it would be easier to get out of the house than in. I simply had to find the coal chute lever and use something to hold it in place.

Nausea washed over me once I realized the pulley was nonfunctioning. How would I get out? In my panic, I reached my hand out to steady myself and made contact with a metal chest. I looked at the piece of furniture and yanked the top drawer open. My gut was telling me this was where I'd discover the paper. I almost whimpered when all I found was the owner's manual for the washing machine. I was ready to rip those instructions to pieces when a sheet of paper fell out from between the pages. I skimmed the handwritten notes. They contained dates and names, witnesses and a description of Iola's former career as a private duty nurse. I felt almost giddy, as if I'd swallowed two glasses of champagne.

I had almost gotten through the notes when I heard a garage door open. Since her garage was detached, I wasn't sure if it was Felicity, but my heart began to beat loud enough to drown out the sound of the garage door closing. I had to get out of there without her knowing anyone had snooped. I prayed I could find the strength to pull the chute open and get myself out.

Sometimes prayers aren't answered. It wouldn't budge.

I heard keys rattling and imagined them sliding into the lock and twisting, just as my stomach twisted. Felicity was home.

I pulled the light cord and the basement went black. The darkness magnified her steps as she entered into the house.

With only a glimmer of light from the streetlights, I felt around for somewhere to hide. I stumbled upon a door, which led to a small room.

I ducked inside and pulled out a penlight from my purse. It spread just enough brightness to see I was in a pantry, which was loaded with cans of soup, vegetables and baking supplies. No way out, though, except the way I came in. Panic made my thoughts spiral into nonsense. Maybe Felicity didn't know I was there. Maybe I could stay in the pantry until she went to bed. Then find something to pry the coal chute open and make my escape.

The cold reality of no escape hit me and I stumbled against a broom and dustpan. They crashed into the pantry door.

I froze for a second. Then dug into my purse for my gun like a rabbit escaping from a hunter, moaning as I recalled leaving it at home. Who needed a gun when having dinner with a cop?

Felicity's footsteps ended outside the pantry and she called to me. "I know you're here, Claire. I saw your car. You better come out."

Note to self. If there's a next time, park farther away.

I flattened myself against one of the pantry walls and using my penlight, made my way past the flour and sugar bags, to an aerosol can of non-stick cooking spray. Not much of a weapon, but better than nothing. If only Felicity would stick her head inside the pantry, I could spray it in her face.

Unless she had a gun. *Of course she had a gun.* My best option was to provoke her, not enough to shoot me, but enough to get closer to me. "I found the information you and Charlotte were going to use to blackmail Iola Taylor."

No response.

"Did Charlotte talk you into it?"

A sharp laugh. "Charlotte? She was loyal, but that woman was about as smart as a mushroom."

I took the cap off the non-stick spray as quietly as possible. "You took the folder. Were you with Charlotte when she killed your brother?"

"Enough talking. Come out, Claire."

I could picture the gun in Felicity's hand. Probably one of Marco's. "If you tell me how you got the papers on Iola, I'll come out."

I heard her annoyed sigh. "Very well. You'll never live to tell anyone. Charlotte saw the folder, but it didn't occur to her how useful the information could be. We argued about it. She didn't want to hurt anybody else. She didn't understand Iola Taylor could help me. That the woman hated my brother too. And she had been with him just before he died." Her voice softened, became wistful. "You know, I have talent. Real talent. I could have been famous." She paused and her voice hardened with hatred. "George ridiculed me, discouraged anybody from working with me. He forced me into the background. He deserved to die."

I found applesauce cups. "So you and Charlotte killed him?"

"It didn't start out that way. We went to see him. To ask him if he would put in a word for me with an agent.

When we got there, he was woozy, bleeding from the head. We helped him into a chair. Charlotte was even going to call 911. But first, I wanted to ask him about helping me. Know what he did? The bastard laughed. He laughed at me."

I trembled as I held the spray in one hand and the applesauce cups in the other. It was hard to breathe. I needed to keep her talking. "That was so cruel of him."

"Charlotte and I tied him up so he could really think about helping me. Instead, he demanded we let him go. Then he called me a talentless, third-rate writer without the ingenuity to survive on my own. Yes, that's what my dear brother thought of me."

"He must have been a terrible brother. So what did you do then?" Maybe if I showed her some sympathy, she wouldn't shoot me.

"I picked up a manila folder just to hit him with. I was too close, though, and it slashed his face. I didn't realize how sharp those edges are." Her voice sounded distant, removed. "You know, it felt good to see him hurt. So I cut him. Again and again. He begged Charlotte to call 911 but she just stood there, watching until he called her a hideous swine. She grabbed some newspaper, wadded it up and shoved it in his mouth. Then she grabbed Iola's folder and was ready to slice into his arms. The paper on Iola fell out and I stopped her. Right away, I knew what to do with that information. We probably would have left him with just the cuts I'd made, except he managed to kick Charlotte and knocked her down. I handed her another folder and told her to go for it. We really weren't planning to kill him. We just got…carried away." She released a long breath. "Now come out."

I jumped out, my hand on the nozzle of the can, spraying for all I was worth. With my zigzag method, I managed to hit her. She howled and clutched at her face with one hand. I threw the applesauce containers at her, hoping she'd drop her weapon.

Instead she fired wildly. I screamed and my shoulder jerked back as if someone had hit me with a rock. Following that was a burning feeling and I realized a bullet went into my arm. I ducked behind the door fearing she'd bolt toward me. The combination of non-stick spray and spilled applesauce must have made the floor treacherous and I heard a thud followed quickly by another. Then, silence.

My arm was going numb and immobile. I ripped open a roll of paper towels and pressed them against my right arm to slow the bleeding. Then with my good arm, I grabbed a family-size can of peaches to use as defense. It wasn't necessary. Felicity was out cold lying near a metal stool, the gun an inch from her splayed hand. I scooped up the gun, preparing to call 911 before I became too lightheaded from losing blood.

The next thing I knew, Corrigan was kneeling beside me while the EMT's prepared to load me into an ambulance.

"Where's Felicity?" I croaked.

"Dead. Looks like she hit the stool here and then the concrete." He stroked my hair. "Thank God, you'll be all right."

I winced as the EMTs raised the gurney. "The paper on Iola." I felt my mind drifting away. "I found it."

"We'll talk about it at the hospital. I'll meet you there."

***

The doctor had bandaged my arm from my elbow to my shoulder. Standing by my hospital bed was my father, Aunt Lena, and Corrigan.

My father squeezed my hand. His voice was thick. "Love you, Claire."

"Love you more, Dad."

My aunt pointed to a plate with a fat éclair sitting on the bed table. "I brought you that in case the food here is awful. You need to eat."

My aunt nudged my dad. "Okay Frank, let's wait outside. Brian and Claire should have some time alone." She hustled him out the hospital room door.

Corrigan's smile was warm enough to heat the room. He leaned over and kissed me softly on the lips. That was better than any pain medicine.

"I'm glad you found me at Felicity's."

"Not half as glad as I am. After you called, I was furious. Then I figured I better go see what exactly you were up to. You know, in case you needed some help. When I got there, the door was open. I found you and Felicity. And the information about Iola." He shook his head. "I had to turn the facts page in as evidence. I bet it won't be long before her career is down the tubes."

"I'm ready to give you my statement."

"Okay." He pulled out his notebook and pen. "First, another kiss."

Afterwards, I ran through what Felicity had told me about her brother's murder. I felt too drained to include Iola's part. That could wait until later. Corrigan assured me he'd stick around.

Chapter Thirty-Five

It had been about two weeks since Felicity shot me. My arm was healing, but I still needed to keep it in the sling. This made a less-than-stylish accompaniment to my maid-of-honor dress. That was fine, though, since I told myself all eyes would be on Aunt Lena.

I was right. When she walked down the aisle in her dress with the flamboyant taffeta rose perched at her bosom rivaling her bouquet there was never a more radiant bride. She and Ed, *Uncle* Ed, were so adorable standing at the altar, both so nervous they swayed, almost synchronized with each other.

As they said their vows, I dabbed at my eyes, and glanced at my dad, who was sniffling. If I wasn't mistaken, he was stealing glances at Suzy.

While everyone waited for the couple outside the church, I remarked to Dad, "This may be the first time I've seen Ed without a toothpick in his mouth."

"Yeah, now he's a married man. Wonder if Lena will make him give up those things."

Suzy tugged on my father's arm. "I hope not. Marriage shouldn't mean you surrender what makes you,

you." She and Dad exchanged a look that made me think I'd better not throw out my only-wear-at-weddings shoes.

While the marriage ceremony was dignified and lovely, the reception was loud and raucous. Almost everyone knew everyone else, making it more fun than I imagined it would be. Angie's nephew was the leader of the wedding band and they performed music with a heavy disco beat. People were throwing down moves I had never seen before. I imagined aspirin would be in great demand the following morning.

The three-tiered wedding cake Angie made was, in a word, exquisite. It looked as if it was made from spun sugar by fairies. People remember the cake and the food. I must say, Suzy and my dad rose to new heights to make the dinner buffet memorable. I'd been of little help with my injury so could take no credit.

After a heart-bursting round of the Tarantella, my aunt tasted the baked ziti. Her face still red from the dance, she cornered me. "I saw Frank and Angie and *that woman* set up for the food." She made a face. "What caterer did you hire?"

"It wasn't a caterer. It was *that woman*, Suzy. She wanted to do something nice for you so she and my dad did it all."

My aunt's eyes narrowed. "She did that for me? Why?"

"Because she's a good person. You need to get to know her."

"We'll see. If she cooks like that, maybe she's not all bad."

I didn't dare add that, from my observation of my dad and Suzy, Aunt Lena may need to acquaint herself better with Suzy sooner rather than later. The groom, my new uncle, came over. He whisked my aunt away for a dance. They glided across the dance floor, so well matched, a rigatoni-shaped Ginger to a wiry, down-to-earth Fred. I learned later Lena had gone for private dance lessons after the contest fiasco.

I looked around to see my date, Corrigan, dashing in his groomsman suit, talking with Gino, who had arrived back in Cleveland just two days ago. Already, he'd been to the office where we discussed his taking back the business, such as it was.

My insides sank every time I thought about what to do next. I had cleared Iola's name as far as George Dixon's murder, but with the crashing of her career, she never paid me. Even her advance check bounced. With no money and no options, Gino took pity on me and offered me my old position. I have until Monday to give him my answer. I'll be turning his offer down. It's too much like a step back for me. My future feels like a road they started building but stopped when the money ran out.

I shook off my low mood. This was supposed to be a happy time.

My aunt was preparing to throw her bouquet. I had no intention of being jostled by the other single ladies, so I stood back. The drum roll began and the bride tossed the flowers.

They landed right in the bend of my arm. While everyone laughed and applauded, I glanced over at Corrigan and he looked my way. Our eyes met.

Recipes...

My mother used to make the following recipe when I was young. She thought of it as a kid's meal. To this day I still enjoy it.

Fettucini con Ricotta e Latte

4 servings

1 stick butter
1 lb ricotta cheese
6 tablespoons whole milk
2 tablespoons chopped fresh Italian parsley
1 large garlic clove, minced (optional)
Salt and pepper to taste
1 lb fettuccini
Grated Romano Pecorino cheese for topping

Melt butter in heavy small saucepan over medium heat. Add garlic if using and saute 1-2 minutes. Combine ricotta, milk, parsley, and melted butter in large bowl. Season with salt and pepper.

Cook fettuccini in large pot of boiling, salted water. Stir occasionally. Cook until al dente (just tender but still firm to bite). Drain, saving some of the pasta water in case pasta mixture is too dry.

Toss pasta with ricotta mixture and serve immediately.

This next recipe I make when I'm feeling like I deserve a special treat. It's fast with no fuss. It's also very rich, so you may want to cut it in small bars.

CD's Yummy Bars

Makes 70 bars

1 package Devil's Food Cake Mix
¼ cup water
2 eggs
¼ cup butter
¼ cup packed brown sugar
10 oz. jar maraschino cherries without the stems, drained well, chopped
Vanilla frosting (I use canned. Don't tell anyone. You can make yours from scratch, though.)
4 oz. unsweetened chocolate. Do NOT use semi-sweet

Preheat oven to 375 degrees F. Combine half the cake mix (dry mix), the water, eggs, butter, and brown sugar in mixing bowl; mix thoroughly. Blend in remaining cake mix. Stir in chopped cherries. Spread in greased and floured jelly roll pan (15 1/2x10 1/2x1 inch). Bake 20-25 minutes. Cool.

Prepare frosting mix. Or open the can. Spread on cake.

Melt chocolate and carefully spread evenly over the frosting. Chill.

Cut into 1 ½ inch squares before the chocolate is completely hard.

Dear Reader,

If you enjoyed this book, please recommend it to a friend. Even lend your copy to them!

Reviews are always welcome. They help other readers discover your favorite books. If you do write one for The Terrified Detective: Eclairs and Executions, please let Carole know. She'd like to thank you personally. Her email is cmsldfowkes@gmail.com.

Sign up for Carole's Newsletter to get insider information, sneak peeks and freebies, and to be the first to hear when her new book is coming out. Since these newsletters only come out a few times a year, you won't be inundated with them. Also, rest assured, Carole doesn't sell email address.

The link for her Newsletter is:
http://eepurl.com/8xC5L.

For more information on Carole, visit her website:
www.carolefowkes.com.

If you liked this fourth book in the Terrified Detective cozy mystery series, make sure you check out Books One, Two, and Three which are available now.

Plateful of Murder

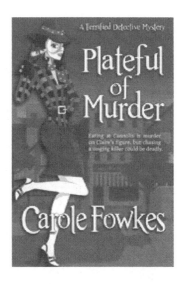

Claire DeNardo is scared of a lot of things. Ordinary objects like roller coasters and men's hairpieces make her knees knock loud enough to be a band's rhythm section. Unfortunately, the only job Claire can find is working for her Uncle Gino in his seedy detective agency. Until now, her cases have all been middle-aged men with trophy wives who needed watching.

But when Gino retires and leaves her in charge, Claire quickly gets swept up in a murder case despite her fears. Both the client who hired her and the handsome police detective want her off the case. When the wrong person is charged, it's up to the terrified detective to summon all the courage she can to find the true killer.

Killer Cannoli

Private Investigator Claire DeNardo visits her Aunt Lena's café, *Cannoli's,* and discovers a romance brewing between her aunt and a new customer. Claire's suspicions that he's lying about his identity prove solid when he's found dead at the café. Claire ignores the warnings of Police Detective Brian Corrigan and delves into the dead man's life. In the process she realizes her aunt may unwittingly possess what the killer wants. And it's not her tiramisu recipe.

Bake Me a Murder

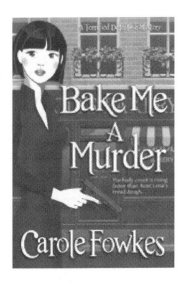

Private Investigator Claire DeNardo reluctantly takes on a case presented by her part-time employee, Ed. Ed's cousin, Merle, is searching for his former girlfriend, a topless dancer who ran with a rough crowd. But it's too late. The woman has been killed and Merle, who is now Claire's client, is arrested. When Claire digs into the victim's past, she uncovers a thriving illegal drug trade. Her fears about this case double when she learns about the mobster who is behind the unlawful business. All this while dodging Police Detective Brian Corrigan's determined efforts to get her off the case and into his arms.

Acknowledgements

First, I want to thank my husband, Greg, for his support and his great ideas. I'm eternally grateful to Joanne for her encouragement and her patience in reading and re-reading my script. Nikki and Jack were invaluable with their advice and knowledge. Rae-Dawn lent her enthusiasm and expertise to my efforts. My appreciation also goes out to Nancy for her great editing skills. Finally, an enormous thank you goes to Kathleen for her assistance, ideas, and plain old talent. She made the publishing of this book possible.

22165643R00150

Made in the USA
Columbia, SC
27 July 2018